Buy Buy Baby

Helen MacKinven

cranachan

For my babies, Ross and Lewis, who have grown into men that make me proud to be their mum.

CAROL

I DON'T JUST TALK TO THE DOG, I answer back for him too.

'It's only 11% proof so dinnae give me that look.' Jinky's stare held steady as I topped up my glass. 'And it's Friday night so give me a break, will you?'

'Fair enough.'

Was it any worse than talking to yourself? Jinky crept back to his basket; I didn't need the dog's approval. The wine helped to take the edge off things and encouraged me to reach for the notebook. It was balanced on top of a higgledy-piggledy stack of two unopened credit card statements, an overdue electricity bill, a menu for Domino's, an Argos catalogue and last week's copy of the *Shawbriggs Herald*.

I'd promised my bereavement counsellor Charlotte that I would start keeping a journal of my thoughts and feelings. But now that I wasn't a mum anymore, there was nothing to write about; every day was much the same for me. I was a hamster on a plastic wheel, spinning round and round on the boring cycle of life.

My best pal, Elaine, gave me a fridge magnet of a retro cartoon with a 1950s housewife and the caption, "*A clean house is a sign of a wasted life.*" The state of my kitchen was proof that I took it to heart, like everything else.

'Why can ah never find a pen when ah need one Jinky?'

'Maybe if you tidied up it would help!'

'Who rattled your cage?'

I raked through the junk drawer, tossing aside an old phone charger and a handful of dead batteries, to find a pen that worked. After another gulp of wine and a satisfying chew on the pen's gnawed end, I was ready.

FRIDAY 11TH FEB 2011

Dear Journal

On telly you see folk in group therapy and they do introductions round the room, like when they're at an AA meeting. It feels a bit like that, so here goes... My name's Carol - but I'm NOT an alcoholic. I'm drinking wine cos I've had a good day. Mind you, when I think about it, I drink wine when I've had a bad day too. Anyway, this isn't about how much booze I drink, it's about me writing it down in black and white that today was a GOOD one and that's VERY unusual.

I laughed out loud for the first time in over two years. It felt weird to smile without forcing it. I probably should've guessed something special was going to happen cos my horoscope in The Sun said, *"A welcome change is in the air and may well take you into new territory"*.

I looked down at the dog. 'This isnae the beginning or end of ma story Jinky.'

'Is that a fact?'

Jinky trotted past with no sign of shared excitement. The dog

2

stretched out its scrawny body and slumped to the floor, letting his tongue hang out like a rasher of bacon. It was pointless trying to inspire a stupid mutt.

'Thirsty work.'

'So you keep telling me.'

If Jinky was a pedigree dog he'd have more class and would understand. I stuck another bottle of wine into the fridge; I needed the wine to fuel my pen.

Let me tell you a wee bit about me. I've got a love it or hate it laugh. It seems so long since I've heard it; I'd forgotten how it sounded. Even though I was the teacher's pet, it got me into trouble at school all the time. Elaine used to say that I laughed like a donkey out of breath. Dan said I had a great laugh. He couldn't believe that I'd found his joke so funny. He didn't realise that no one had dared to tell me a joke since my boy Ben died.

Writing Ben's name reminded me that I'd been logged into the Broken Cord forum. The computer was still switched on in the dining room; I'd shifted it from the box room. When I'd first moved in, I toyed with calling the box room 'the study', it didn't sound right when I said it the first time to Elaine. Nobody likes a show off.

There was another reason to move the computer from the box room; I could often see Moira Farrell's American Tan tights drying on the whirligig. My neighbour's tights were the same colour as the fake-tanned legs of my ex-husband's girlfriend. The computer couldn't stay there. A view of damp double gussets and a reminder of legs like Mahogany Tart's weren't images I wanted to live with.

I didn't want to share my news with the forum. The journal,

3

the second bottle of wine and my scabby rescue dog were enough company. The BT advert is a lot of guff, it's not always good to talk.

At work in the florist, my boss Isobel talks, and I listen. Most days, the forum was the only time that I chatted to anyone, if you could call typing stuff online chatting. But like germs, some things should not be shared, and meeting Dan was one of them.

Every weekend me and Elaine do a swap, she gives me her copy of the *Shawbriggs Herald* and I give her this week's edition of Natter along with any other mags I've bought. I don't really need to bother reading the newspaper cos Elaine tells me all the juicy bits when she visits. She reads it cover to cover and knows every snippet of Shawbriggs news worth knowing.

But for once, I'll have a bit of news for Elaine that's about ME. The thing is, cos we've known each other for yonks, I never have anything to tell her about me that she doesn't already know. I hardly ever socialise these days and if I do go anywhere apart from work, then it's usually with her. There's no chance of a mystery man entering my life without her knowing about it. And I bet she'll be sorry that she missed meeting Dan. He's really handsome. He must be six feet plus with broad shoulders and he looks like he might have played rugby when he was younger. I bet he's well-toned underneath his wintry gear, although I still think he'd be soft and cuddly, in a gentle but powerful, kind of way. His accent might be English or just posh Edinburgh, I'm not sure. He was wearing a battered Berghaus jacket and faded jeans so his clothes didn't give much away about him either. Even when my ex-husband Steve wore jeans, he always had on a smart shirt or leather jacket. Everything is sharp about Steve, his clothes and his features. Mum always said that if he was chocolate, he'd eat himself. Unlike Steve, there's nothing flashy about Dan. He's got big eyes the colour of treacle toffee and their warmth matched his smile. Anyone can tell that Dan's got a trustworthy face.

I didn't post anything about my day on the forum and I won't tell mum when she calls tonight about meeting Dan, cos she'd only worry about me speaking to a strange man. Her imagination would run wild. She watches even more telly than me!

I must thank Mum for the notebook cos I think I'll really enjoy writing this journal. She sent me it in one of her 'Helping Hand' packages. Last month's efforts to *help* included 180 decaffeinated teabags cos she thinks cutting out caffeine will help me sleep at night. The Tetley teabags were a BOGOF offer at the Co-op, and the pair of hand knitted lime green bed socks was sold in aid of Guide Dogs for the Blind - so how could she say no? I know she feels guilty about living up north after all that's happened to me, but I can't believe that she honestly thinks these parcels will make any difference. At 42 years old, there are some things you've got to deal with yourself.

Charlotte could be right; the journal might help. Most nights I'm sitting here on my own, logged in to Broken Cord, catching up with the soaps or trawling eBay. I suppose that keeping a journal will be something different to do and, to be honest, I need to get my spending under control cos the debts are really mounting up now. I'm not daft; I know I don't need a pair of electric blue Jimmy Choo sling backs. Posh high heels aren't much good for a shift working at the florist, but it's so easy to get caught up in the bidding. There's such a buzz when you outbid everyone else and you win the item. Then, when you slip the shoes on for the first time, you're transported somewhere else, it's like Dorothy's ruby slippers in the Wizard of Oz. I feel as if I'm buying my own wee bit of magic, but I know I need to stop buying shoes and bags that never leave my bedroom. Even if writing in a journal only keeps me off eBay for a while, then it's all for the good. Well, it's worth a try I suppose!

P.S. I've not finished the second bottle of wine. I know when to stop.

In the Daisy Chain, I spend most of my time in the back shop, leaving Isobel out front to deal with the customers. The teeny weeny room is a bit like a cave. It needs to be cool and not too bright to make the blooms last longer. The air is always solid with the smell of bitter greenery, not sweet floral aromas. Unlike most customers, I know that there is no point in putting your nose to the rose. These days, with all the artificial growing conditions, the flowers lose their scent – they smell of nothing: Parfum de Zilch.

Other folk might complain about the claustrophobic space, the constant chill and the gloomy light through the skanky net curtain. Even on the best of Scottish summer days, rarely a smidgen of syrupy sunshine reaches the back shop, but I never whine about my work area. No one could call me a Moaning Minnie.

In the front shop, there is too much air to breathe in, without being overwhelmed. The startling daylight from the shop's full length windows is an even bigger problem; it leaves me feeling completely exposed. Naked. It was a recurring nightmare – me, starkers, with only chrome buckets of carnations and chrysanthemums to hide behind. There was no question about it, and certainly no complaints from Isobel, the back shop suits me just fine.

Sometimes, if Isobel is out delivering orders in her van, I can go for hours without speaking to anyone. The leaf-green Citroën Berlingo has a massive chain of daisies painted over its bodywork, and the vehicle is as well-known as its driver. Isobel seems to know every other passing pedestrian and spends most of the time driving with one hand, so she can wave and toot the horn. Peering over the steering wheel, she can be seen around Shawbriggs most days, flashing her big horse teeth. At least her unfortunate gnashers are framed with a smile so sincere, not even a plastic surgeon could remove it.

Since Ben died, I no longer deal with the public. It's easy to avoid the small town banter, if I plan my day carefully. I've spent the last couple of years fine tuning my timetable, making sure I avoid clashing with the comings and goings of my next door neighbours, the Farrells at number 20. I save my chatting time for the online forum.

I could usually manage a half-hearted nod to the other dog walkers on the woodland trail. And if I was feeling really generous, I sometimes made a withdrawal from the bank of prepared phrases I had at the ready: 'Braw night, eh?', 'That rain's no stopped all day', and 'Aye, it's dreich but the forecast says it should clear up for the weekend.'

Only for the regulars though; even weans know about stranger danger. I remembered the boy and his cat on the telly adverts from the 70s warning us not to speak to strangers. *"Charley says never go anywhere with men or ladies you don't know."*

When I'd turned the corner and bumped into him, I didn't have time to psyche myself up to speak to anyone, certainly not an unfamiliar face. His sudden appearance was followed by a streak of amber. The furry shape shot past me before disappearing into the thick undergrowth. I thought at first that it was a fox, but it was shorter and faster than any fox I'd ever seen and it was wearing a pink collar. The high-pitched squeals confirmed that it was only a Jack Russell on the hunt for rabbits. Without a second to restrain him, Jinky's skinny frame bounded off to join the pursuit, leaving me face-to-face with a stranger.

I tested my dog's recall. 'Jinky!' There was nothing but a rustle of bushes, no sign of him. 'Jinky!' It was times like these when I really grudged keeping Ben's dog. I should've taken him back to the rescue centre after Ben died.

'I'd save your breath. Roxy's not a quitter so we could be in for a bit of a wait if your dog sticks with her. Sorry.'

He approached me and pointed at the blackened wooden bench a few steps along the gravel path.

'We might as well take it easy while we pretend that we're in charge of our dogs. By the way, my name's Dan.'

His hand was as big as a shovel, and he scooped up mine into his powerful grasp. They were ideal strangler's hands, complete with hairy tarantula fingers that could crawl across a neck to make a velvet choker necklace. Dan's move was so sudden, that I had no option but to submit to his spontaneous gesture. But I quickly withdrew from his grip, as if the warmth of his skin had scalded me, through my fleecy glove.

It was a firm handshake, nothing more. My dad Roy would have been impressed by Dan's strong grip. Roy claimed that a dead fish handshake was poofy. Dan was anything but limp-wristed. I peeled off my glove, to find a ragged cuticle to tug and tear with my teeth.

'Don't worry, I don't bite.' He took a step back and raised his hands in surrender. 'Unless you want me to!' To my surprise, his raised eyebrows and cheesy Colgate grin made me smile and I sat next to him on the bench.

'You don't think we should go after them?' I asked, turning my head in the direction of the bushes.

'Nah, I'm happy to wait here. Are you?' asked Dan.

'Eh, okay. Ah'll give it a couple of minutes.' I didn't realise I was chewing on my chapped lips until I tasted blood.

'So you're a Celtic fan then?' asked Dan. He seemed to be glowing like the boy in the Ready Brek advert.

'Eh?' I asked.

'Jinky, wee Jimmy Johnstone, *the* Celtic legend?'

'Ah see what you mean.' I stuttered, sounding like an eedjit. 'Actually, ah'm no keen on fitba, ma son picked the dug's name.'

I was sitting out in the open, on a well-used path; there was no need to worry. *Get a grip,* I told myself. I looked behind me at the dense woodland. Maybe I was right to be cautious? Although the simple truth was, I knew nothing about this man. I considered the facts:

He said his name was Dan.

Dan was a complete stranger.

He was friendly.

Dan was a potential rapist.

He had made no attempt to move from the bench and lure me behind the screen of nearby trees. *Calm down.* And then Dan sprung to his feet. I felt my insides clench and my breathing quicken. Was this the point when I should run? Yell and tell, just like I'd taught Ben. Should I try and find Jinky first or leave him behind? Like sparks from a Catherine Wheel, my options flew into the air, but I didn't get time to act on any of them. The two dogs raced back towards us, circling the bench together in frenzied laps.

'Roxy! What the hell have you got this time? Drop it now!' Dan bent down to wrestle a brown sphere of spikes from the terrier's mouth. Prizing open her jaws, Dan eased the prickly ball out and laid it down gently on the grass. Dan clipped Roxy's lead back on and clapped her head.

'There's no point in me getting mad at her. She's a terrier; she can't help herself. And look at that cheeky face, who could resist it?' asked Dan.

Ben would've loved Roxy too.

'Well it looks like the hedgehog will live tae tell the tale so there's nae harm done,' I said.

'Yeah, look - he's already wandered off.'

'Hedgehogs are funny wee things.' I blurted out, hoping it wasn't a stupid comment.

'You're right. I've never figured them out. I mean hedge-*hogs*. Why can't they just share the hedge?' said Dan.

My laugh was what Elaine called a *Tena Lady* laugh, "If you dribble while you giggle, they're the most absorbent pads". My paranoia had been ridiculous. Thank God I hadn't run off and made a fool of myself.

Dan was an animal lover.

Dan was funny.

Dan was a nice guy.

There was no need to remember what Charley says.

I was blessed with a photographic memory, but sometimes it felt more like a curse when I couldn't delete images that I wanted to forget about Ben's accident. But replaying the scene with Dan over and over was, for once, a blessing. I was even grateful to Jinky. Keeping the dog wasn't such a mistake after all. I'd met someone new and they weren't from the Broken Cord forum. Dan was someone who didn't know about Ben and someone who'd made me laugh. Not someone working their way through the stages of grief.

'If half the folk in Shawbriggs are as friendly as you, I've moved to the right area,' said Dan. 'It's lovely round here. But can I ask you a question?'

My eyes followed Dan's. He'd noticed that the bench we'd been sitting on was charred, just like all the branches on the surrounding shrubs and trees.

'Why're all the trees black round here?' asked Dan, rubbing his big paw-like hands along the thick black mould that coated the branches.

'That's caused by the 'angel's share'. It comes fae the distillery's warehouses close by,' I explained. 'A wee bit of the whisky that's stored in the barrel evaporates through the barrels as it matures. The vapours cause a black fungus tae grow and it sticks tae stuff like the trees.'

It was the first time in ages that I felt I had something new and interesting to say. I even let slip that I called the blackened bench my *Angel's Bench*. My chewed lips were bleeding again.

'It sounds like you'd be worth knowing in a pub quiz. We'd make a good team! Is there a local quiz night round here?' asked Dan.

'Eh, ah wouldnae know. Ah dinnae go oot much these days but ah'm sure there'll be something on in one of the pubs in Shawbriggs,' I replied.

I no longer noticed the nip in the evening air; it was wiped out by the heat from my cheeks, as rosy as a Raggedy Ann doll.

'No worries. Leave it with me and I'll let you know what I find out,' said Dan.

As Dan waved goodbye to me and walked off, he said that he hoped we'd see each other out walking our dogs again soon. I waved back and called after him, 'So do I'.

JULIA

MORTGAGE, CAR LOAN, GYM MEMBERSHIP, designer wardrobe: it was a clutter fuck of debts. I literally couldn't afford to miss the deadline. I had until three o'clock to submit an article to Business Scot, one of my key clients, and with my own accounts a mess, I needed this contract to pay the mortgage. Some might say that's what I get for buying a waterfront flat kitted out from BoConcept. I would say fuck you.

I've worked hard to get where I am, so why don't I deserve the finer things in life? I've built up a successful portfolio, but my freelance work depends on my reputation to produce high quality writing. There are no short cuts to credible articles. No one outside my career really understands how tough it is to write for the corporate industries. My readers are smarter than the average bear. They're information-savvy experts; sloppy writing or poor research is unacceptable. So what's the point in putting in long hours if I don't reward myself?

How can a business journalist, with a shelf full of awards, end up with three maxed-out credit cards? If I can write one and a half thousand words on 'Investors look to companies for clues on economy', then why the hell can't I manage my own personal finances? It was embarrassing to say the least. I'd sooner admit that I had to use tweezers on the hairs that sprouted round my nipples than divulge the piss poor state of my bank account.

A bit of pressure can be a good thing, so instead of tackling my workload I lit a cigarette and turned my back on the Clyde and its grey gloom. I clicked open my *Play* inbox, a more exciting prospect than poring over companies' forecasts or reacting to the demands of my *Work* inbox. Ever since I'd created an anonymous email address, on-line dating had become as much of a guilty pleasure as dragging on a Marlboro Light or watching reruns of *Come Dine with Me*.

There was only one new message in the *Play* inbox. Unfortunately it was from Adam, a guy I'd met last week, and who was now nicknamed Dog Breath. Should I open it or just delete it? The date with Dog Breath was an experience I'd rather forget. As soon as I saw him slide off his bar stool and wave, I knew it was a mismatch. He'd clearly lied about his height and build - and even worse - he was wearing mirrored sunglasses, perched on his head, indoors in February.

'Adam?' I hoped not.

'Aye, and you must be Julia.' No shit Sherlock, I almost blurted out, but nodded instead.

'Ah was a wee bit early,' said Dog Breath.

'Looks like you've been here since lunchtime.' I'd clocked several empty pint glasses.

'Very funny. Think you're a comedienne?'

'No. I'm merely observing the fact that you're half pissed already.'

'Ach, you career girls take life too seriously. Chillax.'

Dog Breath leaned over and patted my arm with his clammy hand. 'Dinnae worry. Ah'll get you a double voddy *and* a shot of Sambuca. You'll catch up with me soon.'

There was more culture in a yogurt factory.

Dog Breath obviously didn't understand that getting *slowly* drunk together could've been fun. A bonding experience. The key word is *together;* Dog Breath hadn't worked that out. He raised an arse cheek up from the bar stool.

'Sorry. Ah should stick tae German lager.'

His meaty fart was the fatal blow. It was difficult to decide whether his arse or his breath smelt worse. I wasn't going to wait a minute longer to draw a conclusion. Thank Christ I had a taxi number on speed dial.

Our date had been an unmitigated disaster and I hadn't dared to share the details with anyone yet. My wee sister Lynn and my best friend Kirsty knew I'd started to dabble with the idea of finding Mr Right online. Neither of them had needed to resort to cyberspace to find love, and they had no concept of what was involved. They didn't appreciate the time and effort it took to register with sites, create a profile, email potential men and *then* arrange dates before you even spoke to a guy.

I had a constant onslaught of junk emails, most of them selling Viagra, although a dating agency's advert caught my eye and aroused my curiosity. The *Men2Be* agency promised that only "*discerning professional men*" were on their books. The naff name had initially put me off from registering, but I was keen to test the authenticity of the agency's claim that the men were all highly successful professionals. The steep registration fee of £1500 did make me think twice about signing up. But it seemed a fair price to pay to filter out any undesirables. I was confident Adam's name wouldn't be on their database.

There was no question that it was money that I didn't have; the cost would ultimately put my credit cards way over the limit. The only comforting thought was, that if the dating site bought me access to the right kind of men, then it would be money well spent.

Men2Be's secondary sifting process was a massive questionnaire for prospective members – it was going to take fucking ages to fill in. The online form wanted to know everything from how much I earned, the school I had gone to, the designer labels I favoured, the property I owned, to the car I drove. The dating agency's strict criteria even ruled out any woman who was over a dress size twelve. Thank Christ I'd kept up my gym membership. I had to be a bit creative with a few facts and figures, or I'd never have passed the entry requirements. It wasn't a problem; a good journalist knows how to massage the truth.

Kirsty had even emailed me a dictionary of terms for women's personal ads. But the joke was only funny if I didn't have to cross reference my own profile with the comedy version. It was obvious that if I wrote one thing, it meant something entirely different:

30ish = 38
Adventurous nature = slept with everyone
Athletic build = no tits
Voluptuous = fat bird
Average looking = ugly as a monkey's arse
Gorgeous = pathological liar
Glamorous = high maintenance
Emotionally secure = on medication
Soulful= cries a lot
Contagious smile = does a lot of pills
Outgoing = loud and embarrassing
Fun = annoying
Free spirit = junkie
New age = body hair in all the wrong places
Looking for soul mate = stalker

Passionate = up for it
Sensuous = dirty
Open-minded = desperate

The humorous element of the list wasn't completely lost on me, but it made me overanalyse every single word I chose to describe myself. No one wants to end up a cyber-spinster.

Did I want to sound intelligent or would being too clever put men off?

Did I want to sound fun or should I sound more serious?

Did I want to use a professional photo or would it look as if I was trying too hard?

Reading the variations, anyone would think that there were more sides to me than a Rubik's cube. Updating my profile was the perfect displacement activity.

SCREEN NAME: JOURNOJULES
LOCATION: GLASGOW - CITY OF STYLE
AGE: THIRTY-SOMETHING
SEX: JOURNOJULES - WHAT D'YA THINK?
EMPLOYMENT: FREELANCE BUSINESS JOURNALIST
BODY TYPE: JESSICA RABBIT
LAST BOOK READ: SCOTTISH BUSINESS DIRECTORY
FAVOURITE AUTHOR: VIRGINIA WOOLF

BEST/WORST LIE YOU'VE EVER TOLD:
"IT'S NOT YOU, IT'S ME"

WHAT ARE YOU MOST SCARED OF?
BEING ON A PLANE, ABOUT TO CRASH... AND THE BLOODY BAR IS CLOSED!

TOP THREE THINGS THAT ANNOY YOU:
1. REFORMED SMOKERS
2. PEOPLE WHO EAT WITH THEIR MOUTHS OPEN
3. RUDE SHOP ASSISTANTS

FIVE ITEMS YOU COULDN'T LIVE WITHOUT:
1. MY LIVER
2. SEQUINS
3. MY BLACKBERRY
4. LA PAVONI ESPRESSO MACHINCE
5. MY NEICE HOLLY

The most difficult question to answer on all of the sites had to be, "WHAT ARE YOU LOOKING FOR IN A RELATIONSHIP?"
This was the BIGGY, the question that required the most thoughtful answer.

Over the last few months, I'd tried out a few:

"A guy that makes my nipples peak just by looking at them."

"The total package with all the trimmings."

"A best friend, lover, partner."

"The other half of me."

I toyed with answers for hours. Too slutty? Too tongue-in-cheek? Too corny? Choosing a response was a nightmare. Eventually I decided on an honest answer, minus a key detail.

"The last love of my life."

I'd alluded to seeking a long term partner (without any mention of the 'B' word) and hoped it wasn't too scary a prospect for most men. It was a no-brainer NOT to advertise the whole truth. No man would ever reply to the most honest answer, the bluntest version being, *"Desperately seeking a man to settle down with and start a family"*.

It was certain that even a subtle hint or a coded message

about babies would send any man running for the Campsie Fells at top speed… no matter how smart, attractive and funny they found me.

I didn't have the energy to complete *Men2Be's* questionnaire right now. I took a final pull on my Marlboro and turned my attention back to the *Play* inbox. For a bit of sport, why not hear what Dog Breath had to say for himself? I clicked open his message, subject heading: *2ND CHANCE.*

'Un-fucking-believable!' I crushed the last of my cigarette into the chrome ashtray until it was a pile of tobacco crumbs.

Dog Breath's email almost beat a guy I'd had dinner with last month. After meeting up, he'd sent me an '*Our Date*' message the next morning with some "*useful feedback*".

On reading it, I'd spluttered into my espresso and stained my merino jumper. "*The ideal woman is one who is attractive and intelligent, but doesn't know she is. I hope you don't mind but I gave your e-mail address to a mate of mine - I couldn't figure you out so maybe he'll have better luck with you than me.*"

When I'd told Kirsty, she had to chew on her batik cushion to muffle her screams of despair.

'Eh?! You're kiddin' me on? So, in other words, his ideal woman is one who is insecure? Christ almighty, I'd no idea that wankers like that actually existed!'

'Can you believe the cheek of him? Passing my number along! What an absolute liberty! I mean, *figure me out*, what the fuck am I? A Sudoku puzzle?'

I couldn't wait to share the, *2ND CHANCE?* message from Dog Breath, but I assumed Kirsty would have her head down working on her latest novel; not everyone I knew had a demanding career.

I stretched across my glass desk to reach for my Blackberry and scrolled down to the next name on my contact list – Lynn. The trill of my sister's mobile ringtone quickly changed to a voice mail automaton. I didn't leave a message. For full effect, my tale of internet dating had to be regurgitated on a one-to-one basis.

I pictured Lynn, out and about in Shawbriggs, 'busy' chatting to her neighbours in the cul-de-sacs of Legoland houses on the Woodlea estate. It was a valley of mock-Georgian façades, with a herd of 4x4s grazing outside garages that were too dinky to actually park a car inside. My life was just as busy as Lynn's - my diary was always full. But at times it felt as empty as my sister's garage.

There was no point dwelling on it. Without any more delaying tactics to hand, I grudgingly opened my work files and went online for the latest share prices required for the article.

Half an hour later, I was saved from death-by-numbers thanks to Lynn calling me back.

'What's up sis?'

'You sound out of breath. Have you been to the gym?' I asked.

'Huh! I wish I'd time to wipe my backside properly never mind a session at the gym! I was at Sainsbury's. What do you think I do all day? Work out with a personal trainer in between appointments at the beautician's?'

'Hardly. I just thought with Holly at school, you'd have a minute but I'll call back another time if you're too harassed.' It was hard to fake my disappointment; a quick chat and a sympathetic ear was all I needed.

'Jeez, you're not going in a huff again are you? I've got as many minutes as you need. What's up?'

'It's nothing important. I just wanted to let you hear the latest from my list of online losers.'

'Go on. What's this week's instalment?' enquired Lynn. I imagined her getting comfy on the sofa; feet up and ready to share my pain.

'Well, you know how the date I had with Dog Breath was tragic?' I paused for effect, I'm not known as a drama queen for nothing.

'The one who said on his profile that he was tall but was shorter than you in your ballet pumps? Thank God you didn't wear your platform sandals,' said Lynn.

'Yep, the very man who'd also described himself as "*athletic*" - but that could only be true if playing the Xbox was a sport.'

'Didn't you make it clear you didn't want to see him again? Don't tell me he's been in touch?'

'Uh huh, he emailed me! Are you ready for this? I'm still shaking with rage.'

'Why, what's he done? I told you to be careful…'

'Don't worry, it was just an email but listen to this.' Another pause helped the build-up. "*I should've waited for you before I started drinking. Sorry doll. Any hope of a second chance? I'll make it worth your while next time and don't worry, I've never had a problem with brewer's droop. You look like you could do with a bit of hard-core stress relief to chillax and I'm THE man for the job. I've got just THE power tool you need to fix your problem! LOL.*"

Lynn stifled a snort before surrendering to a bout of laughter.

'Jeez, I think I've just wet myself! I should've kept up those pelvic floor exercises.'

'I'm glad I've given you a giggle but I can't say I found it *that* funny.'

'C'mon sis, as Dog Breath would say, chillax. You're too sensitive these days. And I thought you said it was only a bit of fun when you signed up to the sites?' said Lynn.

'I did, but as sure as shit floats, every weirdo in the West of Scotland seems to find their way into my inbox! Do you think I should change my online profile?' Lynn didn't bother to hold back a sigh, no doubt rolling her eyeballs at the same time.

'No. I think you should stop taking it so seriously or pack it in.'

'Easy for you to say. It's grim meeting anyone new these days. Thirty-eight and I'm nowhere near settled!'

'Thirty-eight's not that old. You've got loads of options, you don't have to rely on the internet,' replied Lynn.

I flopped on to the sofa, throwing a cushion to the floor; aware that I was definitely too old to act like a moody teenager.

'Really? Is that so? Hmm, let's see what my options are... ' I couldn't stop myself from ranting and I counted them out on the fingers of my left hand. 'One: wine bars in reality are *Whine* bars with a '*wh*'. Full of women on girly nights out, whining about being single. Two: pubs. Full of old boozers, or young guys out with their mates. Three: evening classes. Remember I tried salsa dancing?' I didn't wait for an answer. 'Full of desperate single women - and a few even more desperate mature men. Need I go on?'

'I think you've just been unlucky recently.'

'That's an understatement. I think I must be pathologically single.'

'You're exaggerating as usual.'

'I'm not. All I want is to find Mr Right before I become Ms Wrinkly!' I kicked the cushion to the other side of the room.

'Look, I really think you need to lighten up about this whole dating game. You've just had a run of Mr Not-Quite-Rights.'

'No, it's more like a conveyor belt of Mr Got-to-be fucking-joking.'

'I suppose you've had a few time wasters recently. Remember the guy who asked you if the rug matched the curtains. What did you call him again?'

'Goatee Geek. The one who put the 'eek' into geek and had beard-druff that snowed all over the tablecloth.'

Lynn sniggered and I scooped up the cushion, squeezing the life out of it before replacing it on the sofa.

'Yeah, that's the one. I saw this advert for dye that you can get for your hair down under. Can you believe it? Hair dye for your who-ha! They even had a shade called pubic pink! I couldn't stop laughing at the thought of it.'

'It's good to know that my dates with Dog Breath and Goatee Geek provide you with hours of entertainment.' I was tempted to hang up, there's only so much of Lynn's smugness I can take in one go, at this rate I'd be ripping the guts out of the cushion, and it didn't deserve to die.

'Julia, I'm trying to laugh with you, not at you. Look, I'm sorry if I've touched a nerve. How about I organise another get together with the gang from Chris's office and you come over too? A couple of new guys started in the sales team and I could find out if they're single.'

'Thanks, but no thanks. If they're single, it's probably for a bloody good reason. And anyway, I'm still trying to get over your last attempt at matchmaking me with Captain Caveman from Chris's rugby team.'

'Neil wasn't that bad. His sense of humour's just a bit old-fashioned,' said Lynn.

'Old-fashioned? That almost makes him sound endearing! Telling jokes like, "*Scientists have discovered a food that diminishes a woman's sex drive by 90%... It's called a wedding cake!*" It's hardly surprising his fiancée dumped him. And by the way, I can hear you giggling so you clearly do remember how awful he was!'

'Try and see the funny side! Although you're right, Neil was a total prat. Have you got anyone else lined up then?' asked Lynn.

'I'm meeting a guy called Peter this Saturday for dinner and his profile sounds very promising. But so did all the other possibles, *before* I met them in the flesh.'

'Keep an open mind, he can't be any worse!'

'True, unless he's a complete freak, it'll be an improvement. He's a senior partner in a firm of corporate lawyers, so at least he's got to have a brain - which puts him way ahead of the recent contenders. *And* he'll be earning big money!'

'What's the catch? Has he sent you a photo?' asked Lynn. I went over to my computer and clicked on his details, Pete's photo appeared on the screen.

'Yes, and after a few glasses of wine, he has a slight look of Mel Gibson!' I enlarged the photo; he could definitely be described as handsome.

'What long matted hair and the saltire flag painted on his face?' Lynn was the only one of us to find her joke amusing.

'Ha fucking ha! Anyway the main thing is that unlike Neil and the rest of the losers you've tried to pair me up with, he doesn't appear to have any baggage.'

Without exception, since I'd split up with my long-term partner Andrew, every man I'd dated had more baggage than Glasgow Airport's Reclaim Hall, it made it hard to believe that Peter would be any different.

'Well, I want to hear all about it when I see you. Are you coming over on Sunday?' asked Lynn. She must've been in the kitchen as it sounded as if she was unloading the dishwasher. Was it really too much to ask to have her full attention?

'I plan to, and if I'm not too hung-over after my night out, I'll take Holly for a walk again along the woodland trail.'

'Great. Are you free to babysit on a Friday night this month?' asked Lynn. The clanking of pots and pans was really getting on my nerves now.

'Sure, have you got something planned?'

'Not yet but I'd like to go out for dinner with Chris. I hardly see him these days. After the merger with the Edinburgh branch and his promotion, he's got big targets to meet. If he's not away on business, he's working late every night. It's crap.'

'When you're promoted, long hours come with the territory,' I shrugged.

'Don't get me wrong, the money's great - and we'll finally be able to take Holly to Florida this Easter. She doesn't know yet and I can't wait to tell her.'

'Tell me something I don't know!' said Lynn. 'I've got to listen to her constantly harp on that she's the *only* one of her pals that hasn't been yet. As if I believe that *everybody* in her class is going on a holiday costing £4,000 plus spending money!'

'Oh, c'mon Lynn, you can't blame her for using that old line that *everybody's* been. It always worked on Maggie when I tried it.' There was no denying that I could play our mum like a fiddle.

'You always managed to get your own way. Still do! Holly's picked up all your tricks... '

'Well good on her. Stop whinging, it's only money and it'll be worth it to see her face when she meets Minnie Mouse.'

'True, but I'd rather she saw more of her dad at nights.'

'She'll soon learn that you never get what you want without paying the price.'

CAROL

Dear Journal

Since my first entry, not much has happened. It was a really long weekend with Elaine away and I didn't speak to a single soul since I met Dan on Friday night. I was glad to get back to work.

It wasn't a normal Monday at the shop cos today is Valentine's Day. Isobel had a new banner made for the window, "Want your nookie? Get a bouquet!" and it definitely worked. We were run off our feet so the day went ten times faster than Saturday. After dinner my legs were still aching so I only took Jinky out to the swing park and back. It was too dreich and miserable to do his usual route. We'd have ended up absolutely drookit. Jinky looked well miffed when we were back after only 15 minutes, but the big sad eyes only ever worked on Ben. I honestly don't care. I really wasn't up for the same old chit chat from the same old faces. I did wonder if I would bump into Dan again cos I didn't see him with Roxy over the weekend. I'm not sure it would be a good idea to speak to him anyway. I mean, I thought he seemed a nice guy, and it was good to laugh again, but the next day I felt really guilty. It might sound stupid to some folk, but I like to think that Ben is always with me. On Friday it was as if I'd forgotten all about him, cos I was too busy joking around with Dan. My horoscope said, "*You now have Mars in your sign, boosting your ambitions and helping you overcome your fears and reservations.*" It can't be right every day.

I'm so glad that I never told mum about meeting Dan. She'd be disgusted to think I could be out laughing my head off when it's not even two years since Ben died. But I'm looking forward to telling Elaine when she gets back from her romantic weekend away.

The excitement of Valentine's Day wore off years ago for me, but I used to make an effort for Ben. I loved finding soppy novelty gifts like fluffy teddy bears and heart shaped chocolates for my boy. It was just a wee bit of fun between us. He knew the cards and presents were always from me, but he faked surprise every year. It was just like him not to hurt my feelings. He would've been 12 years old this May.

I got post today though, not a Valentine's card obviously, but a parcel. It was my new, (well, new to me) handbag off eBay. It was the highlight of the day.

Even the original tags [RRP £180] came with the bag! Elaine says I'm daft to buy bags and shoes I'll never use, that come from shops I'd never go into. But I got it for £89.50! She doesn't understand. It's pointless trying to explain. She says that just cos I live on the Woodlea estate, doesn't mean that I have to try and fit in with the rest of the snooty mums round here. They'll never see the bags or shoes anyway. I keep telling her that they're not all stuck up. Lynn, who lives a few doors up, is really friendly and her little girl Holly is a sweet wee bairn.

Steve and I only moved over to this side of town for Ben's sake, you know, nicer pals for him and a better school. It didn't matter about taking on a big mortgage. Ben loved this house, but I know I can't afford to bide here much longer now that I'm on my own. I won't miss the Farrells, though.

Just before the accident, Ben got a row from that old git, Eddie Farrell. The bairn had been playing with a new football his dad had given him and was kicking it against the fence. The banging must have annoyed Eddie cos he shouted over that Ben was to pack it in. Ben just ignored him. What harm was he doing? He was only a wee boy playing in his own back garden. When the ball went over the fence, I told Ben not to go asking for it back cos Eddie would eventually throw it over. But the next day, Ben came running into the kitchen with the ball. He was howling. The ball was slashed right through. I should've had words with Eddie, but how could I prove it was him? And we still had to live there, so I didn't want to have a big row over a ball. I bought Ben a new football but he said it wasn't as good as the one Steve had bought him. I didn't know the difference between Adidas and Nike.

When I told Elaine about the carry on she said it was time I grew a pair of bollocks. She's right. I wish I had a second chance; I'd batter Eddie Farrell's door down and stick the burst ball down his throat if I could. No one would ever get to stop my bairn's fun. I didn't know then that I'd never hear Ben kick a ball again. No matter how much I wish for it, I can't have my time with Ben back - and the days without him drag.

'It's been a quick week, eh?' Isobel shouted through to the back shop.

I wasn't just in another room; I was on a different planet. There were tubs of lilies to *condition*, florist-speak for stripping the leaves and trimming the stems, so it was easy to operate on autopilot. It's such a simple task, but that meeting with Dan had already proved to be a distraction. I'd spent hours daydreaming about a man I'd only met for minutes.

'Did you hear me?'

'Eh? Sorry Isobel, what did you say?' I asked.

'I was saying that the week's really flown in. Don't you think so?'

'Aye, ah cannae believe it's Friday already.'

'Up to anything nice this weekend?'

'Not really. Nothing special planned. Ah need tae take Jinky on a decent walk if the rain stops and clear up some leaves fae the garden.'

'Well that's something to look forward to, a bit of fresh air, a bit of fun away from here, eh?'

'Hmm, aye, ah suppose so.' The words stuck like a lump of dry toast in my throat and I kicked at stray leaf cuttings on the floor.

FRIDAY 18TH FEB 2011

Dear Journal

I felt like I was back at school again when I went to Wednesday's counselling session at the health clinic. I wouldn't have been surprised if Charlotte had given me a gold star for starting this journal AND for meeting someone new. It was so embarrassing when she gave me a big bear hug. She kept saying over and over that she was really proud that I was making definite progress. It was nice seeing her so pleased for me though.

She didn't actually say it, but I knew Charlotte was happy that I'm not using the Broken Cord forum now. She said it was good to see me meeting new people. Charlotte says it's the first time she feels I've put energy into helping myself, instead of always trying to help others.

Most nights I could be on the message boards for hours on end, chatting to other parents who've lost a bairn. I found the site when I was looking for a poem for Elaine to read out at Ben's funeral. It came up on a Google search cos it's named after a lovely poem called The Broken Cord.

The poem was smudged with Elaine's tears; I got it framed along with some of the flowers that I pressed from the enormous wreath Isobel made for Ben. His flowers were all done in green, white and gold, the colours of his beloved Glasgow Celtic football club, and Isobel made them into a huge 'B E N'. There were bright yellow chrysanthemums and gerberas, pure white roses and daisies and beautiful emerald green satin ribbons. The flowers faded, but the words of the poem will never lose their colour for me. I've always loved all kinds of poetry and now this is my favourite. It goes like this:

The Broken Cord

We little knew that morning that God
was going to call your name
In life we loved you dearly;
In death we do the same.

It broke our hearts to lose you;
You did not go alone;
For part of us went with you,
The day God called you home.

You left us peaceful memories,
Your love is still our guide;
And though we cannot see you,
You are always at our side.

Our family chain is broken,
And nothing seems the same;
but as God calls us, one by one,
The chain will link again.

Right after Ben died, the forum really helped get me through the tough times. I didn't feel I was alone or going mad and I could say things without being judged and worrying about what Elaine or mum would think. It was mostly me and a couple of other regulars online everyday saying the same things over and over. I can see now that it was dragging me down. Elaine said I needed to switch off the computer and speak to real people, not cyber friends.

I've stopped using the forum for good now anyway cos I found out that Steve is running a memorial football tournament for Broken Cord's funds. I don't want anything to do with the charity if he's involved with them too. I can't tell any of the other members why I'll not be posting any more messages. It's too hurtful and hard to explain my reasons, even to strangers.

Weekends are always hard to cope with, and I couldn't resist logging in to the forum for one last time. I scanned the calendar of events to see that Steve had indeed entered my world again. The gossip was true. There was Steve's name, as bold as ever, broadcasting his love for his dead son. I logged out, and clicked back to my eBay account. The charity was now one member down.

SUNDAY 20TH FEB 2011

The worst day of the week is Sunday. Everyone else will be taking their bairns out, or having family over for dinner, so I just sit tight and wait for Monday. Ever since I admitted that I dreaded the weekends. Elaine always pops round to visit. I showed her my mum's latest 'Helping Hand' package. I knew Elaine would find the 'gift' funny and have a laugh at mum's note to me:

I picked up this 'I love NYC' t-shirt at the church car boot sale last Sunday (although it's news to me that anyone in the village has ever been to New York and I must ask who it was when I'm at the bowling club tomorrow) I thought I could use the t-shirt for gardening but it's a bit snug. I thought you could use it as a night shirt.

Picturing my 68-year-old, size 22 mum squeezed into the size 18 t-shirt was enough to get me and Elaine giggling. Elaine said it was good to hear me laughing again so I suppose my mum's 'Helping Hand' packages aren't a complete waste of time.

We took Jinky out along the woodland trail. Elaine likes dogs about as much as me and that's not much! Getting a dog was to please Ben. Elaine said that the trip to the dog pound was literally a guilt trip. She was right. After me and Steve split up, I would've done anything to cheer Ben up - even rehoming a smelly border collie cross-breed. No wonder it had been a long term resident at the SSPCA centre. Jinky was what the staff called a "sticky" dog, meaning he was stuck with them at the Cardonald dog home. I'd have left him stuck there for good, but Ben was always too soft hearted and he was determined to give Jinky a second chance. He insisted on calling the mutt 'Jinky' after Jimmy Johnstone "Celtic's greatest ever player". I knew he was quoting his dad, and it hurt that he still idolised him, but I'd promised Ben that he could pick the dog's name. The woman at the centre warned me that Jinky was about two years old and I'd likely have him long after Ben had left home. She was right after all.

Elaine and I blethered as we traipsed along the woodland path. Dan was up ahead; he waved at us then bent to pat Jinky who'd bounded up to the bench. I was glad I'd worn a woolly scarf to hide the mottled rash that would be wrapping itself around my neck. I wore shyness like a favourite perfume.

'Just keep walking, dinnae dare give him eye contact,' warned Elaine, quickening her pace. 'He's obviously high on something. Trust me. Drugs are everywhere these days, even in Shawbriggs.'

I couldn't help but giggle and I waved back at Dan.

'Ah'm no kiddin'. These nutters can be dangerous. He could steal Jinky.'

'It'd be ma lucky day then!'

I waved again as we got nearer the bench.

'What're you playing at? Dinnae encourage him!' shrieked

Elaine.

'It's fine, relax. Ah know him.'

Dan stood up and curtseyed theatrically. Jinky cocked his leg against the bench to create a puddle of steaming pee. I looked on with shame; Jinky had no respect for my special seat.

'Good afternoon ladies, the pleasure's all mine.' Once again I couldn't fail to melt under the warmth of his charming smile. 'Just when I thought I'd never see you again, you appear before me with an equally lovely lady.'

'Ah cannae smell drink but ah told you he was high on something,' mumbled Elaine tugging Jinky away from Roxy who was sniffing round her rear end.

'Please excuse my dog, she has no manners. Allow me to introduce myself, I'm Dan.'

At the mention of good manners, I squirmed with embarrassment. Jinky was taking deep, satisfying sniffs at the crotch of Dan's jeans. Dan ignored Elaine's efforts to yank Jinky away and attempted a handshake. Elaine responded with a quick nod and a clipped 'Hiya.' I stepped forward to pat Roxy.

The wee dog coiled its body around my legs; nuzzling in to lap up any affection on offer.

'Roxy's obviously pleased to see you. So am I,' said Dan. His eyes locked on me and Elaine couldn't fail to notice my mouth grow from a newborn smile to a fully grown grin.

'Will we see you again soon?' asked Dan.

'Probably, ah walk Jinky most nights.' The heat radiating from my cheeks took the edge off the wintry chill, but it wasn't enough to thaw Elaine's icy stare as she rubbed her chubby hands together. I got the message.

'Ah suppose we should make a move. Elaine's going out with her hubby for dinner soon,' I said.

'What about you? Anybody waiting to take you out for

dinner?' asked Dan.

'Me? No, ah've nothing tae rush home for,' I replied.

'Well, if you fancy going out for a meal one night, or if you hear of a quiz night… Here, I'll give you my number.'

'We need tae get going,' said Elaine.

Dan reached into his jacket and scribbled eleven digits across an old receipt for petrol. It was a scrap of creased paper or a prized possession, depending on whose hand it was in.

'Bye for now then,' said Dan.

All the way home, I held the square of white paper so tightly that the ink transferred to my palm, leaving Dan's imprint on me.

'What the hell was aw that aboot? Going for a meal and being on a quiz team. Who is this joker?' asked Elaine.

'Ah've met him before. He's a nice guy.'

'And how would you know? You dinnae know him from Adam!'

'Elaine, ah'm no a stupid wee lassie anymore. Ah dinnae need you tae tell me who ah can talk tae,' I replied, trying hard to sound calmer than I sounded.

'Dinnae need me tae look out for you these days, eh?'

'Ah never said ah dinnae need you but we're no bairns anymore. Ah know who ah can trust.'

'Ah wish that was true,' muttered Elaine.

I kept my mouth shut as Elaine lumbered back along the path. She was wearing more layers than a Polar explorer and could pass as Frosty the Snowman's wife.

'C'mon, let's get back. It's cold enough tae freeze the balls off a pool table,' said Elaine.

'Do you like ma new jacket?' she asked.

'Aye, the colour suits you.'

'Thanks. Folk think that wearing white makes big girls look bigger, but that's not actually true.'

I'd stopped noticing how overweight Elaine was a long time ago. It had been years since Elaine had asked, *"Does my bum look big in this?"* There was no point, it did. It was big and Elaine knew it.

'Ah suppose it's like saying dogs shouldn't wear collars cos it makes them look furry,' I said.

'Exactly. Why should ah wear black tae try and make me look slimmer? Looking big and looking terrible is not the same thing. Ah mean you can paint a house black but it'll still be a house.'

Elaine claimed that her husband John preferred big women as there was, *"more cushion for yer pushin"*. Too much information. Considering John was more Pillsbury Doughboy than Playboy Adonis, him and Elaine naked together wasn't something I wanted to picture. Ever.

My best pal maintained that she was born with the fat gene and blamed her roly-poly mum, convincing herself that there was no use in fighting genetics. Her whole family had big bones - with a lot of meat on them. Elaine was literally my biggest and best friend.

After we finished at high school, Elaine had been desperate to leave Portcullen and escape to the city. Her big sister, Jill, had moved down to Glasgow years before. Elaine couldn't wait to follow and experience the glamorous Glasgow that Jill had bragged of on her trips home. She begged me, the home bird, to spread my wings and move to Glasgow too. Without a better idea or job prospects in my small fishing hometown, I agreed to fly the nest to do the same Business Admin course as Elaine at the City College.

On the first day of our course, we clung to each other like lifeboats in a raging storm. Elaine had levered her backside from the chair and bravely introduced us both to the rest of the class. This was greeted by sniggers at her broad "teuchter" accent and the squeals of her seat.

As quick as we could, we shook off our Doric accent and picked up a *Weegie* twang. The only thing that stayed the same was Elaine's weight. She hated college from the first day to the last, finally admitting that a desk job was not for her. I had come to Glasgow with my best pal and, over the years, I worked hard to make sure that our childhood friendship survived long after the college course, my marriage to Steve and Elaine being godmother to Ben.

When Ben was born, Elaine loved him as much, or even more than, any doting auntie ever could. There was no question that Elaine was a solid friend in every respect and became the loyal keeper of my secrets. Only Elaine knew about Steve and the true cause of Ben's accident.

MONDAY 21ST FEB 2011

Elaine's just phoned me and I don't know what her problem is. My horoscope was spot-on today. The stars said, "*If you didn't know who was on your side and who wasn't, you're about to find out*". Elaine's been nagging me for months to try and get out and meet people. But when I do meet someone she gives me a hard time about being careful and not getting involved with a man I don't know. How am I supposed to get to know Dan unless I go out with him? She was the one who'd suggested trying internet dating. I've had a look at a few sites but I've never actually signed up. It just didn't feel right. I tried to write a profile once but when the site asked me to fill in, "What do you have on your bedside table?" The answer, "A photo of my dead son Ben", was enough to tell me I wasn't ready to go ahead. I could've lied but that's just not me. If I'd told the truth, God only knows what kind of man that would have attracted. I don't want a new man anyway, not after Steve. I only want my son back. I was meant to be a mum; that's the only thing missing in my life. A new friend might be a good idea though, so I'd like to meet up with Dan. Just as friends, honest! A posh guy as funny and braw looking as Dan would never be interested in me.

At least Dan doesn't know about Ben. He's not making any judgement about me being ready to meet someone, unlike Elaine who always thinks she knows what's best for me. If I had used dating sites, then anyone I met online would be a stranger, until I actually talked to them face-to-face. It makes more sense to trust someone I've met in the flesh. At least this way, I've seen Dan's not a sleazy old perv. He might be someone I could have a laugh with. I could do with a wee bit of fun now and again.

Charlotte's been telling me for ages that until I put my grief down, I can't pick anything else up. Maybe it's okay to let go now and then? It's alright for Elaine; she goes home to John and has loads of other pals. I've told her umpteen times that I'm not looking for romance, just maybe a new friend to talk to. I've been through a lot but that doesn't make me completely stupid or insensitive. After Ben died, I was like a robot for months. Nothing that anyone says or does could upset me after the pain I've felt. But it still hurts when Elaine talks down to me. After what happened with Steve, you'd think that she would know that I'd never let a man have power over me again.

JULIA

EVERYONE AND EVERYTHING WAS PREGNANT. Mother bloody Nature was ready to give birth to another new season and all around me, greenery was budding, as ripe as my ovaries. A tree had sprouted a fresh shoot that threatened to poke me in the eye. I ripped it from its branch. The shortcut through the thicket was going to maim me and ruin my nubuck boots. Fashion and flora were as compatible as me and Dog Breath.

Holly's corkscrew curls sprang from the Barbie hair bobble that strained to keep the bunch of frizzy hair captive. As focused as a greyhound, Holly didn't pause until she had reached the invisible finish line where we stopped every other weekend to indulge in our forbidden treats.

Now perched on the wooden bench, Holly puffed out balmy breaths and waited impatiently for me to catch up. I wished I had her energy. Wearing woolly Ribena coloured tights, Holly's matchstick legs swayed back and forth. I wondered if she was singing quietly in time to a pop song or if swinging redundant limbs was simply a child's automatic response to loose dangly legs. But how would I know? I only got to study Holly for an hour or so each week.

'According to my watch, it's treat time,' I said.

'Yippidy do da!'

Nudging up to face Holly's button nose, I delved inside my Gucci backpack to fish out the sweets. Holly's cobalt eyes beamed up at me before diving inside the bulging bag of Pick 'n' Mix.

Lynn once accused me of treating Holly like a prized porcelain doll, as if she was covered in layers of fine gauzy tissue paper. I didn't disagree with Lynn, I had fun taking Holly 'out of the box'. Lynn claimed that once I grew tired of my treasured toy, it was easy for me to pack my living doll away again for another week. As the mother, Lynn was left to deal with Holly's tears and tantrums. I'm the auntie, what did she expect? Everyone, including Holly, knew the rules of the game.

'Hey missy! Stop right there. You know the routine, your wee peepers should be shut tight before a lucky dip in the magic bag, and no cheating this week!'

It was the same old repertoire where I used my 'teacher' tone and waggled my finger in front of Holly's face. Holly stuck out her tongue but it disappeared as fast as a lizard's.

'Hey, I saw that.'

It was one of our private rituals that had evolved over the last few years of our afternoons together. This routine was just as daft as the others, but we dutifully played our respective roles, week in, week out.

'And don't go eating all the flying saucers or Black Jacks before I get a chance. They're for me!'

'Okey-dokey!'

I only ever ate Holly's least favourite sweets. I had to watch my figure; sugar was sinful.

I savoured our candy-coated special moments. But, much like any calorie-laden treat, the satisfaction from the sugary taste was short-lived. Wasn't that what a loving relationship was all about?

To escape into a secret world of games and rules that suited both our needs? It was over a year since I'd split up with Andrew and, unlike Holly who accepted who was in charge, he didn't want to play by my rules.

I caught up with Holly at our usual stop-off at the blackened bench. Wiping the seat with my glove, I settled down next to Holly to enjoy the last of the watery winter sun. Today we had more to watch than birds, a guy was walking his terrier. Pausing to rest wasn't an option for the dog, it tugged violently on its leash and lurched forward. The owner bent to unclip the leash; releasing the dog and the pent up oomph pumping inside its taut muscles.

The Jack Russell was quick to bark, and even quicker to chase. Off it shot like a bullet, speeding towards an unseen target that only it could sense. We sat in silence, chewing sweets and enjoying the antics of the excited dog.

The guy stood beside the bench, waiting for his dog to reappear. Holly had her nose in the bag of goodies and I wrapped my arm around her.

'Hello there,' he said.

Holly's head lifted as the guy nodded towards the sweetie bag. 'I can see you're enjoying that! It's years since I've seen a sherbet Dip Dab. I absolutely loved them when I was a wee boy.'

The guy's face lit up at the sight of Holly licking the tangy yellow sherbet off the strawberry flavoured lolly. I cuddled her tighter.

'Me too,' I agreed and held his gaze.

Holly tugged at my sleeve and pulled me closer, her eyes bulged in horror. 'You always say that I've never to speak to strangers!' she hissed in a stage whisper.

The guy smiled at Holly. 'You're quite right and a very smart girl. I'm sorry; I should have introduced myself properly.' He extended his huge right hand towards me. 'My name's Daniel Saunders, but friends call me Dan.'

My pale face took on what the girls on the makeup counter at Fraser's would describe as a "hot pink hue". This guy wasn't a weirdo who eyed up little girls. Jumping to conclusions was a favourite exercise of mine, and one I had to try to control.

'Pleased to meet you Dan, my name's Julia, and this,' I tugged gently on her ponytail, 'is Holly.'

'I'm new to the area but hopefully I won't be a stranger for long.'

Holly watched our prolonged handshake in between dipping into her sherbet. The dog decided it wanted a lick at the lolly too.

'What's your dog's name?' asked Holly.

'Her name's Roxy. Hey cheeky,' Dan swiped playfully at the little terrier, 'leave Holly's sweets alone.'

It sensed a better offer and darted off after a whiff of rabbit. 'Watch that bag or she'll be back to try and steal your sherbet,' warned Dan.

'She'd better not, Dib Dabs are my favourite too,' I said.

'You don't look old enough to be reminiscing,' commented our bench-mate.

'Thanks, I'm flattered, but it doesn't look like I'll get the chance to relive my youth today. I bet that this little madam has beaten me to it.'

'Nope, you're wrong, there's one more left. It was hiding at the bottom of the bag. Would you like it?' said Holly, as she offered Dan the little sachet.

'That's really kind of you but I'll let your mummy have the last one.'

Holly let out a high-pitched giggle, 'She's not my *mum*, she's my auntie!'

As if Roxy's paws were fitted with springs, she bounded in

and out of the long grasses in a tussle with the undergrowth. Holly giggled as Roxy ran rings round an invisible circuit, back towards her master.

'Well, here's *my* wee girl back now so I'll leave you two in peace to enjoy your feast. But before I go, could I please borrow your paper bag Holly?'

'Why?' Holly's puzzled expression searched my face for the answer. I shrugged my shoulders; I was as baffled as she was.

'Well, just in case your Auntie Julia fancies meeting up, she'll need my phone number.'

'Eh, well, go on Angel Face, give Dan the bag,' I instructed. Surely this was as harmless as swapping email addresses on dating sites.

Holly still looked confused until Dan gently prized the paper bag from her grasp and scribbled eleven digits inside a huge letter 'D'.

'And hey, don't go throwing that bag away! It's special now. Will you remember to give it to your Auntie Julia when you've finished your sweets?'

Holly's head rocked back and forth like a nodding dog on a car's parcel shelf.

'Good girl. Bye Holly. Bye Auntie Julia. Call me if you want to go for a coffee… or maybe even something stronger?' Strolling along the woodland pathway, he gave us a fleeting backward wave.

It was time we headed off too, I sighed, loudly.

'What's up?' asked Holly, running her sweetie-stained tongue up and down the illicit lolly.

'Oh, nothing.'

How could I possibly begin to describe my feelings to a seven-year-old? There was a limit to how much we could share. I looked forward to spending time with Holly, our woodland walks, girly shopping sprees, trips to the cinema and cafés. Up until now, our days out had always been enough for me. But not anymore. I was more certain than ever, that despite what Lynn believed, I grudged handing Holly back after a couple of hours of borrowed time.

Like one of my Max Mara dresses, I wore the 'trendy auntie' look perfectly, it suited me. But, the more I spent time with Holly, the more I wondered if I could convincingly pull off a new look? Could I be seen as a mum, not just an auntie? Would the cut of the cloth fit and feel good enough to match the chic persona I was known for? Sure my lifestyle would have to become more high street than high fashion but for the first time, I was seriously prepared to consider substance over style.

And of course my twenty-a-day smoking habit would be a complete no-no. Well, maybe only when the baby was in the room. The flat might have to go in favour of something without a waterfront balcony. That didn't automatically mean moving to somewhere like the Woodlea estate though. I could enjoy a Marlboro Light at the back door instead of the sofa. I could find a ground floor flat in the West End and still live in a classy area. If there's a will, there's a way. There was no question that I'd have to trade Cristal for Cava; it was about time I listened to my screaming overdraft anyway. Deep down, I knew that the days of leading a champagne lifestyle would be over. Hard choices - but they would be worth making. Wouldn't they?

It was only the gagging sound of Holly choking on her lollipop that snapped me out of my daydream. With a few sharp slaps to Holly's back and a reassuring cuddle, I was able to avoid a visit to A&E.

A fistful of fizzy cola bottles and a lollipop was enough to placate Holly. Her jaws got busy and all that was left of her chewy Drumstick lolly was a soggy white stick. Holly simulated a lengthy draw on it; make believe smoking had always been cool, no matter the generation. She exhaled her candy-scented breath into a satisfying smoke-like cloud. The thin February air was perfect to pretend to be Auntie Julia. Her showpiece was wasted on her audience of one. I refused to acknowledge Holly's portrayal of adulthood, best just to ignore it. There was no need to discuss smoking, cigarettes, lung cancer or anything else deemed unsavoury by Lynn or my mum Maggie. Subjects such as illness, disease or even death were not on my agenda. Mum and granny could cover the grim topics with Holly. My time as auntie was supposed to be all fun and no fear. I was not going to be swayed from the programme, not until Holly performed her next trick.

'What's a P.A.N.K.?' asked Holly, reaching up to brush back the highlighted lengths of my hair. Her clammy whisper tickled my ear.

'Why are you whispering? There's no one around.' Without realising, I had automatically used a hushed tone in response.

'Dunno.' Holly was determined not to let it go, 'Is P.A.N.K. a naughty word?'

'I've really no idea. Why, where'd you hear it?' I asked.

'Mum called you a P.A.N.K. when she was talking to granny on the phone this morning, when she was telling her that you were taking me out this afternoon.'

'*Really*? What exactly did she say? Can you remember?' I couldn't hide my intrigue at the discussion aired behind my back.

'Eh, I'm not sure but I think it was something like, "it's great that she gives me a break but even a P.A.N.K. like Julia deserves a day off at the weekend".'

'Hmm, I think we'll head back to the car. The sun's gone now and it's starting to get chilly. C'mon, save the rest of the sweets for after your dinner or your mum'll shoot me.'

We walked hand in hand back to *Gary*, my beloved silver Mini Cooper. I had tried to explain the name to Holly more than once. Holly didn't grasp that Gary Cooper had been a legendry actor, famous for his role in the western *High Noon*. I'd told her that the film was Grandpa Jack's all-time favourite and Gary Cooper was as iconic as my little silver car. But Holly had never known Grandpa Jack or Gary Cooper.

'Can I have one more flying saucer, pleeeease Auntie Julia…?'

'Okay, but that's your absolute limit, you greedy little piglet. Now hide your wee trotters and put your gloves back on.'

Half an hour later, back at her own house, Holly peeled off her winter coat, hat, and gloves and joined her mum in the kitchen.

'I don't want soup.'

'It's home-made,' said Lynn

'I don't care. I'm not hungry!'

'But you must be starving by now…'

A swift finger to my lips was enough to silence my niece's moans. Within minutes, much to Holly's disappointment, we were both sipping the steaming parsnip soup that Lynn ladled into rustic mugs for us.

'You don't always have to make something from scratch every time I visit,' I said.

'It's no bother. I know you hardly ever buy fresh food.'

There was no need for a dig at me. A coffee and a fag was all the nourishment I required during daylight hours. Lynn swanned around her kitchen; her ponytail like a pendulum. I knew better than most that regular sessions of Botox don't come cheap. Was that why Lynn tied her hair back as tight as possible? There was no sign of knitted brows on Lynn's forehead, but maybe that had more to do with her deep sense of smugness than the tightness of her hair band.

Lynn's version of the roles and responsibilities of a stay-at-home mum included making freshly cooked food as a daily task – organic, of course. She acted more like a post-war female who could rustle up a casserole from the recipe pages of her *Woman's Weekly* whilst darning a woollen sock. Where was the progress?

It really bugged me when Lynn described herself as a "full-time mum". She talked as if any woman who had a child AND a job was only a part-time mother, whose love and care stopped whenever they entered the workplace. It was utter bollocks. My career would always be part of my identity and, if I had a child, I wouldn't be prepared to lose that sense of self along with my placenta. There was no need for 'mummy' to be your only job title. My timesheet wouldn't only account for the out-of-office hours, my shift as mummy wouldn't stop when I sat at my desk. I'd be on duty 24/7.

I could make up the terms and conditions of the job to suit myself. Lynn's stay-at-home uniform only varied in colour and texture, according to whatever the Boden catalogue suggested in the '*Outfit Maker*'. Whilst I accepted compromises would have to be made, I made a mental note that if I ever experienced motherhood it didn't require me to give up my career, own a wardrobe full of Boden clothing or rustle up homemade soup within the hour. And under no circumstances would I *ever* wear a velvet Alice band.

'So tell me little sis, what's a P.A.N.K.?' I asked.

My sister raised an eyebrow and glared at Holly.

'It sounds like someone's been telling tales and I can guess who that would be. Holly can hear the grass grow!' Lynn spun round quickly to catch a glimpse of her daughter's eyes grow as large as her soup bowl.

'Well?' I persisted, with my arms folded across my chest and my head cocked to one side.

Lynn looked sheepish and hesitated, 'Okay If you honestly don't know, P.A.N.K stands for someone like you - a Professional Auntie with No Kids.'

'Oh really? So you think you're clever giving me a label?'

'Relax, it's just a bit of fun. It's no big deal.'

'Fun? No big deal eh? You're such a smart arse at times. Have you ever asked yourself if it's a label I'm happy with?'

Holly was hunched over the table, busy smoothing out the creases of the sweetie bag to hand back to me.

'Oooh, you said a naughty word Auntie Julia!'

'You're right Holly, arse is a bad word. Sorry,' I replied.

'And you were naughty at the park.' I shot daggers at Holly but the wee besom continued. 'You're not supposed to speak to a strange man,' giggled Holly, waggling her finger at me, this time she played the teacher.

'Eh? What's this about a strange man?' asked Lynn.

Holly tried sneaking the sweetie bag under the table as if we were swapping notes at school. Unfortunately, Lynn's mischief radar was as highly tuned as a teacher's.

'What are you up to Holly?' Lynn uncurled Holly's fingers from her vice-like grip. A sweaty palm, blotched with blue ink, revealed the mobile number scrawled across the crumpled bag.

'And Dan thought Auntie Julia was my mum!' Holly still found this highly amusing.

'Who is this Dan, would I know him?'

'Relax Lynn, it was just a guy walking his dog who stopped to pass the time of day with us.'

'He gave Auntie Julia his phone number!' squealed Holly.

Behind Lynn's back, I seized the chance to do a quick mime of me smoking, then I placed one finger across my lips and silently mouthed, 'Sssh!!!!' Holly needed no further reminder that our ULTIMATE secret better not slip from her lips. Much to my relief, Holly gave me the thumbs up and a gap-toothed smile. With years of practice, Holly was well versed in her promise never to reveal to her mum or granny that I still smoked. Even more scandalous would be to tell them that it sometimes happened in the presence of the golden child.

'If you want to chat up men, don't do it when you're with Holly. At least she knows not to talk to strangers. Maybe it's just as well you're the auntie and *not* the mum,' snapped Lynn.

Silence hung over us like grimy clouds, heavy with an unshed downpour. Head in her bowl to slurp the dregs of her soup, Holly was too busy to feel the air turn stormy. I jumped off the oak stool at the breakfast bar and scooped up my backpack.

'Where are you going?' asked Holly,' I thought you were going to paint my nails?'

'Sorry babes, I need to go. It's like your mum said, even professional aunties need time to themselves. See you next week. I promise.'

'Okay, but remember, you can't break a promise!' replied an indignant Holly.

'And why don't you go and get your room tidied like you promised *me*?' added Lynn, shoving Holly in the direction of the door, before daring to face me. 'Look, I'm sorry, there's no need to go, mum's popping over soon. Wait a while, she'll want to catch up and you haven't even told me about your date with Peter,' pleaded Lynn.

'I'm seeing her on Wednesday for lunch. Thanks for the home-made soup.'

'Julia hang on...' Lynn stretched her arms out to give me a farewell embrace as normal. I kept moving. An abrupt exit was the only response Lynn was going to get from me.

Spotting Holly take a sneaky peek over the banister, I strode into the hall. For the benefit of my niece, I went from sandpaper to silk and whispered gently, 'Bye Angel Face' as I reached up to plant a kiss on her forehead.

'Bye Auntie Julia!'

I could feel a gurgling cauldron of progesterone bubbling up inside me; fizzing and spitting. I glimpsed into the hall mirror to check my makeup and hair.

It's much easier to keep the tears from starting than it is to stop them after they begin to fall. I held my eyes open wide: biting my tongue and trying not to blink was a tried and tested trick. It didn't work this time. Expensive water resistant mascara is worth every penny.

Reversing *Gary* out of the drive, I caught sight of Holly, waving from her bedroom window. Would she be able to see me dabbing my eyes? Holly wasn't the only spectator. I sped through the estate but had to stop at the junction at the end of the street. Would Lynn's neighbour Carol notice my shoulder-heaving sobs as she crossed the road with her mongrel? I couldn't give a rat's arse; I had too many other things on my mind.

The sense of emptiness at not having my own child had crept up on me over a number of years. It felt as if I'd been lowering myself into a steaming hot bath very, very slowly and the effect of finally lying in it, right up to my chin, wasn't nearly as shocking as if I'd just jumped straight in.

It had taken months to fully express my desire for a baby when I was living with Andrew; hints hadn't been enough. The realisation of what was missing in my life hadn't happened all at once, remarks about motherhood weren't new or unusual. I'd heard it all before, from my mum, Lynn, Rachel at the *Gazette* and other ex-colleagues, and even from my best friend Kirsty. And yet none of them spotted the cracks in the not-the-maternal-type mask I'd worn for years.

When I'd first met Andrew, the chemistry was so powerful

that I could feel his energy without even touching him. Over time that initial fizz had petered out; particularly when I mentioned taking our relationship to "the next stage". I realised that this innocuous phrase from me, was a veiled threat for him. It had the power to turn him from a hot love to a cold companion.

For the three years Andrew and I had been a couple, he'd always made me agree to hold back the dam of pressure to produce. But he was gone - the dam had burst its banks - and there was no chance of curbing my emotions now.

Andrew had been certain that the time wasn't right. After I left the *Gazette* to go freelance, I thought it was ideal as I had more flexibility. A teeny mention here, a tiny suggestion there, of how a baby could complete our world fell on Andrew's cloth ears.

'Can we discuss this some other time.'

'*Now's* the right time.'

'I don't want to discuss it.'

'Why won't you just hear me out?'

'We can't afford it.'

'We can make it work!'

Polar opposites.

'I'm not ready yet!'

'No one's ever ready to be a parent.'

'It's not up for debate.'

'Why can't we talk it through?'

'Just leave it will you!'

Unconsciously, my desire had crossed the point of no return and a subtle, quietly played out battle for a baby had begun.

Andrew's retaliation was as smooth as glass, but it also had a serrated edge that could cut me deep. Sometimes I wondered if his blood was pumped by a generator, not a heart. At dinner parties, his tactics were blatantly obvious, but only to me. He would try to goad me into submission with shrewd references to our focus on career goals and how we loved the freedom to travel the world.

He seemed endlessly amused by making *tick-tock* noises in my ear whenever anyone mentioned starting a family, as if my biological clock was the size of a giant wristwatch. It had been a long running joke that, on the surface, I played along with. It had taken me a while to finally admit the truth and tell him that the *tick-tock* of my body clock was much louder than he imagined. It was a screaming siren that climaxed in a huge row when he picked me up one night at Glasgow Airport.

'What a fucker of a day that was,' I said, flopping into the passenger seat.

'Yeah, that meeting sounded hellish. What a bummer having to get a later flight. You must be knackered.'

'I'm dead on my feet, but I enjoyed the flight back.'

'Am I hearing right? Are you telling me you actually enjoyed a Ryanair flight?'

'Hey, don't get ideas that I'll settle for budget travel this summer! I'd rather walk than fly with them again.'

'So what made the flight bearable?'

'I helped a woman get her baby girl to sleep.'

'Christ almighty. I really am hearing voices! Have I picked up Mother Teresa by accident?'

On the flight back to Glasgow, I'd watched a woman in her early twenties, detaching a bawling baby girl from her hip. I soon found out that I was stuck sitting next to the squirming babe-in-arms. With minutes until take off, the infant was still screaming like a banshee. Stuck in the window seat, I texted Andrew that the flight was about to take-off and, after a crap day, the next fifty minutes were likely to be torture.

Once the seatbelt sign was switched off, the baby's mother tapped me on the shoulder.

'Is there any chance you could hold my wee one for a minute. I'm desperate for the loo.'

'Eh, okay. Sure.'

'Great. I'll only be a minute.'

'Yeah, fine.'

'Don't look so worried. I can't go far!'

Much to my surprise, firm rhythmic pats on the baby's back and a verse of *Hush, Little Baby* worked. The tears stopped and I gently wiped the girl's downy cheeks. By the time the mum had returned, the baby was sleeping soundly on my damp shoulder, snuffling like a piglet on a truffle farm.

'Wow! Thanks. I could tell you're a mum who knows what she's doing,' said the woman.

'Eh, no problem,' I replied, with a smile as wide as a letter box.

For a split second, I'd been filled with a real sense of pride, before I remembered that I wasn't a mum at all. When I landed, I couldn't wait to share my maternal success story with Andrew.

'I'm a natural - isn't that great!' I boasted.

'Whatever makes you happy...?' Andrew replied, reaching across to turn on Radio Clyde's football phone-in show. I swiped at his hand and jabbed the button to switch off the radio.

'Don't patronise me Andrew. I'm NOT happy just holding a stranger's baby! If you don't understand, then what's the point in us staying together?'

I slid out a Marlboro from my packet and let out a long, slow sigh. *Stay calm,* I told myself.

'Can't you wait? You know I don't like you smoking in my car.'

My silver lighter snapped open, but the flame was quickly extinguished before I tossed it back into my handbag. It was too late to retain my composure; even a cigarette's calming power wouldn't work this time.

'No. I can't wait. And yes, I know what *you* want. But it's not all about you! What about what *I* want?'

Instead, I slowly squashed the cigarette between my fingers and let the crumbly remnants sprinkle all over the floor of his precious sports car.

He didn't understand. He would never understand. I was back home in Glasgow, with Andrew next to me, but the landscape had shifted. The realisation meant that someone, or something, had to change. Battle weary, I had to accept that there was no point waiting to see if Andrew would develop paternal feelings. I had invested a lot of time and energy in Andrew; I truly loved him! My business brain told me that I had to speculate to accumulate. Giving him my love was a massive outlay. I really wanted him to be THE ONE. But, a baby was a deal breaker. He hadn't paid out the dividend that was now rightfully mine. An ultimatum was my only option.

'I want a baby to be part of our future Andrew.'

There was no going back. We both knew that.

'That means we don't have a future.'

Andrew dropped me at the entrance to our flat and drove off to stay at his mate's house. All I was left with was a baby sick stain on my suit jacket and an ache in the pit of my womb.

CAROL

I PINNED DAN'S TATTY PETROL RECEIPT to my kitchen memo board. It was surrounded by money off coupons, last year's Tenerife postcard from Elaine, a purse-sized keepsake card 'One step at a time-this is enough' – that Charlotte had given me, along with a post-it with scribbled details of a local yoga class and umpteen snaps of Ben.

Over the last four days, I'd memorised the smudged digits of Dan's mobile number. But I didn't have the guts to make the call; I wished I'd given him my number too. What if he didn't remember me?

What if he didn't actually expect me to ring?

What if he had changed his mind and didn't want to meet up?

I used to get frustrated by Ben's relentless 'what if…' scenarios, day and night, week in, week out.

'What if Jinky got run over, would we get another dog?'

'What if you won the lottery, would we still stay in Shawbriggs?'

'What if you could afford a car, what kind would you buy?'

I'd told him not to waste time wondering about things that might never happen. Now I understood how annoyed Ben must have felt; full to the brim with all those unanswered questions.

It was my turn for the *'what ifs'* to keep me awake at night, and they all revolved around eleven scrawled numbers. There was no comfort from my horoscope either. I rarely questioned Mystic Meg's advice, but it would be daft to ignore *The Sun's* forecast: *"You are likely to be making some impulsive decisions that will turn your life around".* I felt extremely brave one minute, then completely terrified the next.

WEDNESDAY 23RD FEB 2011

Dear Journal

I'm still waiting on a purple patent Fendi tote bag to arrive, but instead I got mum's latest 'Helping Hand' package in the post. It's an ironing board cover with a muscle man's semi-naked torso, "so you won't get 'bored' HA HA HA when you look at the board". I've no idea where she could've bought this in Portcullen and the thought of it being second-hand is disgusting. The cover wasn't in a wrapper, so there's a high chance that someone else has already drooled over the model's six pack. I bet it wasn't just the iron that got steamed up. It gives me the dry boak just thinking about it.

That wasn't the only weird mail, I also got two travel brochures, both addressed to me! I definitely didn't request any; I mean who am I going to go on holiday with? It's years since I've been abroad and that was long before I moved to the Woodlea estate. A while ago, Elaine did say that her and some girls from work were going to start saving for a Hen weekend abroad and I could join them. Would they REALLY want me to go with them? I can only guess that Elaine's filled in my name and address cos she's still nagging me to think about getting away. "It's time," she says, like she's been talking to Charlotte behind my back. Who decides when the time is right to do ordinary things like other ordinary people?

Mind you, I couldn't help flick through the brochures; everyone likes to dream.

But I can't even find the courage to call Dan to meet him for a coffee or a meal, never mind a holiday with women I don't even know. I really wish I had the confidence to go on a Hen weekend, but I don't, not yet anyway. "Small steps" is what Charlotte keeps saying, and a holiday right now would be too big a leap. What's really holding me back is another promise I'd made to Ben, to take him on a foreign holiday, somewhere nice and warm. He loved the sun, but I could never face taking him abroad as a toddler. It seemed so much hassle. Then we moved into the new house in Woodlea and we were overstretched with the cost of the move and decorating. Between that, and separating from Steve, it was always a case of "definitely next year", except that next year never came. Another broken promise, so I really can't face going without him now.

I clicked the phone safely back on the cradle. It was cordless, but that didn't mean it could run away with itself and start making spontaneous calls to new numbers. Not a chance, out of the question, no way José. This phone had all the numbers it would ever need programmed into it already.

Mum was speed dial 1 and Elaine was speed dial 2.

No, this phone wasn't the reckless type. It didn't go dialling unknown names or numbers, unless there was a very good reason.

I was lonely. Surely that was reason enough to call Dan? Why should I be ashamed to admit it? It wasn't an embarrassing disease.

The horoscope was wrong about me being impulsive. Apart from my eBay bids, I wasn't known for spontaneity. It took me three whole days before I decided to call Dan.

Going… going… one more gulp and my hefty glass of wine was gone. With the phone handset in one hand, and the last balloon glass of Asda Frascati refilled within reach, I was ready. Dan answered immediately, and took me by surprise, as if the phone had called him without any involvement from me at all. I'd half hoped he wouldn't answer. Just dialling the number would be enough to make Charlotte proud.

'Is that Dan?' I asked.

'It is indeed.'

'It's Carol. Dae you remember me? Ah met you oot walking, with Jinky, ma dog? And then with ma pal?' My chest was heart-attack tight.

'Of course, I remember you - Carol, the font of all knowledge and my ideal quiz partner.'

He did sound pleased to hear from me and there had been no need to explain who I was. All I had to do now was keep reminding myself to breathe. I was on the phone to Dan; not waiting for the next body blow from Steve.

'Ah'm no so sure ah'd be any use in a pub quiz.'

'No problem. How about we meet up for a meal instead?'

He still wanted to meet up with me; I remembered one of the words from a poster on Charlotte's wall - *fear exceeds reality*.

'If you like curries, the Spice Gourmet on the High Street's supposed tae be nice,' I said, gripping the phone tighter still.

'What man doesn't like a curry? Sounds good to me. Although I bet you've already got plans for the weekend?'

'It's actually ma birthday on Saturday but ah've got nothing planned.'

White lies don't count - and this was only half a white lie. Going to the cinema with Elaine was in truth, nothing special.

'Well, if you don't mind spending your birthday with me, then that would be great,' said Dan.

This was the easy bit. Much harder would be telling Elaine that, for the first time ever, I had a better offer.

In a heartbeat, I agreed to meet Dan.

By the time I came off the phone, we'd arranged to meet on Saturday at seven. I sunk into the sofa, absolutely drained and realised that all those endless *what if* scenarios had been a complete waste of energy.

Flattening out Dan's wrinkled scrap of paper, I tapped a new number into my phone's contact list. I circled Saturday on the calendar I got with a Chinese takeaway; for once I wasn't dreading the weekend's arrival.

Dan was already at the Indian restaurant when I arrived, even though I was ten minutes early. He was wearing a Scotland rugby top and jeans and I was chuffed that I'd worn a straw coloured lamb's wool jumper and jeans too. His scuffed Timberland boots stuck out from underneath the table. Thank God, that I'd swapped the pair of Roberto Cavalli cowboy boots I got on eBay for the Clarks ankle boots that I wore to work. It was best that my expensive shoes and handbags remained as a secret stash at home.

Getting ready had been exhausting; raking out old favourites and rummaging for simple accessories. My magazines advised that *less is more*, so I'd returned the abstract print top to the back of my wardrobe and concentrated on trying to tame my hair instead. But with Dan already in the restaurant, I couldn't slip into the ladies' toilets to try to resurrect my hairdo. Back at home, my straightening irons had made my hair as sleek as a seal. That was half an hour ago. After the rain shower, my hair was like tufts of loft insulation. Why hadn't I put my umbrella back in my bag after it had dried off in the hall? It wasn't as if it was hard to miss. Mum's last birthday gift was a cow print brolly. The shop girl had convinced my mum that it was not only practical and funky, but that it would also make me smile. Practical? Yes, if I remembered to put it in my bag. Funky? It was as funky as a teabag. Capable of making me smile? Anyone with a brain needs more than a novelty umbrella to raise a smile.

It was too late; Dan had seen me and my frizzy hair. But did that matter? My hair hadn't been straightened when he'd seen me on the woodland trail. Au naturale was my usual day-to-day look. With a token smoothing down of my damp bob, I waved back at Dan. He was sitting at a table tucked into a large alcove at the very back of the restaurant.

Dan stood up and greeted me with a warm smile. *I deserve to be happy. I deserve to be happy.* I repeated the affirmation Charlotte had asked me to memorise. I didn't really believe that it would work, but I managed to say it nine times before I reached Dan. Nine - my lucky number and Ben's birthday.

I made a move to join Dan, but Rahul, the head waiter, recognised me and weaved in and out of tables to welcome me with open arms.

'Carol, how lovely to see you my darling. At last you've come to enjoy our exquisite Indian cuisine. I am honoured.'

It had been my job to create a weekly floral arrangement for the Spice Gourmet for the last few years. Every Thursday, when Rahul hobbled in to the Daisy Chain to settle his bill, he called through to the back shop to gently nag me to sample their menu.

By the time I was escorted to Dan's table, I felt like a local celebrity the way Rahul was fussing over me, asking if the table was to my liking. It was all too much. Between Rahul's very public concern for my comfort and Dan's intent gaze, I was in a right tizzy.

There was a family at the table right next to Dan. The foursome included a boisterous baby, squealing and straining for freedom as he grabbed at the mother's laminated dessert menu. Meanwhile, the father was busy chastising a cheeky toddler who was yelling back at him like a football hooligan of the future.

'Rahul, is there any chance of moving us tae a quieter table, please?' I whispered.

'But of course, follow me,' said Rahul as he gave me a nudge and a playful wink in Dan's direction. I would have rather swallowed razor blades than a curry if I could've avoided any more embarrassment.

Once Rahul had relocated us to a more discreet table, I noticed Dan was frowning as he glanced back at the noisy family group.

'Don't you like children?' he asked.

This wasn't the opening line that I'd prepared for. None of the imaginary conversations that I'd practised over and over, featured a direct query about liking bairns - especially before the pakora. This line of questioning wasn't on the menu at all.

I decided it was a now or never answer. Tell him about Ben - and I might never see him again. Or tell him about Ben - and he might just understand. It was too big a part of me to bury; it would always resurface eventually. The question was not *what* to tell him, but *how much*? Before I could respond, Rahul reappeared with the menus, pressing me to try the Murgh Makhani.

'Knock, knock,' asked Rahul, his moustache twitched like a fuzzy grey caterpillar.

I played along obligingly.

'Who's there?'

'Curry,' replied Rahul, fiddling with his black bow tie.

'Curry who?'

'Curry me home, I've eaten too much Murgh Makhani!' Rahul slapped his leg, the sheen from his worn out black trousers gave his thigh a polish that was almost as shiny as his bald head. The other diners stared across at the waiter creased with laughter. No one but Rahul seemed to find his joke funny at all. Feeling his pain at the awkwardness of the moment, I interrupted, 'Rahul, you never telt me entertainment was included with the meal. Ah'd nae idea you were a comedian on the side.'

'And there was me thinking I had a monopoly on corny jokes to make you laugh. Looks like I've got competition,' added Dan, smiling at me.

Rahul took the hint and shuffled off with our food order.

'By the way, I love what you're wearing tonight,' said Dan.

'What, you're kiddin'? This is just an auld thing ah dug out of ma wardrobe,' I beamed, 'and ma hair is a total mess!'

SATURDAY 26TH FEB 2011

Dear Journal

It was the best night out I've had in years. Dan is so funny. After Rahul's rubbish joke, Dan made up for it with his 'Top Ten Curry Songs' that he just made up on the spot. He's so quick-witted. There was Poppadum Preach by Madonna, Korma Chameleon, Tikka Chance On Me, You Can't Curry Love and my favourite: It's Bhuna Hard Day's Night! I laughed so hard, I spat out a bit of naan on to his plate. I was mortified but he just picked it up and ate it! He is so laid back and says that's what he likes about me, that I'm not one of those high maintenance women that runs off to touch up their makeup every five minutes. I'm glad I never wore my designer boots or bothered taking my Mulberry satchel. I doubt whether Dan would know Mulberry from Matalan, but it might have given him the wrong impression about me.

By the end of the night, he knew the real me anyway. He wanted to know all about me and I told him about Portcullen, mum, Elaine and the Daisy Chain. I even ended up telling him about being divorced and Ben dying. He didn't push me for any details, he just listened to as a much as I wanted to tell him. You can tell that he's very tactful, not like some folk. It was a bit risky sharing so much personal stuff but thankfully he didn't go to the loo and not come back.

After telling him about Ben he appreciated why I didn't want to sit next to the bairn in the high chair. He even guessed that I call the black bench at the woodland trail my *Angel's Bench* cos it's where I like to go and think about Ben. I was right to think that he would understand. Dan said it must feel like I've had to learn to live without a limb; that although I was coping, there would always be something missing. He worked out that although I'm someone's daughter, friend, employee, neighbour, the only role I really want back is 'mum' to make me feel whole once more.

Dan said that even if I hadn't told him that it was my birthday today, he'd have guessed that I was Pisces cos it was obvious to him that I have a gentle nature. I was really impressed that he knew all about star signs. He said that I'm a typical Piscean cos I'm friendly, kind, compassionate and sensitive to the feelings of those around me. It's the nicest thing I can remember anyone ever saying to me and one of the best birthdays I've ever had. I think repeating "I deserve to be happy" has worked for me after all. And the best bit of the night was that he got Rahul to bring out a wee cake with a candle on it. It was just a slice of Black Forest gateau (and it wasn't even defrosted properly cos I could taste ice crystals inside) but I still loved it. And Dan knew without me saying a word that I wouldn't want Rahul and the other waiters to sing Happy Birthday, he told Rahul that the celebration was private.

I didn't find out much about him except that he works from home as "a computer geek" and that he's forty-four and has never been married. I wanted to know more, but he seemed happier to listen than do the talking. He said that this was my special night so it should all be about me. Dan was absolutely brilliant to talk to and it was better than all the sessions I've ever had with Charlotte or spending the night on the forum. He thinks that I shouldn't give up on the hope of being a mum again, although Charlotte's never suggested that as a possibility. Dan said it's obvious that I've got a lot to offer a child and that Ben would want his mum to have a new baby to love. He's sure that Ben felt lucky to have had a "yummy mummy" like me, even for a short time. I'd never thought of Ben being lucky, or me being yummy, before tonight.

Three rings and then the phone's answer machine kicked in.

'Carol, it's yer mither. You must be on yer night oot so ah'll get a blether with you the morn.'

I looked at my watch; my sigh woke Jinky who was sleeping at my feet. There was nobody else I could blame for the eggy stink that wafted upwards.

'You dirty devil!'

'You've got a cheek! The night after the curry you farted non-stop!'

A soft kick to his hind would work; Jinky wasn't the only one that had to move. I'd been so caught up in writing the journal that

I'd forgotten to ring mum. Every Sunday at 5.50pm precisely, my mum made herself a cup of tea after *Songs of Praise* and settled back in her La-Z-Boy chair to wait for my phone call.

'Ah'm sorry, ah lost track of the time.'

Hearing my mum's accent was like putting on a pair of comfy slippers, a nice reminder of home.

'Ah just wanted tae ken if you had a braw time last night wi Elaine. The rain was stottin aff the grun up here and a didnae ken if you'd bother tae go oot,' said my mum.

I suddenly remembered telling my mum that my birthday treat was a night at the pictures with Elaine. It would be easier to lie to my mum, than to try and explain about a date with Dan.

'Aye, it was dreich here too but we managed tae get oot for a curry.'

I reckoned that if one half of the story was true, then it didn't matter too much that I'd been with Dan instead of Elaine at the Spice Gourmet.

'Fit did she get ye fir yer birthday?' asked my mum.

'A Bay City Rollers CD,' I replied.

'That's a weird present. Fit would she want tae give ye an auld record like that fir?'

Thinking of all the naff items my mum had sent me as 'Helping Hand' packages made me wonder how she could seriously criticise anyone's choice of gift.

'Do you no remember that me and Elaine thought the Bay City Rollers were braw and we kept sneaking in tae play Jill's records?

'Aye. Foo could ah forget? Yer room was covered in posters.'

'Well, Elaine said it was aboot time ah had ma own copy of *Once Upon a Star.*'

'Jill was daft aboot them. Ah mine she got the bus tae Aberdeen tae see them and came back weering her breeks at half-mast. And then you and Elaine copied her!'

'Aye, but that was the fashion!' I replied.

'And Elaine wis aye pinchin a wee shot of her big sister's tartan scarf and the twa of ye were prancin roond the toon singin, Bye Bye Baby. Aye, how could ah forget?' said my mum.

'Aye we had a laugh. It'll be great tae hear all the auld songs again,' I said.

'Aye, the guid auld days when you twa bairns still lived in the toon. Ah fair miss ye baith.'

Any further need for birthday news was gone as my mum reminisced, the meal at the Spice Gourmet already forgotten.

We had set times for phoning and a set pattern of conversation, I wouldn't be required to say too much more and then I'd be able to get back to writing my journal.

SUNDAY 27TH FEB 2011

Dear Journal

Elaine nipped over before lunch but didn't wait long. Her sister Jill is visiting her later on with her nephew Declan, the teen wolf. She likes to bitch about Jill, but she doesn't realise how lucky she is. Growing up, I'd have loved a brother or sister, and now with dad gone and only mum left, it feels kind of scary that my only family live over two hundred miles away. Phoning mum is not the same, and with no car, it's hard to get up there easily. I don't see her as much as I'd like to. I was pleased to see Elaine even though she'd been a bit crabbit with me on the phone. I think it's cos I'd cancelled the trip to the pictures, but I told her that I'd explain why when she visited.

So when Elaine said, "Well go on, tell me, are you up for it? Are you ready for a bit of excitement?" I blushed. I thought that she'd heard from someone that I was out with Dan at the Spice Gourmet last night. "Don't look so worried, I probably exaggerated some of the stories from the last 'Girls on Tour' trip," Elaine said. That's when the penny dropped, cos then I remembered about the travel brochures arriving and Elaine nagging me to join her and her pals on the Hen weekend.

I tried to tell her that even if I felt *"up for it"*, I couldn't afford a foreign holiday, clothes and spending money - it all adds up. She got really annoyed and kept making big huffy noises. She doesn't realise how much I spend on eBay. I don't show her all the handbags and shoes; she'd laugh at the 6 inch stilettos so most of the stuff I buy is only for my eyes. But it's not just the shopping; there are all the other debts. Elaine must have forgotten that I didn't go back to the Daisy Chain for over a year after Ben died. I couldn't expect Isobel to keep sending me sick pay. Isobel's a good boss but a wee florist business couldn't afford to fund a grieving employee. The pay packets stopped arriving, but the bills didn't. I was lucky Isobel took me back when I was ready and she even lets me get every second Wednesday afternoon off to have my session with Charlotte. The job's good for me but the money isn't. I've never been able to catch up with the debts I ran up over those months off sick. Elaine has no idea how much I really owe.

Elaine blethers on about Declan being moody, but she was more like a teenager sulking with her cuppa tea, flicking through my mags. She read out an article about folk buying bairns abroad instead of adopting in the UK. Elaine says they're all just copying Madonna and Angelina cos it's a fashion statement. It's funny that Elaine tells me what she thinks about EVERYTHING except her not having children is the one thing she NEVER talks about.

I've known Elaine since primary school but I still don't know if she has ever wanted to have a baby herself. I don't even know if she can have one cos she's never said that's she's tried. And I'm too feart to ask.

I mean it's not as if she doesn't like bairns. She loved the very bones of Ben. I asked mum once why she thought Elaine had never had a baby of her own. She just laughed like it was obvious and I was being daft for asking. She said, "Ah've kent Elaine since she was a bairn and she's ower selfish tae be a mither.' Mum might be right cos I can't imagine Elaine giving up her "me time".

When Declan was born, Jill told her that giving birth was like passing a basketball with your bum on fire. Maybe that's what put her off? Or it could be cos John's a lot older than Elaine and he doesn't want a baby or can't have one? It looks like I'll never know cos, if she wanted to tell me, I'd surely know by now.

Elaine said that it's a pity that folk couldn't buy a baby on eBay to save them any hassle. I was glad she didn't have time to take Jinky out with me today, the mood she was in. I didn't bother telling her about the meal with Dan. She never even asked why I didn't go to the pictures.

JULIA

Maggie was so busy yakking, she didn't notice me heading for the booth at the back of La Bonne Auberge. I could hear her before I saw her; I wasn't the only one. Maggie always felt the need to raise her voice when she was on her mobile. She didn't seem to believe that her phone could actually convert the sound of her voice into radio waves unless she bellowed into the handset. I was probably the only one that found it endearing.

In her early sixties, Maggie was still striking and her favourite Jaeger trouser suit gave her an immaculate, understated elegance. In her youth, her hair had been panther black, but now her cropped curls were arctic white. Few women were fortunate enough that their greying locks made them more attractive with age: my mother was one of them and she proved that true style never dates.

Finally finishing her phone call, Maggie sprang to her feet and gave me a warm embrace before launching into her first gentle reproach.

'Hello stranger. I'm surprised I recognised you.'

'Maggie, don't be so dramatic. It's only been a fortnight since we saw each other,' I replied.

'Honest-to-God, I've felt every minute!'

'Who're you trying to kid, the whole restaurant heard you organising your shifts at the charity shop. You're never at home.'

'Well I can't sit around waiting for my eldest daughter to come and visit, can I? It's just lucky that Lynn's always popping in.'

'That's because she's got nothing else to do apart from insulting me!' I held the carte du jour menu like a battle shield.

'Now who's being dramatic? Lynn told me you stormed off in a huff when she called you a P.A.N.K.'

I gave a Wimbledon winning grunt.

'Lynn was only joking. You should know what she's like by now, have a glass of wine and relax,' my mother commanded.

'I've already ordered. The Maître d' recommended a Côtes du Rhône.'

A teenage waitress in a French apron hovered over us anxiously. The waitress paused for Maggie to sample the wine. Maggie nodded at the girl, granting the go-ahead to top up our wine glasses and take our food order. I don't normally eat much at lunchtime, but today I was in the mood for blood. I opted for a rare Rib Eye Steak.

'Maybe you're right about Lynn,' I gave in, 'but she doesn't know when to stop. She more or less said that I was a bad role model for Holly. Did she tell you that?' I asked, knocking back the rest of my glass of wine.

'I think you're overreacting. You know how protective she is with Holly. Don't take it to heart; she's struggling a bit just now so she's probably a bit uptight.'

'What do you mean she's struggling?'

'Well, she says that Chris is hardly at home and I think she's feeling a bit lonely. I know how it feels…' Maggie sighed pointedly.

I refused to nibble at the bait and waited for my mother to carry on.

'You know she always thinks that everyone else is out there doing exciting stuff, when she's stuck at home.'

'Boo hoo!' I rubbed mock tears away with my clenched fists, 'Have you got a hankie to dry my eyes?'

Maggie tutted, but despite her disapproval, I continued. 'I'm sorry Maggie, but it'd be hard to find many women who'd feel sorry for Lynn. I mean c'mon, she's living the dream! Great guy for a husband, doesn't need to work, beautiful daughter, four bedroomed detached house. Do I need to go on?'

Maggie pleated her napkin into a perfect concertina and unfolded it again, layer by layer. She flicked the linen cloth as if she was shooing away an annoying fly.

'Anyway, I hear you've got a couple of new men in your life? Lynn said one of them is called Dan. Is he nice? Is he handsome?' She machine-gunned questions at me. 'Lynn said that Holly was really taken with him, and she was all giggles about him giving you his phone number. Are you going to meet up with him?'

'Maggie, he's just a dog walker who stopped to chat to me and Holly. Sure, he asked me out for a drink but he's definitely not my type. Bloody hell, Lynn really needs to get out more if that's all she's got to talk about.'

'Honest-to-God, what are you two like?' Maggie posed this question as if to an audience. 'At each other's throats one minute, then best buddies the next. I thought you'd be past all this argy-bargy, you're nearly forty for goodness' sake. You'd think you'd have more to worry about than letting your wee sister upset you.'

Sitting proudly, on Maggie's sideboard at home were two photographs in matching frames. One was a demure portrait of me in my black gown and graduation cap and the other was of giggly Lynn in a diamante tiara and a Cinderella wedding dress. The pictures said everything about our different paths. One fell head over heels into domesticity, while the other climbed the career ladder. Once again, I felt cheated that Maggie found it easier to relate to Lynn – her mini-me – and the modern day version of Maggie.'Is this the point where you remind me that, by my age, you'd been married for years with two kids, and how tough it was, back in the day?'

'Well, if you ever have children, I'll remind you that being a housewife isn't an easy option. I should know.'

It was five years since my dad's death, and Maggie had reinvented her social life and seized every opportunity to take advantage of her new found freedom. She never tired of dining out on stories of how difficult it had been for her to bring her girls up while their dad was away on business. She claimed that she felt as if she was a single parent; it was Maggie's all-time favourite moan.

'Even when he was at home, your dad never lifted a finger to help me. I didn't know what a hobby was until…'

'You're making up for lost time now.' I interrupted.

'It's true what they say; good things come to those who wait.'

'If only life was that simple.' I grunted.

'Have you time for a dessert or is this just a quick bite before you shoot off?' enquired Maggie.

'I'm sure I can manage to treat my old mum to two courses. I'm in no hurry today,' I replied.

'Good. And less of the old mum!' Maggie's smile contradicted her tone. Her gesture blew away any whiff of animosity that I might have imagined, allowing us to lighten up and sink back into our usual, comfortable routine.

'You go first,' I said.

'No, you go first and we'll save the best till last,' replied Maggie.

'Oooh, that sounds interesting. Teasing me now eh?' I laughed. 'I feel under a bit of pressure now. What makes you think I've not got something exciting to tell you?'

'Because, much as I love to hear what you've been up to, it's always work, work, work, with you. You never seem to stop,' said Maggie. My workaholic lifestyle was another favourite topic.

'I know, but it's tough right now. Working freelance means I can't take much time off. My flat costs a fortune and, after buying the car, I can't afford to pass up on any chance of work.'

'Julia, everybody likes nice things and I know you work hard to get them but remember, it never did your dad any good. Only a month of retirement before he dropped dead. Not much of a reward for over forty years' hard graft in a job he hated.'

'Yeah, well I do love my job', I replied.

'I know you do and I'm chuffed you're doing well, I just wish you'd get out more and enjoy yourself.' Maggie patted crumbs of pastry from the corners of her mouth with her napkin. 'I know you took a while to get over Andrew but it's time to live a bit again. When was the last time you went out with your friends?'

'I suppose it was a while ago. You're right. I could do with getting out more, but I hardly see the girls from work these days. Rachel keeps in touch, but most of them are all one half of a couple.'

'Look don't snap at me again, but Lynn mentioned that you went on a date with a rich lawyer from Edinburgh. She said he looks like Mel Gibson but she couldn't tell me much more.'

'Sounds like she's already told you enough. And really there's nothing more to say.' I took another large gulp of wine.

'Oh, c'mon, don't torment me. You know I love to hear all the gossip. How did the date go?' asked Maggie.

She leaned forward to suck me into a musky cloud of Youth Dew; her signature scent. It was pungent enough to wipe out the aroma of her salmon en croute. The Estée Lauder perfume had been my dad's standard Christmas gift and I couldn't remember a time when Maggie's dressing table didn't include the fragrance amongst its various lotions and potions. It carried memories as strong as its scent. As a little girl, I loved to pretend I was spraying the slim, ridged bottle with its tiny contracted waist in the middle, just like the hourglass figure that Maggie had maintained. One sniff and I was six years old again, tottering around my mother's bedroom wearing her raffia platform shoes.

'His name's Peter. But don't go buying a mother-of-the-bride outfit yet; it was only the first time we've met, so there's not much to tell.'

'But how did you meet him?' Maggie's forehead was a field of furrowed skin.

Just because Maggie was aware of the concept of internet dating, that didn't mean she would endorse it, and certainly not for her own daughter.

'Eh, he's a friend of Kirsty's.' I lied. 'She was asking after you the last time I saw her.' It was the easiest answer. 'Oh, that's nice. How's Kirsty doing?' asked Maggie.

'Great, but I don't see her that much. We text each other, but it feels like we're not on the same wavelength right now. Her last novel was a huge hit, so things are really hectic with events and stuff. Plus, she's about to launch her latest book. *And* she's got Nick.'

'It's the "*and she's got Nick*" that's upsetting you, isn't it?' asked Maggie. In a split second, I was trapped with nowhere to run.

'Don't forget, I'm your mum. I always know what's really bothering you,' claimed Maggie. She was at the top of her game when it came to maternal intuition.

'Okay, maybe you've got a point. Kirsty wasn't really there for me when Andrew left. She's lived with Nick since uni, so she just doesn't get how I feel about not having a partner.'

My mother topped up my glass of water, deliberately neglecting my wine glass.

'She always sounds so wrapped up in her writing that you wonder if she'd miss Nick if they ever split up,' mused Maggie.

She couldn't resist stirring things a bit and was in no rush to abandon this course of conversation.

'Hmm, yeah you're probably right,' I played with my cutlery, sliding it back and forth across the tablecloth.

'You and I both know that your dad could be a pain in the neck at times, but I do miss him dearly. Like I'm sure you miss Andrew. It's a shame it didn't work out. I honestly thought you were finally settled.'

'I think that's our main course coming.'

I caught another waft of my mother's perfume. It was Christmas 1977 again, and I was overcome by the smell of Youth Dew as Maggie handed out the presents. Santa had brought me my first record player and a 7" vinyl record. I played the number one single by Wings endlessly. I could still picture myself, mouthing *Mull of Kintyre* into my mirrored wardrobe, wearing an itchy jumper that Maggie had knitted for me. It was a Fair Isle jumper, a pattern that was as complex as my future relationships with men.

Andrew was the exception, or so I'd thought. The pattern for our relationship had seemed simple, easy to follow. We loved each other, what more did we need? Nothing. That was until I dropped a stitch that Andrew wasn't prepared to pick up.

Maggie and I had always been able to confide in each other, and yet it seemed like a long time since I had truly expressed my feelings. My mother wasn't going to let the opportunity pass.

'I really liked Andrew. I miss him too.' Maggie looked wistful. 'It's a real pity that you two split up. And he was always good fun to be around. He'd have made a great dad. Don't you think so?'

I imagined Maggie's brain desperately trying to knit together enough loose strands to make sense of what had been bothering me for months.

'Maybe. Who knows? We never really talked about having kids.' I confessed.

Everyone I was close to assumed that I'd been happy enough with sofa-lising instead of socialising. I traded weekends in clubs, downing vodka shots, for quiet nights in with a bottle of Cabernet Sauvignon. And I went from a party animal to waiting for a visit from the stork.

'The steak is delicious. Have a taste,' I urged. A forkful of vampire-red meat wasn't what Maggie wanted from me, but it was all that I was willing to give.

'So, what's your news?' I asked.

'I was hoping you'd ask that soon before I burst with excitement!'

'Good God, don't do that, it'd make a right mess of my Armani!'

It worked. Maggie laughed on cue and our chat shifted gear once again. My mum edged forward in her seat as if a she was ready to leak a state secret.

'Well, go on, don't leave me dangling, what's the next instalment in the *Maggie Davis Show*?' I asked, mirroring my mother's pose.

'Honest-to-God, you'll never guess. But you can have a go,' she teased, with an enigmatic smile.

'Nah, I've no idea what you're up to this time, so I won't even try to guess.'

'Like you said earlier, I'm making up for lost time,' replied Maggie, beaming from ear to ear, and pausing between mouthfuls of salmon. 'Your father would have flipped at the very thought of my plans.'

'That counts for nothing. Dad freaked out when you wanted to get a part-time job, remember?' I could pass comment on him now, not then, not when it might have made a difference.

'He wanted me at home for you and Lynn.'

'And him.'

'There's nothing wrong with putting family life first…'

'And you weren't allowed to get your hair cut short or wear trousers.'

'He just liked a lady to look like one. There's nothing wrong with that either.'

The crusty scab might have healed, but picking at it could easily expose a deep, raw wound. I didn't need to remind Maggie about the oppressive regime that she had lived under all her married life. The scars were still visible, I knew where to look; Lynn and I had them too.

'Anyway, forget about all that. I make all my own choices now. And this will impress you,' said Maggie.

'After this big build up, it better be good,' I challenged her, 'give me a clue at least!'

'Okay, it's something you've already done that I never thought I could ever do.'

'Eugh, that throws up a whole load of very disturbing images about my mum! Yuk!'

The waitress cleared our plates away as I drummed my fingers over my lips. Maggie grinned and savoured the moment, staying mute.

'C'mon, this is torturing me. At least one more clue.'

'Okay, final clue: you did this over twenty years ago.'

My brain did a high speed rewind to visualise a pretentious eighteen-year-old. There I was, crackling like static with exam stress. Bored with school. Fed up living at home. Pissed off with everyone and desperate to start uni. The other images of my teenage social life were far too frightening to recreate with my mother sitting opposite. Going for the most sanitised possibility,

I responded with my safest answer.

'You're going to uni? As a mature student?'

'Don't be daft, no! I'm not clever like you and anyway, what would I do with qualifications at my age?'

'Well how long are we going to play this game? C'mon tell me!' I pleaded.

'Okay. I'm thinking of going to India,' said Maggie, wiping away the revelation with her napkin.

'What? I don't get it? I never went to India!'

Maggie was still too young to play the batty old eccentric. I had no idea what she was talking about. India? After years of holidaying in the Highlands?

'India?' as if repeating it would help me make any sense of this alien concept.

'Well, you went travelling on your own all over the place!' stated Maggie, dismissing the dessert menu. Her appetite had vanished as quickly as her good mood.

'Maggie, I was eighteen, that's what you do at that age and I was with a big crowd of pals, I was never alone. Please don't tell me you've booked and paid for anything yet?'

'Listen to you,' said Maggie. 'Who's the mother now? I never held you back when you wanted to "*see something other than suburbia*" and I've always wanted to go to India.'

'But you've never *ever* said anything about India.'

'That's because you've *never* asked, you were too busy doing your own thing. And I let you. All I ever wanted was to give you roots and wings; you know that was always my aim for you and Lynn. And you chose to fly.'

'But that was different…'

The waitress sheepishly set down our coffees, creating a short-lived pause in my tirade. I wasn't prepared to quit my interrogation yet.

'Maggie, I don't think you realise that the world's a very different place these days.'

'Yes, I do, it's safer. Have you any idea how worried me and your dad were when we couldn't even phone you? Weeks would go by without a cheep from you. There was no such thing as texts or emails. We heard nothing from you.'

'Fair point, but…'

'Look, don't worry, I'll be absolutely fine.'

'I'm not convinced.'

My head shook involuntarily from side to side. 'It's not just your safety I'm concerned about.'

'Julia, I'm a mature woman and I've got a good Scots tongue in my head if I'm stuck,' laughed Maggie.

'Trust me Maggie, I tried a solo holiday after me and Andrew split up. Remember I went island hopping round Greece? Let me tell you, it's no fun sightseeing on your own.'

'If you carry on like this, I'll be glad to get a bit of peace and a break from your nagging. I know now how you must've felt all those years ago with me harping on at you. But you got the chance, I didn't.'

'I never realised you wanted the chance.'

I stirred my coffee senseless until I lost myself in the bottom of the cup; unable to fathom out the person sitting opposite me. This wasn't my mum. This was an extra-terrestrial called Maggie, who claimed to want an Indian adventure. She looked just the same in her creamy, silk blouse and fresh water pearls, but she spoke in a very different language, not the mother tongue at all.

'Honest-to-God, I thought *you* of all people would understand.'

I understood perfectly. Whoever said that "*all good things come to those who wait*" was talking bollocks.

'You're forever saying you've got to make things happen and that's what I've done. It's always worked out for you,' said Maggie.

There was no point in rubbishing my mother's naïve belief that I always got what I wanted. Maggie was right though, I couldn't just sit back and wait. I'd need to take matters into my own hands.

CAROL

I should've asked Elaine face-to-face instead of on the phone.

'Ah thought you'd be happy that ah've taken Charlotte's advice and you'd want tae support me,' I said.

'But yoga's no ma scene. Sorry,' replied Elaine, 'you're on your own this time.'

Playing the guilt card hadn't worked; it was time to use my emergency back-up plan.

'But what aboot the feedback from your appraisal at work?'

'What's me talking too much tae Lisa got tae dae with yoga?' asked Elaine.

'No that bit - the bit when your team leader telt you that there was anger management classes available. Maybe it would dae you good tae try yoga.'

I pictured Elaine at the other end of the phone, with her nostrils flared up like a sweaty racehorse. I didn't dare go as far as also pointing out that any form of exercise, over and above going for a walk with me and Jinky once a week, would also do Elaine good. There's a big difference between being bold and being totally reckless. I wasn't that stupid.

'Aye, ah remember her "constructive idea" but ah dinnae rate a word she says aboot anything. Supposed tae be the team leader? She couldnae lead Jinky on his leash! And as for me having anger management issues, that's me just expressing maself. Ah'm a big girl with a big personality. And trust me Carol, she knows nothing aboot personality. She's got the personality of a shop dummy!'

'So there's nae chance of you giving it a go?'

'Ah'd rather be hit by a train than dae yoga in public. Ah'm sorry Carol, dinnae ever say that ah'm no there for you, but ah'm allergic tae Lycra.'

Subject closed. Elaine's only offer of support was to drive me to the class and wait with me until it started. It would have to be a solo mission.

Two days later, I poked my nose into the GP room of the community centre. It was jammed full of yogier-than-thou women settling their buttocks on to their rubber mats. Elaine grunted in disgust. I rubbed my clammy palms down the side of my jogging trousers.

'Look at that bunch of tree huggers. Dae you think they remove the pole from their arses before the class starts? Ah telt you that you should've gone tae jazzercize instead,' said Elaine.

'Ah'll see you in an hour.' I slunk into the room, leaving Elaine standing at the door with only a draught for company.

There was one free spot at the back, and my trainers squeaked like a mouse with its tail in a trap as I tiptoed across the wooden floor. All gooey and smiley, the teacher introduced herself as Jamelia. It was going to be fine.

'Spiral your fingers inward and let the energy shoot out of your fingertips,' instructed Jamelia, in a soothing voice.

Attempting to balance on one leg, with the other leg lifted

high into the air, was much harder than I'd imagined. None of the other women seemed to have the same problem holding the poses. Charlotte's *try-something-new* advice had let me down this time. It actually had the opposite effect: trying to concentrate and calm my mind was stressful.

Up front, Jamelia was demonstrating the 'Marichyasana III' to the class. 'The seated twist is just what you need to stretch and strengthen your spine, and it's great for massaging your internal organs as well. The *mar-ee-chee-ahs-anna* literally means a ray of light of the sun or moon.'

'Which in Sanskrit translates as a torturous twisty pose with your butt cheeks spread,' whispered the friendly face next to me.

'By the way, I'm Pam.'

I raised myself up from my yoga mat, sticky with sweat and smiled back. 'Hiya, ah'm Carol.'

'Ssh!' hissed the woman lying next to us.

Too late for hushed meditation, my movement meant a fart slipped out, and it wasn't a silent one. The other women were distracted from the discomfort of 'Marichyasana III' by me letting one go. The yogic calm was now completely destroyed.

Pam attempted to smother her sniggers and ignore the bomb I'd dropped. But a few of the women couldn't hold back their 'thank-God-that-wasn't-me' giggle.

I wished I could evaporate into thin air. Would it be more embarrassing to just run out of the room? Elaine wouldn't be there to take me home. It was too far to walk and I had no money for a bus or taxi. I was stuck. But I reminded myself, worse things happened. Nobody had died.

'Forget about it. It happens to the best of us,' said Pam.

I managed to give Pam a weak smile, a grin so tight it could cut off my circulation.

Jamelia, a true professional, was obviously well used to such outbursts. She casually walked across the room and gave me a gentle pat on my shoulder.

'Don't worry about it', soothed Jamelia, 'After all, and for good reason, *let go* is a more common mantra in yoga than *hold it in*.'

Everything was going to be fine.

TUESDAY 1ST MARCH 2011

Dear Journal

I was fine without Elaine at yoga, even after what happened. I couldn't face telling Dan or Charlotte that I gave up on yoga after the first night, so I've already decided that I'll give it another try. Jamelia and Pam said they hoped to see me again next week too. I planned to tell Elaine about my wee incident in class, and maybe have a laugh about it, but she was in a rubbish mood. She didn't seem happy when I told her about my night out with Dan either. I know I wasn't going to tell her but I couldn't help myself. She was flicking through this week's mags, and read out another story about adopting babies from China. Before I could stop myself, it slipped out that Dan said I had a lot to offer a baby. Elaine nearly fell off the couch and choked on her biscuit. I don't mind admitting that I was really upset by her reaction.

I told her about us going for a curry and how hilarious Dan was, but she didn't think that any of his curry jokes were funny. All she kept saying was that he didn't know anything about me or what I'd been through. I explained that I'd already told him about Ben's death, but she said that was only half the story. She kept repeating that I shouldn't get involved with a complete stranger and that he has no right to advise me on stuff he knows nothing about. I tried to tell her that I'm not stupid and that I wouldn't be jumping on the internet to adopt a Chinese bairn, without thinking it through. It didn't seem enough for her though. She asked me not to see Dan again, cos she doesn't think he's good for me. She said that he's not qualified to be filling my head with ridiculous ideas. But what is so ridiculous about me being a mum again? I was a great mum and Elaine knows that. Elaine doesn't understand, she's never been a mum and she's never been on her own. Ever since Ben died, I've always thought that if he'd had to go, then I wished that I'd been under those car wheels with him. But that night, having the meal with Dan and laughing at his cheesy jokes, was the first time that I've felt glad to be alive in a very long time. Surely Elaine doesn't grudge me that?

Lunchtime at work couldn't come quick enough. I hadn't brought in home baking since Ben died.

'Try this; it's a mood lifter on a plate.' I said. Isobel inhaled the bitter-sweet smell of cocoa as I handed her a slab of chocolate cake.

Bursting out the sides of her green nylon tabard, Isobel set her breasts on the florist's work station like two bulging shopping bags. She swallowed the chocolate cake, sticky with fudge, with the same level of satisfaction as if she'd just gone down on one of the Chippendales.

My boss had the perfect expression of bliss on her face. Like a meditating Buddha, Isobel wore a serene smile; complete with a chocolate moustache.

'Aw, I've just died and gone to heaven,' Isobel sighed. Like a fresh bruise, a blush bloomed across Isobel's plump cheeks. 'Oh, doll, I didn't mean to offend, I'm sorry.'

'You're fine Isobel, nothing tae apologise for,' I said.

While she licked her lips to hoover up the last chocolate

crumbs, Isobel shared what she'd witnessed during her daily stakeout of Shawbriggs from the front of the shop.

'Do you remember how mad you were when you realised Elaine knew about Steve and his affair with Mahogany Tart?' asked Isobel.

'Aye, ah wish she'd warned me.'

'Well, that's why I decided to tell you myself before you heard it from somebody else.'

'Thanks.' I snatched up the nearest flowers.

'Kimberly's pregnant,' said Isobel.

I couldn't look Isobel in the eye. *Stay calm*, don't stop to think. Isobel waited as I snipped away frantically at a bunch of roses. She swept away the stalks that fell to the shop floor, before patting me gently on the arm.

'I'm sorry doll. How about I make us a wee cuppa tea?'

Isobel busied herself with filling the plastic kettle. Only the chinking of mugs and clipping of foliage filled the silence, until at last the steaming kettle clicked and the red light went off. I kept cutting the stems down, inch after inch. All I had left of the bunch was half a dozen flower heads. One by one, I ripped out the petals, the floral confetti drifted to the floor. The petals lay muddied and crushed of colour, destroyed by the sole of my boot. It was the most satisfying floral display I had ever created.

A few moments before I had been upbeat, breathing in chocolate fumes and surrounded by colour - now I was as low as the trodden snips and shavings of floral mess. Wiping my eyes, a trickle of blood ran down my fingers. A rose thorn had only made a small nick, but the cut felt much deeper.

Isobel had spotted Kimberly across the street. Mahogany Tart worked at Street Beach, the tanning salon opposite the Daisy Chain. Flashing teeth and tits, Kimberly was often seen darting in and out of the shop unit. That was another reason why I lurked around the back shop making up the orders.

Before working in Street Beach, Kimberly had a job in the lounge bar at the Norwood House Hotel, the one that Steve managed just outside town. Steve had got her to babysit Ben when he was eighteen months old, after I'd moaned that he'd never taken me out for a drink or a meal since Ben was born. The first night that Kimberly was our babysitter, I'd crashed out on the couch within minutes of us getting home; the wine hit me hard after so long being teetotal. When I'd rolled over and crashed on to the floor, I panicked, realising that Steve wasn't home and I was drunk and alone in charge of Ben. It still makes me queasy to think about how long Steve took to give Kimberly a lift home, even though she only lived a couple of miles away.

Kimberly was nineteen when the affair started. I was changing Ben's dirty nappies. Whilst Kimberly's pert breasts bounced up and down the bar for Steve's amusement, mine sagged and leaked all over the bed sheets. Kimberly wore midriff tops, whatever the season, to show off her taut tummy. I was at home, desperately massaging an Avon Stretch Mark Smoother into my jelly belly.

Years later, in a drunken phone call one night, Elaine admitted to me that, along with the rest of Shawbriggs, she had known about Steve and Kimberly. Elaine didn't know how to tell me and she'd hoped that I would figure it out for myself. There had been plenty of clues; I didn't need to be Sherlock.

THURSDAY 3ᴿᴰ MARCH 2011

Dear Journal

Yesterday I texted Elaine and asked her to give me a ring, but her reply said she was going round to Jill's and would call later on. I wondered if she knew that Kimberly was pregnant and I wanted to talk to her. She must have forgotten to phone me and I didn't want to make a big deal about it, not after her going on about adopting babies the last time she was here. She might even think I knew all along and that's why I've been researching the adoption sites. But I honestly didn't know that Kimberly was pregnant. Isobel tried to make me laugh by saying she knew something was up when Kimberly's tan had faded from mahogany to pine. She called Kimberly a pot-bellied pig but I couldn't laugh along with her.

Mum phoned last night to see if the latest 'Helping Hand' package had arrived, but she'd be the last person I could talk to about Steve and Kimberly. I haven't used their names with mum since the accident cos it only makes her cry. And when I hear mum cry, it only makes me cry too.

Mum's parcel was furry insoles for my wellies to keep me warm when I'm walking Jinky. It gave me an idea cos Dan said that he'd meet me anytime to take the dogs to the park. I'm glad I was brave enough to ring him cos he is so good to talk to. I feel like I can tell him anything. I know Elaine would be mad, but I couldn't help telling him about Steve's affair and that Kimberly is pregnant. He knew right away that something had upset me and he totally understood why. I even told him that I'd been looking at adoption sites about getting a foreign bairn and that Elaine thinks it's a terrible idea. He said I'd be mad not to follow up the chance of being a mum again and that I shouldn't listen to Elaine. Dan thinks Elaine's very domineering; she can be a bit bossy I suppose. According to Dan, some folk enjoy helping victims. He thinks that maybe I'm not as needy as I used to be and that's why Elaine's annoyed. He might be right, but it's a shame Elaine doesn't even want to hear about the adoption idea. When I told Dan, he said I was being really positive about looking into all the possibilities. He did warn me though that adoption comes with lots of complications and I shouldn't rush into anything without thinking it all through. By the time we'd walked the dogs to my *Angel's Bench*, he'd promised me that he'd help me. I've not to bother telling Elaine anymore about it cos she's obviously not interested. He told me to leave it with him as Dan's sure that there's a quicker, easier and safer way than trying to adopt a foreign bairn and that he'll look into other ideas for me. I just wish Elaine understood and cared as much as Dan does.

JULIA

At Peter's suggestion, and as part of my "culinary education", our previous dates had both been to the Rogano restaurant.

'It's the only restaurant I'm happy to eat in if I have to come through to Glasgow. Sweetheart, you'll love it.'

Peter didn't bother to discover that I had actually dined there before on several occasions and knew a bit about its history.

'It's a Glasgow institution,' said Peter.

'Yeah, so is Barlinne Jail,' I replied.

'Ha, very good, Julia.' He rolled his eyes. 'This restaurant deserves respect; we're not in Pizza Express. Rogano is a wonderful survivor from the days when the Cunard Line steamed in and out of Glasgow. Art Deco was at its peak, and time was made for things that mattered, like dining out. The food is, of course, the highlight, but the outstanding decor, the crisp linen, sparkling glasses and gleaming cutlery all contribute to what is undeniably one of life's little luxuries.'

Even though Peter was engrossed in his tribute, he still managed to multi-task, keeping one eye on me and the other on his vibrating Blackberry. So much for respect.

'You can't dine at the Rogano and not experience the chilled natural oysters, on the half shell, Rockefeller style, of course,' urged Peter. 'They taste like a deep breath of ocean air. He winked. 'And there's the added bonus of them being an aphrodisiac.'

'No thanks, I'll give them a miss. I've tried oysters before and it was like eating salty snot.'

'Salty snot? I like a woman with a sense of humour but seriously, sweetheart, you may well have eaten oysters before but you've never had them at the *Rogano*.'

How did he know? Peter ordered the oysters for me; I had as much free will as a three-year-old. Next he would be asking the waiter for crayons so I could colour in my placemat. Then again, I was at the Rogano, not Pizza Express, as he kept reminding me.

Not taking me seriously was a serious mistake. After our second seafood rendezvous, I wondered if there were any obvious signs of a connection between us. At the outset, I'd found Peter to be reasonably interesting and that had been enough to go on, for starters. He definitely wasn't Dog Breath, Goatee Geek or Captain Caveman. That had to be worth something. And he definitely wasn't Andrew either. It was still early days. Passionate fireworks might follow, even though the quick grope we'd shared didn't give a hint that there was a spark of sexual chemistry awaiting ignition. And I wasn't fired up by romance when Peter whispered that he always carried a condom and not to worry, he never ever had unprotected sex.

I'd shagged Andrew on our first date, and it was months since I'd had sex, but Peter's arrogance made me determined to make him wait. There was no doubt he'd expect it tonight. Three dates was long enough to test him, but as I put the finishing touches to my makeup, the face staring back at me didn't look excited by the prospect.

Peter had offered to pick me up from my flat; it seemed a good idea at the time. Now I wasn't so sure. I immediately regretted buzzing him upstairs to wait for me while I straightened my hair.

I leaned out from my bedroom door; Peter stood with his hands behind his back, on sentry duty at the window overlooking the street.

'I'll only be another few minutes. Switch on the telly if you like.'

'No thanks. I only watch the news.' No point in asking him about last night's *Eastenders* then. '*And* I need to keep an eye on the Aston Martin.'

'It'll be fine. You're in Glasgow, not Baghdad!' I called through.

'Hmm, sweetheart, you just don't understand. That beautiful machine out there isn't *just* a car. It's an Aston Martin DB9, a thoroughbred sports car with GT levels of comfort and refinement. It combines the Aston Martin's unique character with an uncompromising design philosophy: the DB9 is a synthesis of traditional craftsmanship, high-tech manufacturing and modern components using the finest materials.'

Jesus wept. Much as I loved my Mini Cooper, this was way too much information for me to digest with any show of enthusiasm. Thank Christ he had his back to me and couldn't see my eyes glaze over. It was going to be a long night.

Peter had sniffed the air theatrically when I let him inside the flat. And, hungry or not, I decided this would be our third and final date. He was in an exclusive apartment on the River Clyde, but anyone would think that Peter had crossed the water and entered a ned-infested tower block in downtown Govan. Peter lived less than fifty miles away in a townhouse in Merchiston Gardens, one of the most upmarket areas in Edinburgh and, although it was much further away from me in social status, a visit to my home was hardly slumming it.

'Did you hear that the Edinburgh and Glasgow tourist boards were competing for visitors? So Glasgow came up with the

slogan: *Glasgow - why wait until one o'clock to hear a gun go off?*'
Peter's guffaw echoed round the room. His jokes were wearing as
thin as my patience.

He glanced at his TAG watch. Would he query my membership
to *Men2Be* and discover my exaggerated claims of wealth? He
was the type who'd grass me up, although if Peter was a prime
example of *Men2Be's* most eligible bachelors, the agency could
stick their membership where it hurts.

Within minutes of Peter wandering around my private space,
I felt an uneasy sense of violation crawl up my legs, like that of a
slug, leaving behind its slimy trail.

'Not a lover of the classics then?'

Peter's eyebrows twitched as he scanned the spines of books
he plucked from shelves, silently grading my literary taste,
before turning to my work station to flick through my copy of
Le Raconteur. The business supplement from *The Times* seemed
the only reading matter to meet his approval. When I heard him
arrive, I'd stashed this week's copy of *HELLO!* under the sofa's
cushion. Now I wish I hadn't bothered, I'd have enjoyed seeing
his snooty face crumple in disgust.

Peter stopped at the riverside window to take in the view of
the Clyde with the Finneston Crane in the foreground. Even the
powerful symbol of Glasgow's industrial heartland wasn't enough
to hold his gaze for long. The only things in the flat that seemed
to interest him for more than a few seconds were the numerous
photos of Holly that he picked up and scrutinised.

He studied each one, but instead of feeling proud that he
seemed so taken with the images, I felt disturbed. The snap shot
he lingered over the longest, was the one of Holly as she ran
across the suede-like sand on the beach at Millport, waving at
me, as I held the camera, snap happy.

'Minnie Mouse,' sighed Peter quietly under his breath. 'Very cute.'

'Pardon?' Did my ears need syringed? Had I heard him correctly? Had he actually referred to Holly's Minnie Mouse pants? Surely not.

I snatched up the photo frame and examined it closely for the first time. I'd definitely heard Peter say, "cute". No doubt. Was his comment merely a voiced observation? Or was there more to it? Stop. *Stop it!* Don't give it head-space. But the repugnant idea clung to my brain, like a barnacle.

Peter ignored my query and continued to prattle on, 'I'm actually quite adept at photography.'

'Really? So photography is another one of your many gifts.' He also had a gift for shielding himself against blatant sarcasm.

'Yes, I suppose it's true to say that I am a man of many talents. Where was the photo taken?'

'Millport.'

Sixty minutes from Glasgow on the Ayrshire coast, Millport was stuck in a 1950s time warp, and that was part of its appeal. Even when Lynn and I were Holly's age, the Ritz Café on the promenade was old-fashioned. We'd stand on tippy toes to peek over the glass fronted counter, in awe of the back wall, lined with shelves of sweetie jars, all the colours of the rainbow, a synthetic paradise. Maggie and Jack would nag us to make a choice from the menu before we settled inside a booth with our feast. Our mottled, bare legs stuck to the tomato-red vinyl of the banquettes. And even though we still shivered after our dook in the sea, we sat at the glossy Formica tables, lapping at 99s or delving head first into Knickerbocker Glories, enjoying every last lick.

The glamour of the palm trees along the front, and the ostentatious Victorian villas sitting proudly around the bay, made the little seaside town seem as exotic to me then, as it was to head off to Mauritius now. Almost thirty years later, I'd no naïve allusions that my memories would be as golden as Millport's sandy beaches, but I still wanted Holly to enjoy the faded charms of the resort, just as Maggie and Jack had done with me and Lynn.

I took Holly to Millport on the May bank holiday, when she was almost three. Surprisingly, the weather had turned for the better by the time we'd left Largs behind, in the wake of the ferry. A paddle in the sea at the beach at Kames Bay had been irresistible for the excited toddler, and I let Holly strip off to her pants to splash around freely. My snap shot of a special day out showed a semi-naked Holly giggling with uninhibited joy. The photo was my all-time favourite and I'd never before doubted my judgement in openly displaying the photo in my home.

Now, I wanted to paint a vest over the teeny nipples that stood erect on the elfin figure. I couldn't prove anything, but there was a difference between politeness and downright intrusion into the private life of a young girl. From a man who'd never met Holly before, one too many questions about my niece made me anxious to have him out of my home. Was it my problem for even thinking that Peter might have inappropriate thoughts about Holly? Did it say more about me than him? I wasn't one to ignore my intuitions; they'd never let me down yet. I had to end the date, right here, right now, and I couldn't bear listening to any more of his guff.

'Ah, the west coast, one of the most dramatic coastlines in Britain. I've often passed The Cumbraes when I've sailed up the Firth of Clyde. Never been to Millport myself though. Do you fancy taking Holly back to that beach and I could update the photo for you?'

'Millport's not really your kind of place Peter.'

'I wouldn't disagree with you, sweetheart. But you have to suffer for your art. You get nothing for nothing in this world. A smart girl like you should know that by now.'

'Listen Peter, I need to go to the bathroom before we go. And I might be a while.'

Peter couldn't fail to hear me repeatedly flush the toilet and he was pacing up and down when I emerged.

'This is so embarrassing. I'm really sorry to spoil tonight but I seem to be suffering from a bad case of the shits,' I said.

'Oh.'

I guessed that learning about a lady's diarrhoea in such an uncouth manner would be unacceptable for one of *Men2Be's* "discerning gentlemen".

Smart girls should know that by now.

'I think it might be safer if we called it a night. I wouldn't want to risk your Aston Martin's upholstery. Although I suppose I could sit on a plastic bag. The leather seats will wipe clean, won't they?'

'Oh no. Travelling is not a good idea if your plumbing's playing up. I think it's best if you stay at home.'

'Yeah, you're right I suppose. I'm worried that my piles might start bleeding again.'

On *Men2Be*, Peter was the 'platinum package', a good looking, successful professional with more disposable income than he knew how to handle. But it didn't compensate for the fact that he gave me the heebie-jeebies. It was what might be lurking *under* the surface of Peter's polished exterior that troubled me most. For all I knew, his alternative online profile could be Paedo Pete.

My fake ass-plosion worked a treat; he couldn't get out my flat quick enough. He was so far up his own arse, I was willing to bet that when he orgasmed, he screamed out his own name. At least, I consoled myself; I'd never need to put my theory to the test. Within minutes, Paedo Pete was hurtling back along the M8 in his precious Aston Martin, miles away from ever getting near

Holly, even in a photo frame.

But it wasn't easy to scrub thoughts of Peter as Paedo Pete from my mind when I next saw Holly.

'Look Auntie Julia. All different colours. I did them all myself!' declared Holly, pushing her painted finger nails proudly under my nose.

'Wow! They're gorgeous.' I mock munched Holly's fingers, gobbling them up, one by one.

'Yummy,yummy! Like a bag of Tooty Frootie sweeties. Have you ever tried them?'

'Nope, can we get some today?' asked Holly, tugging at my arm.

'We could try Granny's Sookers in the west end. Tootie Frooties are like Skittles,' I explained. 'I usually order them online from a retro sweetie shop.'

'What's a retro sweetie shop?' asked Holly.

It's a shop for old people. Like me and your mum.'

'You spend far too much time on the internet,' interrupted Lynn, 'And, as for you,' she said, pointing her finger at Holly, 'no more sweets today. You've had your quota!'

Aw, pleaseeee,'the high pitched appeal came from me.

'You're worse than a child. But I mean it, you shouldn't keep feeding her rubbish every weekend,' warned Lynn.

'God almighty, don't be such a party pooper! It's only once a week and anyway they're fruity so they're good for you,' I smirked. Holly copied me.

'Yeah, and my teacher says that you're meant to have your five a day,' said Holly.

'Jeez, what a double act. Go on the pair of you and leave me in peace for at least an hour,' pleaded Lynn, shooing us out the kitchen door.

'We'll probably be longer than an hour. I'm hoping to visit Maggie after we've been shopping,' I replied.

'Great, I'll get my ironing done then. See you later. Enjoy yourselves, but go easy on the sweets!'

Lynn had more chance of being hit by an asteroid whilst claiming a lottery win, than expecting me to take heed of her warning to avoid a confectionary binge. A trip to Granny's Sookers, produced a packet of Parma Violets, two chocolate bananas, a Sherbet Fountain, a handful of Anglo Bubblies and some Tooty Frooties. Once Holly had satisfied her sweet tooth, it was time to visit Maggie and before long, we were parked outside my mum's Victorian villa. No sooner had the wrought iron gate clacked shut, Maggie was striding down the path to meet us.

'C'mon in you two. What a surprise!' Maggie reached down to sweep up Holly, cocooning her in the feathery softness of her cashmere cardigan.

'Ouch, you're squeezing me too hard granny!' squealed Holly.

'Sorry, my pet lamb.' Maggie wasn't for setting Holly free. 'I love you so much I just want to cuddle you tight.' Still holding her close, anyone would think Maggie hadn't seen Holly for years, instead of a matter of days. Finally, she released her. 'What's happened to your tongue? It's dark purple!'

'That'll be the Parma Violets,' I answered, sinking into the small chintz sofa that Maggie had wedged into the recess of the dining kitchen. I patted the space beside me, inviting Holly to join me. Instead she perched herself on the stool at the breakfast bar.

'Lynn will kill you!' said Maggie. 'You know she's not supposed to get junk food.' I waved her threat away.

'Chill. The purple will have faded by the time we get back.'

'I doubt it,' muttered Maggie, as she filled up the kettle

automatically. There was no need to ask me if I would like a cup of coffee. Still with her back to me, Maggie asked if I'd been out again with Peter since our first date.

'Hmm,' was all the detail I was willing to offer Maggie. I jumped up from the sofa to get the mugs out, hoping that looking busy might defuse Maggie's desire for further information. No such luck. I should have known that Maggie's thirst for gossip would never be satisfied by a mere mumble. Sure enough, Maggie continued, asking me where we had gone for dinner and if we'd planned another date. What was the best way to fob her off? Would it be enough to say that Peter had exposed himself as an insufferable snob who had the emotional depth of a puddle?

My mother's phone rang and Maggie had to let the 'boy meets girl' interrogation drop. I wasn't prepared to discuss the real reasons why I never wanted to see the creepy bastard again.

Maggie finished her call, and it came as no surprise that she was determined to get more information out of me.

'Oh c'mon, spill the beans! You know I love to hear the gossip.'

Honestly, you don't want to hear all the *gory* details.' With Holly's innocence still in my mind, I used the best, but most ironic, diversionary tactic.

'It just didn't work out between us and the details are not for *you-know-who's* little ears,' I muttered and nodded in Holly's direction.

'Message received and understood,' said Maggie, with a wink.

I knew that Maggie would be keen to update me about her travels. I moved the conversation seamlessly on to Maggie's trip.

'So,' I asked, 'what's the latest on India?'

'Did Lynn not tell you? I'm thinking of Europe instead,' replied Maggie.

'No, she didn't say a word. When did you tell her this?' I asked, leaning over the breakfast bar as if I was a Philadelphia lawyer questioning a courtroom witness.

'Oh, I don't know, maybe last week. I thought she'd have mentioned it to you earlier.'

'She probably assumed I knew. Why didn't you call or pop over to tell me?' My tone was as shrill as the kettle's whistle, I was last to know as usual.

'You're always so busy. I don't like to bother you with every little snippet.'

'Travel plans that change continent aren't just a wee snippet Maggie. I'd call that a big deal.'

'Honest-to-God, *chill*, as you'd say to me. It's only a passing thought, so there's no need to look so miffed.' Maggie handed me a mug of coffee and shook her head.

'But if you're serious about this trip, you'll need to put more than a passing thought into where you're going. What happened to your claim that it was a lifelong ambition to go to India?'

'The India dream's still real, but maybe not for my first trip. I might have a trial run with a jaunt to Eastern Europe.'

'First trip?' I choked, causing my coffee to splutter down the front of my roll neck sweater. 'Shit!' as I made frenzied wipes with a nearby tea towel.

Julia, language!' Maggie cocked her head in Holly's direction. I ignored my mother's reprimand and carried on regardless.

'How many trips are you planning?' It was a boardroom voice used within a cosy kitchen, I didn't care that I sounded abrasive.

As if Holly was umpiring at centre court, and from her vantage point at the breakfast bar, her head went back and forth following our animated exchange.

'And now that I've heard about couch surfing I might be able to afford a few more trips,' said Maggie.

'What the hell is couch surfing?'

'Well, Jean, you know, the neighbour that does a shift with me in the charity shop? Her granddaughter, Amy, is going travelling for a year when she finishes her degree. Jean says that Amy can only afford it because she'll sleep on other people's sofas for free. Couch surfing is a great way to meet new people and…'

'Whoa, stop, I've heard enough. Have you lost the bloody plot?' I yelled, forgetting to temper my disapproval, never mind my choice of words.

'Now Julia, there's no need for that tone and mind your language in front of Holly! This is why I talk to Lynn more than you about my plans. She never speaks to me like that.' Maggie banged her mug of coffee down; it lapped over the edge, and leaked across the pale granite work surface, turning a white envelope Kenco brown. 'See what you've made me do?' cried Maggie, blotting the envelope frantically with kitchen roll. 'If you're not going to support me, then maybe we should draw a line under this topic before we fall out.'

Holly jumped down off the stool and, in her haste, she toppled on to the terracotta tiles. Maggie and I rushed over to the bundle of flowery leggings and lilac fleece, nudging each other roughly in the race to reach Holly first.

'Oh my God, are you okay my pet lamb?' cooed her granny, rocking Holly in her arms, whilst I pushed my way into the huddle of hugs.

'Can I go home now?' whispered Holly.

Fifteen minutes later, I was striding through Lynn's back door as she emerged from the utility room behind a heaving basket of folded clothes.

'Jeez! You gave me a right fright there, I wasn't expecting you back so early,' Lynn set the laundry down on the kitchen table and scanned the room, seeking out evidence of Holly. 'Where's Holly?' Lynn's eyes bulged like a tree frog's. The back door was still open letting the dreary gloom of the late afternoon creep across the threshold like a toxic gas. 'Where is she? Is everything okay?' Lynn blurted, but didn't wait for an answer, 'Well tell me?'

'Oh, so mum phoned?' I replied.

'No, why, what's happened? Why would mum phone?' Lynn's voice quivered.

'It was nothing, she's fine now. Calm down, Holly's just messing around outside with the torch light on my key ring,' I answered.

Like a coiled spring, Lynn leapt past me, huffing and puffing with every step. Seconds later, Holly was dispatched upstairs to her room and Lynn was tapping speed dial 'No 1' into the hall's cordless phone. All Lynn seemed to say down the phone was repeated, 'Uh, huhs'.

The conversation eventually ended with a pantomime performance of, 'Well thanks mum, as long as *you're* sure she's okay.'

Lynn came back into the kitchen with the finale of, 'Yes, *I'll* speak to her. Don't you worry.'

By the time Lynn had replaced the handset I was tying my fringed scarf and heading for the back door. Lynn moved quickly to block my path, 'I want a word about what happened at mum's.'

'Nothing worth talking about happened at mum's. You want a word? Okay, no worries, here's three. Don't. Patronise. Me.' I side-stepped my sister and pulled on the door handle.

'Julia,' Lynn's hand lightly held my sleeve, 'Let's not argue again…'

'Well don't lecture me then,' I sighed, 'I'm the big sister, the one that's supposed to give *you* advice.'

'That's the problem; this is one area where *I* know more than you. She's your *niece*, not one of your pals and I think you should remember that', snapped Lynn. So much for not wanting to argue. 'You might be the smart career girl but sometimes I doubt you're as clever as everyone thinks.'

'I obviously am stupid because I still don't know what the hell this is all about, care to enlighten me? It's not about the sweets is it?'

'No - or the bad language that mum told me about. But if I need to spell it out, I will. Mum said Holly was hurt when she left earlier.'

'What? For Christ's sake, we both checked her after her fall and she was fine. There wasn't a scratch on her.'

'You really don't have a clue do you? I'm not talking about any physical damage; I'm talking about having to witness her granny and auntie arguing. She's not used to confrontation. It upset her.'

'Well, maybe it's time for her to learn or she'll never survive in the real world,' I said.

'And suddenly you're the expert on parenting? It's probably a blessing that you're not a mum,' she spat, 'I'd pity your child.'

Behind Lynn, there was a fridge magnet with a photo of a cute baby on it. Its face was covered in pasta sauce and it was eating spaghetti with its hands. The caption underneath read, *'It's just a phase – so don't miss it!'* The feeling inside me wasn't just a passing phase, the twinge of need to be a mother had developed into a permanent ache.

'That was a low blow,' I took a deep breath. 'So according to you, I wouldn't make a good mum. Does it feel good to rubbish me?'

Lynn shook her head like a disappointed school teacher.

'I wish you could see how smug you look right now, but trust me, it doesn't suit you!'

'Jeez, calm down Julia. I don't know why you're getting so wound up. You're not even thinking about being a mum anyway. I mean, you're not even in a relationship. I thought you wanted a partner, not a baby.'

'And how would you know? You're too busy playing happy families to know what I want.' My finger jabbed the fridge magnet.

'That's not fair. I've always been there for you if you needed to talk.'

'There's no point in trying to explain. You wouldn't understand, let's just leave it at that. Tell Holly I said bye.'

And for the second time in as many weeks, I left Lynn's house without our usual goodbye hug.

Sniffing back hot tears, I crunched down the gravel driveway. This time, I wouldn't dare look up at Holly's bedroom window to see her wave goodbye; an affectionate gesture would be too much to handle.

I thrust my hands inside my coat pocket, searching for a hankie. But all I found was a crumpled ball with rough edges. It was a crunched up sweetie bag – the one that Dan had scribbled his mobile number on. In the same way as I respected my gut feeling with Peter, I refused to ignore what was surely a sign. Life is full of signs; the trick is to know how to read them. Smoothing out the creases in the sweetie bag, I realised that I hadn't thought about Dan since meeting him and his dog. Without pausing for a moment's reflection, I decided to make the call.

Lynn and Maggie might not believe I have maternal instincts, but Dan had thought I looked like the real deal when he saw me with Holly. Me being Holly's mum wasn't a ridiculous idea to Dan. He might even have found it attractive. There was no denying that he had been keen to meet up with me. I badly needed a drink, with someone who wanted to talk *to* me not at me.

It wasn't a bad idea, Kirsty was away to a book festival down south, and I hadn't spoken to any of my ex-colleagues on the *Gazette* in months. I was adamant that Peter would be my last foray into the disastrous world of internet dating. My chances of finding a playmate at short notice on a Saturday night were remote. I could trawl through the contacts on my mobile, but none seemed as attractive as someone who hadn't heard it all before, or even at all. Dan was as good a choice as any to provide a listening ear; I had nothing to lose by giving him a call. He'd said he was new to the Shawbriggs area, so he might be as desperate as me for some company and a Saturday night drink or two.

Just as I was tapping in the digits, I stopped. Yes, it felt good to respond to instincts but I wasn't that impulsive or completely irresponsible. 'Operation Drinking Buddy' required some preliminary research before I could begin my mission. I wouldn't ring his number until I'd Googled him. It was my golden rule before meeting any new guy. A man might tell you some things about himself, and then there was Google to tell you plenty more.

So who is Dan Saunders really? According to the internet, Dan Saunders of ProTech is an Information and Technology Services Consultant and Contractor. I viewed LinkedIn, the business networking site; he had fifty-four connections in the IT industry. That was good enough for me. No cosmic thunderbolt struck me with seedy revelations of crimes and convictions. A brief online search was all it took to convince myself that it was perfectly safe to pick up the phone and dial.

I was right to believe in fate; Dan answered immediately and was eager to meet me within the hour.

'Of course I remember meeting the lovely Auntie Julia with the sweet tooth and this time…,' Dan paused. 'I'll provide the treats.'

'Thanks, but I'm sure you suggested meeting up for something stronger than wine gums!' I said.

'If that's what you'd prefer, Auntie Julia. I aim to please.'

'*Auntie Julia* makes me sound like a frumpy, old agony aunt.'

Dan's laugh instantly cheered me up.

'You're definitely not frumpy or old.'

I checked my reflection in the mirror, in the right light; I could easily pass for twenty-eight, not thirty-eight.

'Thank you, I don't need to feel any worse today.'

A sigh slipped out as I rummaged in my handbag for my cigarettes.

'By the sounds of things, you could do with an agony aunt. Well you're in luck. Uncle Dan's a great listener.'

'That's good to know Uncle Dan, but there's something I need you to agree to before we meet… ' I made him wait. 'Make mine a double G & T if you get there first.'

'It would be my pleasure.'

Dan's laugh was infectious. Within minutes, we'd arranged to meet later in the west end and I sang along to the radio on my way home.

Dropping *Gary* off at the car park beneath my flat, I swithered momentarily about changing my outfit, then reminded myself that this wasn't a proper date. I honestly wasn't interested in men right now, and that included Dan. I wanted someone to talk to, not sleep with. My shagging knickers and balconette bra stayed behind in the undies drawer. I was back out of the door with just a swift comb of my hair, a squirt of deodorant and a splash of Coco Mademoiselle.

It made sense to call Dan. This wasn't a date. I simply wanted company. Nothing more.

That night, I got the alcohol and the company I craved. With more spirit in me than a distillery, my mind spoke the sober truth. What had started as me letting a trickle of my feelings escape about Lynn's criticism, ended up as a torrent of emotions about my fear of never becoming a mother. My intuition had indeed been correct; the sweetie bag had stayed in my pocket for a reason. A good listener is not someone who has nothing to say. And Dan offered me a very interesting solution.

CAROL

Dear Journal

Dan texted and asked me to meet him at my *Angel's Bench* for a walk with the dogs tomorrow night. I sent a text back that I was sorry I couldn't make it cos I had my yoga class. He replied that he'll miss seeing my smile and filled the whole screen with rows of sad faces. When Isobel came through to the back shop, I must've been grinning like an eejit and she asked if I was alright. I laughed and she said I was either going mad or getting back to my old self. Isobel joked that she didn't know which one would be easiest to work with. It does feel as if I've lightened up since meeting Dan. I think that's why Isobel asked me to take the order for a funeral this afternoon when she was on her tea break. Up until now, all I did was make the wreaths and even then, if a customer wanted something like *SON* spelt out in chrysanthemums, Isobel would make sure that I was busy doing another order and she'd do it instead. She's a good soul. And even though I'd ask folk to come back later if Isobel was out delivering in the van, she never once gave me a hard time for not taking their funeral order there and then. She was right to let me take the order today cos I'd no problem dealing with the customer. Maybe I'll start going back out front again cos it can get a bit lonely with just the flowers for company.

Isobel once bought a huge encyclopaedia of flowers at a car boot sale but she never looks at it. I like flicking through it when we're quiet. I pick a different flower and try to learn its Latin name and memorise all the information. When it's only me and the flowers in the shop, I often wonder what kind of flower the people I know would be.

Once, I heard Isobel's hubby, Big Joe, call her sweet pea when he popped in to the shop. No one but Joe would seriously call her sweet pea, not with her dumpy figure and teeth two sizes too big for her face. No, she could never be described as delicate and fragile like a sweet pea. But anyone who knows her like I do would say that she is gentle and sensitive, so a sweet pea isn't far off the mark. I asked her once what kind of flower she thought suited her best. After a few minutes and a couple of choccy digestives, she replied that she was more like a dandelion - impossible to get rid of, full of enthusiasm when she was young but blowing in the wind now that she was old and spreading.

I can spend ages matching people to flowers. I've got everybody sussed now. Elaine's a full bodied rose - once you get past the thorns she can be quite kind really. My mum's name is Lily, but she's more of a bright orange gerbera cos she's naturally chirpy and always tries her best to perk me up. Dan would be a corn poppy. There's a lot more to poppies than just Remembrance Day. I bet lots of folk don't know that the poppy is actually a weed and can be poisonous to grazing animals. We don't use poppies in the shop; they're rubbish as cut flowers cos their petals fall off too quickly. But I love them even though their beauty doesn't last long. The poppy suits Dan cos it's vivid and bright, plus parts of the flower were once used to heal aches and pains, so he's definitely a corn poppy or papaver rhoeas, its Sunday name.

I used to wish my flower match was an exotic orchid or a trendy bird of paradise. In reality, I've always felt more like a wilting carnation for sale from a petrol station. Although when I told Dan that I worked in a florist, he said he could picture me there with my warm smiley face like a cheery yellow sunflower. It's one of the nicest things anyone has ever said to me. It's rotten not being able to see Dan sooner, especially when he said he has a plan that could solve my problem.

It was a good thing I gave flowers a lot of thought, as there is no question about it, men can't pick the right flowers without help. The wrong flowers send the wrong message. It was up to me to help our male customers get it right.

The questions were always much the same.

'Excuse me, but could you tell me which flowers would be good as an apology?' or 'Which bunch would be a nice thank you gift?' The most common query by far was, 'Can you tell me the best flowers for saying "I love you"?'

I'd thought I'd heard them all before, but I was thrown when a customer caught me singing to myself, the guy's question was a new one for me.

'Eh, ah was wondering, which flowers make you feel happy? Y'see ma girlfriend needs cheering up.'

Thanks to Dan, the answer was obvious and my choice was spot on. Uplifting, joyful yellow - the colour of dreams come true.

'Sunflowers make me happy.'

'Ta, ah'll take a bunch of those then,' replied the customer.

A job well done.

Earlier, a female customer had asked for subtle flowers for an elderly friend who was ill. If flowers could speak, then the gentle pastel shades of the freesias that I chose for a hand-tied bouquet whispered "get well soon" in a soothing tone.

I was back in my stride, busy putting the finishing touches to a new display for the Daisy Chain's window, when I spotted my neighbour Lynn crossing the road to enter the shop. Lynn paused to admire the white calla lilies with slender grasses and iridescent resin crystals I'd arranged in a goldfish-like bowl.

'Hi Carol, you're looking well,' said Lynn.

'Thanks,' I replied. 'You too. Are you looking for something special today?'

'Yeah, I love that arrangement in your window, something like that would look good for the swishing party I'm having.'

In *Natter*, I'd read an article on how to organise a clothes swapping party known as 'swishing'. The magazine feature explained that the art of swishing involved getting your friends together to swap clothes and socialise at the same time. Everyone had to bring along at least one good quality item of clothing, or an accessory, to pass on.

'Only family and friends are invited. I've not asked neighbours, I mean you've got to draw the line somewhere, eh?' said Lynn.

'Ah know what you mean.' I hoped Lynn didn't expect an actual example of my non-existent experience of hosting parties.

'But it'd be good if you could make it. Are you free next Wednesday?'

'Eh, thanks for the invite, it's just that ah wouldn't know anybody else so...' I hesitated.

'Oh, but you soon will. It's only a small get together and

they're a really friendly bunch. Bring along a friend too if you like,' said Lynn.

'Eh, thanks but ah'm still no sure. Y'see ah've never been tae a swishing party before.'

It was tempting to tinker with the arrangement of lilies, anything to avoid eyeballing Lynn.

'That's not a problem. It's all about saving money, saving the planet and it's an excuse for a party. Don't worry there'll be lots of virgins there.'

'It's been a long time since ah could call maself a virgin.'

Lynn laughed as if my feeble joke was the funniest thing she'd heard in years, maybe she didn't get out much either.

'Just like the rest of us then! Trust me; you'll have a great night. It'll be a good laugh.'

'Eh, well, ah suppose ah could come for a wee while.'

I pictured all the designer shoes and bags that I could bring along to impress Lynn's friends. For once, my upmarket accessories could be dug out of my bulging wardrobe, dusted down and openly admired.

'Brilliant. I've got another reason for the gathering but I can't tell you yet, it's still a secret, but all will be revealed on Wednesday night.'

Elaine hadn't been round at the weekend to do our swap of the *Shawbriggs Herald* for *Natter* and I'd missed catching up on news. I couldn't remember the last time I had an invite to pass on to Elaine, but when I texted her later during my tea break, she got straight back to me.

**No thx. Ur
skinny neighbour
wouldn't want 2 swap
her size 8 stuff with me
X**

Panic rose like bile from my stomach. Surely Elaine didn't think I was trying to show her up because of her outsize clothes? Just to make sure she wasn't offended, I quickly texted back.

Accessories fit evry1 +
I really want U 2 come 2 :-)
xxx

She didn't reply and after ten endless minutes, I dialled Elaine's number. My new self-confidence was now as shrivelled as an old walnut. No matter how I worded the invite, Elaine wasn't for changing her mind.

'Carol, leave it will you? Ah dinnae want tae go tae your posh pal's party.'

'Honestly, she's no that posh and she says that her pals are really nice,' I said.

'Maybe you're right but ah'm no interested. End. Of. Story.'

The conversation was one of the most tense we'd ever had, Elaine was as stubborn as a skelf stuck under the skin. I gave it one last go to persuade her.

'Ah'd feel better aboot going if you went too. You know ah get nervous meeting new folk,' I said.

'Here's an idea, if you're quick, you could get a last minute appointment with the spine doctor at the Royal Infirmary,' said Elaine. I gripped the phone.

'Elaine, please dinnae wind me up.'

'You'll be fine. And you dinnae need me there tae enjoy yourself. Go tae the party, it'll dae you good. They'll love you and they'll love your Jimmy Choo heels too!'

Elaine's backhanded compliment was like a slap that throbbed long after the phone call.

By the time Wednesday night arrived, I stood on Lynn's doorstep, feeling as if my insides were in a Kenwood mixer. Repeated ringing of the bell brought no one to the door. I pressed my ear against the wooden door; the yakety yak leaked outside. It was definitely the right day and time, and yet no one answered the door. Maybe I should just go home? Too late. The door sprung open and there was Holly in her pyjamas.

'I'll get my mum,' said Holly. She shuffled off in her Minnie Mouse slippers.

'Thanks pet.'

'*Muuum*, a lady's at the door.'

'Who is it?' asked Lynn, shouting down the hall.

'The one with the shaggy dog. From the wee house at the end of the street, you know, the one with the red door?' yelled Holly.

Holly looked me up and down, whilst blowing spit bubbles. The picture of innocence wasn't as cute up close as I had imagined. Lynn emerged from the kitchen carrying a platter of bite-sized canapés.

'Thanks for coming. Oh, and sorry about keeping you on the doorstep. Welcome to the madhouse!'

No turning back now. I walked up the hall as awkwardly as a newborn giraffe and hung my jacket on a coat hook.

'Go through to the lounge, I'll be in in a minute, just need to fire up the oven,' said Lynn.

My tummy growled like a Rottweiler. Lynn must've heard it cos she added, 'There'll be a light buffet later.'

Edging into the room, my shyness clung to me like a wet shower curtain. The lounge was wall-to-wall with Mumzillas. Their rowdy rabbiting quietened to mere muttering as they eyed up the new arrival. My fixed grin was beginning to fade. Was I supposed to announce my arrival with words too? At last, a cheery voice threw me a lifeline.

'Hello dear, you must be Carol. I'm Maggie by the way. There's a space here if you like,' the older woman squished up to make space for me on the sofa beside her.

It was a friendly crowd like Lynn had promised.

Nothing to worry about after all.

A large glass of wine helped calm my nerves. It was all going well until I overheard Lynn's friend Annie, bitching in the kitchen. As soon as I could, I escaped and ran all the way home.

WEDNESDAY 9TH MARCH 2011

Dear Journal

I'm so glad to be home after Lynn's swishing party. I was even happy to see Jinky waiting behind the kitchen door for me. Whether I want it or not, I always get a great welcome from him. I can see why folk talk about a dog being man's best friend and tonight I needed one.

About ten women were at the party, including Lynn and her sister Julia, and Lynn's mum, Maggie. She was really friendly - thank God. It turns out that Maggie was there to swap her ladylike clothes for more casual stuff cos she's planning on going travelling soon. I was impressed at how brave she is; I could never imagine my mum or me going abroad on our own. I recognised a few of the women who've been in the Daisy Chain before, but it didn't make much difference. I didn't belong there. I took along one of my favourite bags, a genuine Louis Vuitton that I'd got off eBay for £185. An iconic brand, its luxurious style and classic shape make it a top choice in designer bags. I explained that it goes with any outfit, but the way they gawped at me, it was obvious that they didn't think someone working in a florist knew about style, or that they could ever afford it. One of Lynn's pals called Nicola (who has huge fake boobs) asked me if I'd used it much and another one asked me if I had the original dust bag. They didn't believe that the bag was authentic. They passed it round like they were handling stolen goods. Nobody wanted to swap anything for it, and the only one who seemed interested in it was Julia. She'd brought along a beautiful silk Hermes scarf that some guy she'd met recently bought her; she said she felt like an air stewardess when she wore it. I couldn't see me wearing it either so I ended up bringing my designer bag back home with me.

Not managing to swap the bag wasn't the only reason that it was a rubbish night. When I went to the kitchen for another glass of wine, one of Lynn's pals called Annie (grey suede Boden buckle handbag, acrylic nails) was telling Julia that she felt sorry for me cos of Ben's death. I don't know how she knows that I'm his mum, maybe Lynn's told her. I froze when they mentioned Ben's accident and I pretended I was checking my hair in the hall mirror. I shouldn't have been surprised, Isobel shares any juicy gossip she hears in the shop and if I've missed something then Elaine fills in the gaps. Shawbriggs isn't a big place, and stories sprout legs as they race around town.

This isn't the first time I've overheard folk talking about Ben, but it was the next bit that made me get my coat and leave. Annie said to Julia that although it was a real shame about Ben, at least the wee boy's dad has moved on and is having a new baby with his girlfriend. Annie knows her from going into Street Beach and seemingly Kimberly and Steve are both thrilled. She told the others that she'd seen a photo of Steve and Kimberly at an award ceremony run by the local paper. They all agreed with Annie that something good had come out of something tragic - and wasn't Steve a great guy raising money for Broken Cord? Their praise was enough to make me want to vomit.

Before I threw up the stuffed mushrooms I'd wolfed from the buffet, I made my excuse to leave. Lynn asked me to hang on for a few more minutes so that she could make her big announcement. After her telling us all why swishing is a great idea, she giggled that, if she was honest, then she really only wanted to have the party to swap some of her size 8 clothes for bigger stuff cos she's pregnant! Elaine's plus size clothes would've come in handy after all. And I've got a good idea now why Elaine didn't pop in at the weekend to bring me last week's *Shawbriggs Herald*.

By the time I ran home, let Jinky out for a pee and opened a bottle of red wine, I had two texts. One from Dan.

Missed u
Did u have a
good time
at the party? x

And one from Elaine.

Hope u swapped handbag 4 a
1 night stand with a hunky stud
would be more use 2 u!
L O L x

There was also a rambling message on my answer machine from my mum.

'Carol, it's me, yer mither. Fit like this week? Ah jist wanted tae phone tae let ye ken that ah've sent ye a wee package the day.

Oh and tae let ye know that Mrs MacWatt's gaun tae be a great-granny again this simmer. That'll be nine grandchildren and two great-grandchildren she'll hae! Ah'm going tae start knittin fir the bairn. There's nothing tae beat hand knittin and ye can never have ower mony matinee jackets. Ah've bought lovely 4 ply lemon wool. Ye canna gang wrang with that colour. And ah got three baas fir the price o twa.'

There was a brief silence on the tape followed by a long sigh from my mum. 'Ah hope everything's alright doon there. Ye know me, ah worry about ye. And ah didn't think ye'd be oot on a Wednesday night. Ye never said anything aboot going oot. Can ye phone me when you get back in? Then ah'll be able tae relax and settle doon now tae watch...' Then the tape ran out.

I replayed the message three times; mum's lilting voice was as comforting as a cuddle. I wasn't sure which message pleased me most; at least there were three people on the planet thinking about me tonight.

Elaine's "L O L x" banter was real and sincere. Not like the 'friends' I'd spent time with tonight. A true friend, she was trying to spare me from seeing the news in the local paper. She was probably too scared to go with me to the party and risk seeing me upset in public. Elaine was still on my side, and so was Dan. Was it the red wine that gave me a warm glow? Or was it that Dan's message ended with "x" too? Whatever the reason it felt good.

It was well after ten o'clock, my mum always waited for the news headlines before bedding down each night. Should I wake her? Or leave my mum anxious about me not calling back? Another hefty gulp of wine might help me decide. If I phoned, I risked blurting out the news of Steve and Kimberly. My mum would be more upset by a long distance sobbing session than me not returning her call. I returned the phone to its cradle.

It wasn't too late to text; no one could hear me sniff or see my false smile.

**Didn't swap handbag 4 stud
or new pals!
u were right not 2 go
xxx**

That would satisfy Elaine for tonight. There was no need to tell her that I knew about Kimberly's pregnancy or Steve being in the *Shawbriggs Herald*.

**Hi Dan
Can't wait to see u
& hear ur plan 2 help me
x**

Eventually I'd tell them all about Kimberly and Lynn being pregnant, but not tonight, and not by text. Only Jinky heard me sobbing, as I fired balled up tissues on to the floor.

'Ah'll tidy them up later.'

'Rather you than me. You're making one helluva mess!'

The damp hankies lay around me as if I'd been pelted with snowballs. My eyes were screwed shut and yet they still leaked tears on to Jinky's matted fur as I nuzzled into the mutt's neck. The dog was straining to be released from my grip; I couldn't blame him.

'Go on then, beat it. You're crap company anyway!'

'You're no exactly a party animal yourself.'

Jinky jumped down from the sofa and slinked back to the kitchen as I refilled my glass. The wine bottle was soon as empty as my heart.

A few clicks of the mouse were all it took to reveal the details of this year's overall winner of the 'Shine On' award. There was Steve, as bold as a bullock, with his arm round Kimberly: half the brain and twice the boobs.

The front page article broadcast that the 'Shawbriggs Stars' awards recognised the outstanding service given by people who were "shining examples" to the community.

"Through their commitment to helping others in the spirit of 'Service above Self', they provide a significant contribution to the wider community. The 'Shine On' Trophy is a special honour given by the judging panel each year to the person who has made an exceptional, long-term commitment to charity. The Shawbriggs Herald is delighted to reward Steve Walker's tireless efforts in raising thousands of pounds for 'Broken Cord', the national bereavement charity for parents who have tragically lost a child."

The feature went on to say that Steve's own son, Ben had sadly died in a road accident at the age of nine, leaving his father devastated. No mention of me, his mum.

"In the three years since, Steve, general manager of the Norwood House Hotel, and his partner Kimberly McKechnie (pictured alongside our 'star'), have organised a calendar of fundraising events at the popular local hotel. Steve, modest as ever, told us, "It wasn't all selfless. Keeping busy running the charity events has been a lifesaving coping mechanism for me. They've helped me get through every dad's worst nightmare, but the bonus is that the events have given a much needed boost to a fantastic charity's funds."

The news piece ended with a link to Broken Cord's website for more information on Steve's fundraising ideas. It was irresistible. A single click and Steve's face invaded my screen once more. Under his smug grin, there was a lengthy interview with Broken Cord's best loved champion. He was happy to share his top tip for other bereaved dads dealing with the aftermath of a heart breaking accident: *"Take a moment right now to forgive someone for something they have done whether it's real or imagined.*

Forgiveness has to start somewhere... Why not let it start with you?"

'Forgive you? Never ever ever. Not as long as I live!' Spittle sprayed across the screen and I wiped some from my chin.

I hurled my wine glass at the wall, the glass bounced once off the pine bookcase, scarring the soft wood, before the slender neck broke clean off on to the laminate floor. The wine ran down the wall like tears, travelling along the lines of the embossed wallpaper, mapping out a dead end route.

I woke up on the couch – still in last night's clothes. My tongue stuck like Velcro to the roof of my mouth and I staggered to the bathroom. I ran my tongue across the fur that coated my teeth. My poisoned liver had punished me. The skin under each eye was puffy and tinged with yellowish grey bruises. No amount of mint mouth wash or citrus zest soap could make me feel fresh.

Later at work, my washed-out face was enough of a hint, Isobel tiptoed round me as she prepared to go out on a delivery.

'It must have been *some* party last night doll.'

My weak smile wasn't enough to satisfy Isobel's natural nosiness. I couldn't admit that nearly all of the alcohol had been consumed at home alone. A urine sample from me could be served in a bar with a paper parasol and a swizzle stick.

'It turned into a bit of a celebration, cos you know ma neighbour Lynn, well she's pregnant.'

'Lynn Gordon. Aye, I know her mum too. Aw, Maggie'll be chuffed to bits. That's lovely.'

'Aye. Another new baby...'

'Well, as long as you had a good time and your neighbour didn't drink as much as you did! Isobel gently patted me on the shoulder. 'I'll leave you in peace with your hangover.'

My plan was to skip dinner for an hour of sleep before

meeting Dan at six o'clock. I needed to hear his plan with a clear head. Resting was a sensible idea, but when I got back home I couldn't ignore the chunks of broken glass lying on the floor. And I couldn't pretend I wasn't embarrassed to see red wine stains on the magnolia wallpaper. There was no way that I'd be able to relax with the dregs of my weepy outburst taunting me. The power nap would have to wait until I'd hauled the bookcase free from the wall to wipe away any trace of my fit of rage.

I ran a finger across the layer of grime on the skirting board. The filthy woodwork would make my mum weep.

Reaching down with a duster, I discovered a *Matchbox* racing car underneath the bookcase. Ben must have sent the car careering along the floor years ago, to crash and lie forgotten in the dust. I picked up the scuffed metal car and rubbed it tenderly with the cloth; there would be no chance of a peaceful sleep. The yellow duster smelt musty, but it served the purpose well as I used it to mop up my tears.

By five minutes to six I'd made it to my *Angel's Bench*. When I closed my eyes, there was a kaleidoscope of colours: dancing neon patterns in their own private disco.I kept my eyes screwed shut and clenched each and every body part to concentrate, hard. I wished the arms of the bench would somehow wrap me in a tight cuddle – like Ben used to do when I reached up to his cabin bed to kiss him goodnight.

It was no use. The energy used up in tensing every muscle in my body was wasted. The blackened wood of the bench was as lifeless as before. My hands curled into balled fists and my fingernails carved out crescent moons into my palms. But no matter how hard I dug into the skin, the pain brought no relief.

In the distance the Fuzzy-Felt shape of Roxy, with Dan following, became clearer with each step. Dan was smiling and waving at me as Jinky sprinted ahead to meet them.

By the time we'd walked round the woodland trail, Dan had shared his plan with me. Maybe it was the dryness from my almighty hangover that stopped my tongue forming the words to respond; I was in shock and totally speechless at his solution.

'I realise that it's a radical idea and you'll need time to take it all in but, if you think about it, it makes perfect sense. Do you really see yourself pushing a pram with a Chinese baby along Main Street?' Not waiting for an answer Dan continued. 'It wouldn't feel right, and it wouldn't look right. The baby would never really belong to you. It would never compare to it being your own and you know that.'

As we reached the exit, Dan stopped and bent down to put Roxy back on the lead. When he straightened up, he kept talking, as if he didn't expect a reply from me.

'I don't want to pressure you and I understand that you need time to think, but time's actually your biggest enemy. I know you've considered ideas like foreign adoption and sure, there are other alternatives. Do as much research into your options as you want, but I can promise you that you'll come back to the same conclusion. I'm offering you the easiest, cheapest, and most importantly, the safest answer to your problem.'

'What dae you mean safest? The adoption agencies are legal...' I interrupted, aware that the ground beneath me no longer felt solid.

'Carol, the agencies might very well be regulated but you have no idea what kind of baby you'd be getting or where it's come from.' Dan shook his head slowly from side to side.

'For all you'd know, the child could be riddled with disease.' Dan paused, long enough for me to picture babies will all sorts of deformities. 'Do you really want to take the chance of adopting a medical nightmare? Haven't you been through enough?'

He was right. I couldn't cope with that scenario. Overnight, Dan's tone had gone from friendly to business-like; I was struggling to keep up with the swift change of gear. Listening to his logic made my head hurt. The pain would ease eventually, but my heart would never recover, not now that Steve was replacing Ben with a new baby. He had robbed me of a child and no one else seemed able to help except Dan.

He understood my suffering, and was giving me a chance to be a mother again. I'd feel the same mum-to-be joy as Kimberly. Dan must've lost someone really close to him in the past. It was obvious that he knew that the biggest tragedy of death was what was left unfulfilled, and the many things I had still wanted to do with my son. Ben hadn't been able to cheat death, but if I had another child, I could pass on a legacy. I accepted Dan's logic. I could never be described as beautiful, but with Dan's help, I *could* make something beautiful.

"God always helps those who help themselves" was one of my mum's favourite sayings. What was so wrong in considering Dan's solution? He was right; I needed time to think it through. And yet there was no doubt that it was what I wanted, it was just a case of how much it was going to cost me, on every level.

My heart and head galloped ahead; I needed to rein myself in.

'Think about it,' said Dan, cutting through the thick silence between us. 'But not for too long.'

'When do I need to give you my answer?' I rubbed at the tightness in my forehead, in between swipes at Jinky. The mutt barked at me in a plea to keep moving.

'I've got a new job down south and I'll be moving away at the end of the month. If you want to go through with my suggestion, you'll need to let me know soon.'

If Elaine had been here, she'd have given me a sweaty upper lip alert. Even though the nippy March air was biting at my face,

I tugged to loosen the hand knitted bouclé scarf that my mum had sent down last winter. The curls of the multi-coloured yarns threatened to strangle me and I clawed at the scarf to free my throat.

'How soon?' I asked.

'By Sunday at the latest. And remember, this is strictly between me and *you*.' As Dan stepped forward and leaned into my face, the warmth of the word '*you*' clashed with the chilly air. Yet the word still felt bitterly cold.

JULIA

When I'd called Dan about meeting for a drink, my first thought was to meet in my usual haunt, Oran Mor in the city's west end. The converted church overlooking the Botanic Gardens was a safe choice. But I'd paused and instead suggested meeting in Jinty McGuinty's in cobbled Ashton Lane, nearer the university. Jinty's would be a heaving mass of Saturday night punters, but I assumed that Dan would feel more comfortable amongst the traditional Celtic tunes, than the restored grandeur of Oran Mor.

During the day, Jinty's was a dusty, brooding old boozer where the likes of James Joyce would have been comfortable sharing his wisdom. It was a very different scene in the evenings when the dark walls vibrated with music from Clannad to the Cranberries; only the very lucky were able to secure one of the prized wooden snugs to escape the crush. Amazingly, as I pushed through the crowded bar, there was Dan, casually muscling his way into a corner table that had just been vacated. He was holding aloft a small tray with a bottle of beer, a large gin garnished with a wedge of lime and a bottle of tonic water.

Dan wasn't dressed in the tatty Berghaus jacket and worn-out jeans I'd last seen him wearing. Instead he had on a stylish woollen reefer jacket and dark-wash jeans topped with a purple gingham shirt. Dan wouldn't have looked out of place at Oran Mor after all. He waved over and winked at me, he seemed much sharper than I'd remembered in every respect. I was glad I'd made the call.

The glug, glug, glug of Dan pouring the tonic water into my glass was the most satisfying sound I'd heard all day.

'You sounded like you needed this.' Handing me the glass, Dan picked up his and extended it towards me, faking an exaggerated Irish accent, 'Slainte. Here's to being single… drinking doubles… and seeing triple!'

It was the most fitting toast Dan could have delivered. The chink-chink of glass on glass was almost as pleasing as the glug, glug, glug had been a minute earlier. My shoulders dropped by inches as I took a greedy gulp of gin before I took my coat off.

'So,' he brushed his hands through his salt and pepper hair. 'Apart from being Auntie Julia, what else d'you get up to?'

'Is this the point where I can reinvent my life to sound way more exciting than it really is?'

I peeled off my Burberry trench coat and unleashed my emotions along with the belt. Dan had kindly presented me with the gift of a straightforward opener, but I didn't want to talk about work or even play tonight. Lately it seemed that all I could contribute to a conversation centred round career or dating disasters. As interesting and entertaining as the topics might be to some, I'd no intention of discussing either *Business Scot* or men like Paedo Pete.

'I don't believe you'll need to embellish the truth. So, what d'you like to do if you're not working?' asked Dan.

'Truth? Right now, all I'd really like to do is to stay on speaking terms with my only sister and my mother.'

'Ah, that explains the need for a stiff drink. I'm all ears.'

My resolve to play it cool wasn't as strong as the gin. What started as a flippant remark ended up with me telling Dan all about my row with Lynn and her accusation that I was a poor role model for Holly. Dan had little more to do than listen and was soon aware of the rocky relationship I had with my sister. Listening to my moans, I couldn't deny that they reeked of underlying competitiveness.

I was an achiever, of that there was no doubt. Finishing sixth year as the high school dux, I could have shone in any chosen profession and had left Lynn a difficult act to follow. Lynn had never shown any desire to excel academically and, wearing jelly shoes, leg warmers and a ra-ra skirt she drifted through school in a cloud of Elnett hairspray. By sixteen, with Princess Diana blue eye shadow, Miami Vice rolled-up jacket sleeves and a side ponytail, she washed up as a receptionist on the shores of the local Volkswagen car dealership. A couple of years later, Lynn bragged that Chris strutted out of the showroom, not only swinging the keys to a flame-red Corrado hatchback coupé but also a date with her and a free AA Great Britain Road Atlas. My sister's life was mapped out before he'd changed gear in the Corrado. That night in our teenage bedroom, she'd replayed the toe-curling patter Chris had inflicted on her.

'Did you know that Volkswagen have a tradition of naming cars after winds? They named the Corrado after the Spanish word for 'wind current'. And 'Corrado' comes from the Spanish verb 'Correr', which means to run.'

I bet Lynn's undivided attention was lapped up like warm milk by Chris.

'None of the boys I know even drive; never mind having their own car. I've never had a ride in a Corrado before. I've always wondered what it'd be like,' Lynn had told him.

'No need to wonder anymore, babe.' Lynn said that Chris's

wink promised exactly the kind of ride she was hoping for.

Once she'd taken up residence in the passenger seat, Lynn had boasted that she was confident that she'd put the brakes on Chris's days of dating any other girls. And sure enough, after eighteen months of seeing Lynn, Chris traded in his Corrado for a family friendly Caramac coloured Passat. I was there when he rolled up in his new car to take Lynn for a run.

'So what does Passat mean? Is it the name for a wind too?' Lynn had asked. Chris mumbled something about Passat meaning 'trade wind' before he added loudly that he considered the boring workhorse a different definition of Passat:

Pretty
Ass
Sexy
Sport
Auto
Turbo

'Oh, right, I see what you mean,' Lynn had tried to sound convincing, but it was all that she could muster as she took a seat in the dullest of cars next to the dullest of men.

And yet, she'd beaten me in the first round of the 'Who Dates Wins' contest. Years later, she was still streaks ahead. Lynn didn't just have the cuddly toy to take home to her mock-Georgian detached villa; she had a walking talking living doll. Holly.

Lynn had competed in the dating game and she had won the prize that mattered most. For all my career successes, I hadn't even come close to sniffing the scent of Johnson's Baby Powder. Winning gracefully is easy. Losing gracefully is much harder. I tried my best to always smile and congratulate the winner, telling Lynn how happy I was for her. I attended baby showers and christenings and listened with interest at repeated re-tellings of the birth stories. I even fawned over the 12-week baby scans when the fuzzy shapes looked more alien than human. I helped out at birthday parties and sat through school shows. Smiling all the while. No matter how much it hurt. I was a champ at disguising my tears as tears of joy, and remembering to smile, even if it was through gritted teeth.

The theory was great but there's no such thing as a good loser, there's just a loser.

Lynn was the outright winner.

No question.

No steward's enquiry.

Lynn was a mum. Fact.

No studying, no exams, no degree was required for this achievement.

I couldn't dispute Lynn had beaten me hands down. Several swigs of gin later, I found myself admitting that if Dan scratched the surface of my career woman veneer, there was a wannabe breast-feeding mother and toddler committee member underneath.

Was it the ambience of the setting? Or the copious amount of gin that Dan made sure was flowing? Or simply a burning need to offload on someone? Whatever it was, Dan's ears were roasted by the time I'd described how unsuccessful 'PLAN A' had been so far.

Dan discovered that my 'PLAN A' involved ticking four boxes:

1. Establish a respected career in journalism √
2. Buy a trendy exclusive harbour front flat √
3. Marry my soul mate/man of my dreams
4. Give birth to a baby

Numbers 1 and 2 had been relatively easy to achieve.

Unfortunately, my freelance work was unpredictable, and I had a hefty mortgage, which along with my expensive tastes meant I'd racked up huge amounts of debt. But I was proud that the first two boxes had been ticked. It was only numbers 3 and 4 that were proving to be beyond my reach. The stuff of dreams. Just like my top secret fantasy to marry my very own Mr Darcy. But who wouldn't? Rich, gorgeous, even with mutton-chops, a sensitive yet brooding sort of man, that takes such good care of his little sister AND he's absolutely devoted to Elizabeth. Every woman's ideal man.

Never mind Mr Darcy, there wasn't even a Mr in my life. Or even Andrew. Dan listened patiently to my story of breaking up with Andrew and my ultimatum about having a baby.

'I honestly thought he was 'The One', I said. 'I felt so empty when he left.'

'That's because he took your future with him.' Dan sympathised.

'Exacatamundo!'

'A smart woman like you knows what she wants and doesn't settle for second best. That guy just didn't measure up.'

'Don't even get me started on the rest of the dickheads I've dated since Andrew.'

But I did get started and found it difficult to stop. And, as a perfect example, I told him about my recent dating fiasco with Paedo Pete and my suspicions of his interest in kiddie porn.

'Dirty bastard. Guys like that should have their balls cut off with a rusty knife!'

'I couldn't have put it better myself.'

'With losers like Andrew and creeps like Pete out there, it's no wonder you're pissed off.' Dan leaned forward in his seat, and gently took my hand. 'Julia, I hope you don't mind me saying it but if I was you, I'd start to think outside the box.'

I had to accept that PLAN A had failed me so far. Dan assured me that he had an alternative plan. A superior, alternative plan. It could be my PLAN B.

In the heady fug of the pub, Dan's PLAN B sounded entirely logical and reasonable. Dan texted me the next day to see if I'd considered his suggestion. Was it the hangover that made my head pound like a migraine on steroids? Or it was the daunting reality of Dan's proposal?

Spontaneously calling Dan to meet up for a drink wasn't difficult. Acting on instinct and making things happen was what I did best. But committing to his PLAN B was something else entirely. If I made a rash decision now, then I would pay the penalty for the rest of my life.

Deadlines dictated my business life. I was well used to their demand for quick thinking but I'd never before been faced with anything so life-changing. Finishing my relationship with Andrew had taken me months of wavering between the pros and cons before I finally gave him the ultimatum of baby or break up. Being on the receiving end didn't feel any easier.

A second opinion helped but, even through the haze of a hangover, I remembered that part of the deal was that Dan insisted on absolute secrecy. He'd been very clear that if there was the slightest whiff of anyone else knowing about his proposition then the whole thing was off.

Stick with PLAN A?

I had no PLAN B.

Not until I met Dan.

Agree to Dan's PLAN B?

Not a simple choice.

There was nothing easy about consenting to Dan's idea. Business-like or not, this was the hardest decision I'd ever faced in my life. Grappling with my options, was like trying to put up an umbrella in a hurricane. Every time I turned to face another direction, a new path, a different route, the torrential rain battered my judgement call and I was swept off my feet, unable to stand tall and move forward.

When stuck with a work assignment, I found that the answer always came to me when I least expected it and the best thing to do was to distract myself. Keep busy and eventually I'd find a way through the tangled knot of emotional algae that had clogged up my mind. Two paracetamol might help too. The phone's piercing ring certainly didn't.

'Are you free on Wednesday?' asked Lynn.

'Depends. Why?'

'Well I thought you might want to come to my swishing party.'

'Thanks, but I never go out on days ending in 'y'.'

'Very funny. Mum's coming and a few friends.'

'It's the "few friends" bit that puts me off. I'd rather stay at home and backcomb my muff than listen to their school-gate gossip all night.'

'That's a bit harsh. They're a good laugh when you get to know them.'

'I'll take your word for it. And I've got a deadline to meet.'

This time, I wasn't lying, not that it would mean anything to Lynn. Emptying her laundry basket was pressure in her world.

'I told mum you'd be there but if it'd kill you to socialise with *my* friends then forget…'

'What time on Wednesday?'

Days later, I found myself sitting between Maggie and Lynn's neighbour, Carol, at my first swishing party. Lynn promised that there would be a buffet later, I decided to skip it. A night like this meant that alcohol counted as a major food group. It was the only way to endure Lynn's catty clique.

'Would you like a glass of wine?' asked Lynn.

'Of course, I'm surprised you need to ask.'

'Well, you know the house rules here: first glass is served to you, after that, help yourself.'

'Suits me. I hope you're well stocked up.'

It was on one of my DIY wine refills that I encountered Annie, pointing out the other guests in the lounge for the benefit of her new recruit on the PTA of Shawbriggs Primary School.

'Yes, that's Nicola.' Annie raised a pencilled eyebrow. 'She's been divorced twice; poor thing can't seem to hold on to a man, even after the implants...'

Measuring only 5.2 on the Bitchter scale, this was a pitiful effort by Annie. Elbowing my way past the duo to reach the wine, Annie widened the space to include me. She clearly couldn't resist inflaming another pair of ears with the latest hot gossip that she was eager to share.

'I mean, she waited a while after the accident.' Annie lowered her voice. 'But you can't really blame Kimberly for wanting a baby of her own. She said Steve's over the moon,' murmured Annie.

I'd have cheerfully chewed off my right leg in exchange for a cigarette, but I had to make do with stabbing at a black olive. I winced at its saltiness. Annie turned her head and scanned the room as if she was a surveillance camera, prodding my arm as she did so.

'Do you know Carol?' asked Annie. 'She lives in one of the only semis on the estate. I think the family next door to her are called Farrell or maybe it's Fraser...' Not waiting on a response, Annie prattled on, ignoring the fact that my face must've looked like I was stuck on *The Times* crossword.

'I suppose the planners make the developers build a couple of semis, but it's only got a single garage and no conservatory. And even though it's the size of a doll's house, I don't know how she can afford the mortgage on her own - she only works in the Daisy Chain.' I stabbed another olive as Annie continued. 'Anyway, you know about Lynn's neighbour's wee boy don't you?' Stretching up to my ear, Annie whispered and nodded sideways at the wall between the kitchen and lounge, as if Carol and her family history were so apparent that it could be revealed through walls.

'Eh, yes, you mean about him being knocked down and killed? What about it?' There was no stopping Annie now.

'Well, his dad's girlfriend, that's Kimberly. She's as tanned as a Florida granny with all the free sun bed sessions but I blame Jordan for influencing girls like Kimberly. Do you know her?'

'Who? Kimberly or Jordan?' My exasperated sigh only resulted in Annie pausing to slowly explain as if I had special needs. 'I'm talking about Kimberly, not Jordan the page three model. Kimberly was desperate for a baby but he, that's Steve, wouldn't let her in case it upset Carol. That's the wee boy's mum, you know Carol, Lynn's neighbour?'

I was trapped and only a large guzzle of wine took the edge off Annie's long-winded account of Carol's misfortune.

'Well, it wasn't as if it was Kimberly's fault, you can blame her for a lot of things but not the boy getting knocked down. So why should she suffer?' Annie puffed up. 'And I mean, Steve is entitled to be a dad again. Don't get me wrong, I feel really sorry for Carol, I mean it must be terrible losing a child, but life goes on, eh?'

The only escape from the relentless onslaught was to nod and agree, although I was sorely tempted to spit the slimy olive pit in Annie's smug face as an alternative.

'Yeah, life goes on...' I said, as I manoeuvred myself towards the hall, only to see Carol talking to Lynn and being ushered back into the living room. I followed Carol back to the squishy sofa and noticed Lynn rounding up her posse and hustling everyone else back from the kitchen.

Lynn waved a stripy knitted dress in the air.

'Attention ladies! This is an emergency swap. Who'd like this stunning Boden, size 8 dress?'

Even with my glass of wine topped up, I realised that surviving the swishing was going to be as challenging as a Japanese endurance test.

As expected, the room full of women stopped their chit chat to hear out their hostess's plea. Lynn held court and revelled in the moment.

'You see unless I make a few swaps tonight, my clothes will need to be very, *very* stretchy to fit over my ever-growing 'bump'.' She gently patted her tiny tummy. I sat wedged into the sofa between Maggie and Carol, the only ones not to jump as if they'd been zapped by a 500,000-volt stun gun.

'Did you know she was pregnant?' I asked, leaning across Carol to confront Maggie.

'No, she never said a word and, to be honest, I'm quite surprised. I didn't think she saw Chris often enough.' Maggie rolled her eyes in the direction of Chris who had reappeared after settling Holly in bed. Poking his head round the door frame, he caught his mother-in-law's stare and waved over with a cast-iron smile.

'Brilliant news, eh?' Chris snatched his leather jacket from the cupboard under the stairs with 'See you later!' as his parting shot. He topped it off with a cheeky wink, all charm and confidence as ever. Chris hadn't developed the paunch, wrinkles or baldness that most of his mates had acquired, and I had to admit that he was wearing well. I couldn't help admiring my brother-in-law's tight rear end in his Armani jeans and I remembered Lynn, aged nineteen, being keen to see what lay beneath the denim.

'Off out *again*?' To no one in particular, Maggie stretched the word 'again' across the room, like an elastic band about to snap under the strain.

'What are you getting at Maggie?' I whispered.

'Nothing. I hope,' answered Maggie, turning away from further investigation.

There was no chance for additional probing, not here and not now. Carol, Maggie and me were trapped as an audience for Lynn, the Queen of the Night, surrounded by all of her yummy mummy pals, hugging, kissing, swooning and smooching like a gush of cheerleaders. Annie pinged her crystal wine glass with her false nail. Flicking back her shiny auburn mane like a show pony, Annie adjusted her tiny tits back into position in her jersey wrap dress. The power plates at her private gym had done wonders for her post baby tummy and she slowly smoothed out the creases of the Boden 'fun' floral print dress.

'How about giving three cheers for Lynn being such a clever girl? Hip hip...' invited Annie, arms extending, clapping like a performing sea lion.

'Hooray!'

Lynn's pals cuddled and clung to her like pubes on a bar of soap. Maggie struggled to nudge her way through the tight knit group to hug her daughter amongst the huddle of hormones.

'Cheers, to us, the yummy mummies!' cried Lynn, as the tinkle of glasses ricocheted round the room.

Only Carol and I stayed seated and mute.

Maggie's yummyness might have faded a bit over the years, but she looked happy to be knotted within the cluster of motherhood. From outside the circle, Carol and I looked on with fixed synthetic smiles. We were the only ones in the room that couldn't answer to a call of: Mum, Mother, Maw, Mom,Ma, Mammy, Mamma or Mummy.

No designer handbag or scarf could be swapped to allow us to go home wearing one of those, the priceless labels of motherhood. For every woman who is unhappy with her stretch marks, there is another woman who wishes she had them.

'Congratulations Julia!' gushed Annie.

'Eh?' I had no idea what she was wittering on about now.

Mwah, mwah. Annie planted two air kisses on my flushed face.

'On being an auntie again! You must be thrilled.'

'Yeah, delighted,' I agreed through gritted teeth.

Satisfied, Annie moved on to spread the love elsewhere.

'Listen to Annie the fanny,' I said to Carol under my breath, not caring if she noticed my slurred speech. 'Clever girl? She's pregnant for fuck's sake. It's not like she's just discovered the cure for cancer!'

Carol followed my lead and drained her balloon wine glass in one almighty gulp.

'You cannae take the miracle of a new life for granted,' said Carol.

'Yeah, you're right. It is a bloody miracle - the immaculate conception.'

Maggie's return stopped me mid-rant and saved Carol from any further exchanges.

Lynn's fawning fans had finally calmed their enthusiasm and the hostess was redirecting her attention to the 'swishing' element of the evening. It seemed that Maggie was satisfied that her youngest daughter had basked sufficiently, and she revelled in telling Lynn's friends about her proposed trip to tour Eastern Europe's high spots. She rifled through her jute Marks and Spencer bag-for-life, pulling out its contents with as much flourish as a magician producing a rabbit from a hat. Her rummaging produced a Jane Shilton handbag that she could be persuaded to swap for a pair of comfortable size 10 trousers, suitable for a granny on tour.

'I know vintage is all the rage right now. So, would any of you ladies be interested in a classic 1970s leather handbag?'

'Sorry. The only trousers I've got are Capri pants. Maybe Carol's got something that would suit you,' suggested Annie. 'Oh sorry, just ignore me, I'm talking rubbish, Carol's much bigger than a size 10.'

Face-to-face, Annie's remark was a more impressive 6.7 on the Bitchter scale. The room went quiet.

'I think it's time for the buffet,' announced Lynn. Peace was restored. Until Lynn decided to add some entertainment to accompany the crab and mango crostinis.

'Girls, wait till you hear about Julia's date with Goatee Geek, it's hilarious!' cried Lynn.

'It's not *that* funny,' I said.

'Let us decide,' commanded Annie. 'We all love a good giggle. Carry on with the story Lynn!'

'I bet I can guess the ending. All men are bastards,' added Nicola, slapping her thigh.

Heads nodded dutifully and Lynn moved to the centre of the room. It was impossible to pull the plug on Lynn's surge of highly charged amusement; my sister was in full flow.

'And on that theme, Nicola, wait 'til you hear about Dog Breath!'

After several minutes of Lynn entertaining her pals with tales of my ill-fated matchmaking, she summoned me to update them all on my recent exploit, Peter.

'Surely this new man can't be any worse. So tell us, how's it going with Peter?'

For a split second, I wondered how Lynn would feel if I actually told Maggie, Annie the fanny, her assorted clique and neighbour Carol the real reason why I'd dumped Peter. There was no doubt that they'd choke on their home-baked courgette chips if I shared my fears and the fact that I now referred to Peter as Paedo Pete.

I guessed that a made-up version of events would shut them up. I downed the dregs of my wine and told the women that the reason I'd dumped Peter became clear to me after an evening's exploration in his nether regions.

'Let me tell you ladies, by the end of the date, I'd literally grasped the fact that Peter's online profile should realistically be described as 'No Meat Pete'. If his dick was as big as his ego then I would've had a great time.'

I could've heard an ant crawl over cotton wool.

Just for good measure, and for maximum shock value, I added, 'Having sex with Peter felt like I was inserting a tampon. God bless the Rampant Rabbit, eh girls?'

Maggie tutted.

'Julia, I think we've heard enough.'

Result.

They didn't need to know that I never got as far as touching Peter's cock, even under cloth, but talking dirty to this prudish mob meant that I was spared. Not one of Lynn's assembled gang of 'swishers' dared to ask for more details. Carol sucked blood from the cuticles she'd been biting at all night and looked like she'd rather set herself alight than hear anymore.

'It's such a shame you've not been lucky in love. I'm only glad I met Simon when I was young enough. I couldn't imagine not having kids,' Annie gently patted my wrist. The unwanted Hermes silk scarf which I'd brought to swap slipped off the coffee table and lay in a crumpled heap on the floor.

This was no longer a *swishing* party but a *pity* party for me and Carol. Everyone there knew about Carol's dead son and her ex-husband's girlfriend being pregnant, which meant her being childless was not up for ridicule. With no such excuse, I was fair game and thrown into an arena where Lynn, mingled amongst her band of merry women to laugh at me, not with me.

Reaching for my handbag, I could hear tinny snatches of the *Pink Panther* theme tune coming from my mobile again. Each time the tune had played earlier, I'd chosen to ignore it. There was no point in answering a call when I couldn't speak freely anyway, but I couldn't deny that I was intrigued to find out who had been trying to call me repeatedly.

Four missed calls: Three from Kirsty. One from Dan.

If it was urgent, I reckoned that they'd eventually call back. After one too many glasses of red wine, it was best not to answer. If I had, then the result would be one of slurred speech and thought. The two unanswered calls could wait until tomorrow, but the consumed alcohol hadn't entirely affected my clear thinking. Considerably patronised and slightly pissed, it was time to leave the party.

'Julia, don't forget to take back your scarf. You might want to wear it on your next date,' called Annie.

Or even better, I could use it to wrap around Annie's neck, to twist and tighten it until her head popped.

'It was really nice to meet you. Take care and all the best,' added Carol.

'Thanks. You too,' I replied.

You make your own luck. Did Carol know that too?

Dan's offer was the best, and possibly the only, offer I might get for a very long time. This was my first and last swishing party. The only thing that I was planning to swap now was being childless for childbearing. But I vowed that I'd never, ever, be seen in head-to-toe Boden.

CAROL

WITHOUT MY CONTACT LENSES, I half-shut my eyes in a Clint Eastwood squint and strained to make sense of the blurry digits on my alarm clock. I'd wrestled with damp sheets until I finally admitted defeat and fumbled for my glasses. Flicking on my bedside lamp, I wasn't surprised that I'd woken at three in the morning: the dead hour.

I'd learnt about the dead hour in a medical magazine as I waited for my appointment outside Charlotte's office. The article claimed that the sixty minutes between 3 am and 4 am is known as the dead hour because this is when most people die in their sleep in hospitals. Did Charlotte know about the magazine's content? Was it a good idea to leave references to death lying around when most of Charlotte's clients were there for grief counselling and some were suicidal? I decided to get rid of the magazine on my next visit; it seemed the right thing to do.

At 3.03am, I was wide awake, no danger of falling victim to the dead hour. With only the tick-tock from the clock in the hall for company, the memories of how dark those days had been after Ben's death marched across my mind. Things were different now; it felt as if I'd been given a torch, to shine a light in a new direction. I could be a mum again. But it would come at a price.

It would cost £10,000.

Money that I didn't have.

Money that I would somehow have to raise.

A price I was prepared to pay.

It's my best chance. I don't have months or even years to adopt from abroad. Dan's right; no Chinese baby would ever feel like my own.

The stress of attempting foreign adoption and its possible failure was much harder to face than accepting Dan's offer. It was a fact that I now accepted and had to act on. My heart pounded under the cotton of my nightshirt and even in the chill of my unheated bedroom I felt my oxters were clammy with fresh sweat.

Stumbling through the empty house I went into the dining room, somewhere I could always find company. I switched the computer on, my source of guidance and guilt. I now realised that the hours spent searching and shopping brought me pain, not pleasure. The Microsoft melody always made me think of a cool breeze on a hot summer's day and had a calming effect. I went through my list of favourite adoption agency websites and eBay 'watch' items, and began to click delete, delete, delete…

These sites or sales could not help me. But Dan could.

FRIDAY 11TH MARCH 2011

Dear Journal

I can't sleep. I feel like I've got a tight rubber band pressing round my head constantly. How could anyone sleep when their brain is spinning and their head is aching? Mum knew right away that I'm stressed when I phoned her back last night. She doesn't need to see my face to tell that I'm worried and tense. It made me smile when she said, "Ah'm no as green as a cabbage, ah ken when you're upset" but it made me homesick too. I tried my best to sound chirpy when I thanked her for the latest 'Helping Hand' package. She'd sent me a 'Grow Your Own Chilli Plant' kit that a neighbour had brought back from their holidays. She's never liked spicy food and added that we should all stick to traditional food cos our stomachs aren't meant for foreign stuff. Her final word of wisdom was that, "foreign food should bide in foreign countries." Imagine me visiting Portcullen with a wee brown bairn? What would mum and her friends say to my face or behind my back? How could I ever have believed that a Chinese bairn would be easily accepted and loved, when mum can't even bring herself to try foreign food? I went quiet and I must've sounded scunnered cos she asked again if I was feeling okay. But I couldn't explain how I was really feeling.

I phoned Elaine back and she said I seemed a bit fed up as well. I told her that I'd too much wine at the swishing party and I was paying for it now. She said the party couldn't have been bad. I couldn't stop myself from telling her that I overheard Lynn's pal blethering about Kimberly being pregnant with Steve's bairn. She went silent, then finally admitted that she knew about the pregnancy already. It would have been better to have heard it from her than Isobel. Elaine's supposed to be my best friend so you'd think she'd make sure that she told me before anyone else did. It was another case of déjà vu; she knew about Steve's affair but never told me. It doesn't matter anymore anyway. I'm going to have my own bairn now.

I only need to find the money. I won't pretend that I wasn't hurt when Dan started talking about money, like he was doing some sort of business deal with me. I thought we were getting on really well and could be friends. Okay, if I'm being totally honest, I was hoping that we might end up as more than just friends. So when he explained his idea, I wasn't really prepared for it to be like wanting to buy something you can't afford. I'd always loved bidding for stuff from eBay and shopping on QVC, but I'm not used to negotiating money deals with folk I know- especially not for sperm! But when I got back from our walk, I sat and thought about it and I realised that I couldn't expect Dan to do something like this for nothing. I mean, I should have guessed that he would never fancy me and want to get together. I was kidding myself that we could have had a future, but I do believe he cares about me.

I suppose it wasn't a total shock when Dan asked for money. It's not as if we are a couple or lifelong friends, so why shouldn't he want paid? All those hours searching the internet were time wasted. Dan's right. There's not a single site that offers a quicker, cheaper way to get pregnant. His way is the best way. Compared to adopting and trying to get a sperm donor through a clinic, this is hassle free. No checks on my age or background and no waiting time. The one problem is that Dan's given me a deadline. I've to let him know if I want to go ahead by Sunday, but I've no idea yet how to get the money. The only thing I'm sure about is that Steve robbed me of the only child I had and I'm not going to let ANYONE rob me of the chance to be a mum again.

It's only money. I'll do whatever it takes to get it. If it means I have to buy a baby, then I will.

Saturday at the shop was usually the busiest day of the week although today was much quieter than normal. It was always like this in the run up to Mother's Day. Folk saved their usual floral purchases and waited to give or receive a bouquet on Hallmark's favourite day of the year. Two weeks tomorrow women all over Scotland would be accepting gifts and cards from their children, young and old.

My most precious Mother's Day present was the handprint painting that Ben had made in Primary One. The teacher had laminated the colourful splashes made by his tiny fingers to accompany the words of a poem:

> *I miss you when we're not together*
> *I'm growing up so fast*
> *See how big I've gotten*
> *Since you saw me last?*
> *As I grow, I'll change a lot,*
> *The years will fly right by.*
> *You'll wonder how I grew so quick*
> *When and where and why?*
> *So look upon these handprints*
> *That are hanging on your wall*
> *And memories will come back of me,*
> *When I was very small.*

The first year after Ben died; I created a Mother's Day shrine with all the cards and trinkets from previous years with the handprint painting and poem taking centre stage on the mantelpiece. It didn't help.

When I was pregnant with Ben, Steve had given me flowers and a card signed by *The Bump*. Much as I tried not to, I couldn't stop wondering if Kimberly would receive a card and flowers on the twenty seventh of March from her Bump.

I didn't grudge Kimberly celebrating Mother's Day; let her be showered with gifts. It would only be a matter of time before Steve gave her an occasional slap on the face. And not long after that it would turn into a regular punch to the stomach, with a kick to the ribs for a bit of variety. Like a helium balloon, Kimberly should enjoy his inflated affection before it lost its bounce.

Steve was usually careful not to leave traces of his abuse on my body; most of my scars were invisible. But the memories of every slap, punch, kick, burn and bite never faded. There was the time I was supposed to wait in the kitchen, ready to reheat Steve's dinner whenever he returned from work. His shift had ended hours before but he usually spent the rest of the time on one side of the hotel bar, with Kimberly pulling pints on the other. That particular night I had dared to go for a bath, instead of waiting in the kitchen. I thought I had enough time. I was wrong. Kimberly had a night off and Steve came home earlier than expected. My miscalculation meant having my head repeatedly dunked in the herbal scented water when he caught me chin deep in bubbles. Even years later, I don't enjoy a bath.

When Steve's heavy drinking first started to interfere with family life I was younger and still optimistic. I was convinced that I could make him change because he loved me and Ben. But pleading and pleasing him hadn't been enough to encourage Steve to come home, lay off the booze and spend quality time with his wife and son.

I felt like a single parent long before Steve and I divorced. I'd once been floored by a bad case of gastric flu and had spent the day trying to amuse Ben between bouts of vomiting. After the seventh batch of sickness, exhausted and near hysterical, I experienced a moment of madness. Desperate for Steve to come home and help out, and with a surge of nervous energy, I found myself dragging Ben into the car. I was sure that when Steve saw how ill I was he'd be ashamed at not coming straight home after work.

Gagging on a bubble of vomit, I drove the four miles from our home to the hotel. He never took the car when he was on a late shift so he could have a drink with the punters. I travelled with his dinner on a tray on the passenger seat: steak pie, tatties and carrots sweating under cling film. My hands clenched the steering wheel, imagining it was Steve's scrawny neck, as Ben sat in his car seat in the back, firing questions at me.

'Mummy, it's bedtime, where're we going?'

'Mummy, why've you got daddy's dinner in the car?'

'Mummy, why're you crying?'

I couldn't give Ben answers that he would understand and ignored him until we arrived. I stormed into the bar with my three-year-old son by my side, my knuckles white from gripping the tray and Ben's tiny hand.

'Mummy you're hurting me!'

I released my grasp and took a deep breath.

'You've forgotten your way home, again…' I called to the crowd of men at the bar. Steve looked round and his jaw dropped in amazement. I'd psyched myself up so much that I continued,

'So ah've brought your dinner.'

Kimberly at least had the decency to look shamefaced on his behalf but Steve's drinking buddies laughed so hard, lager sprayed everywhere.

'Isn't she well trained, lads?' asked Steve.

I got a round of applause from the regulars and a slap from Steve when he finally got home, quickly followed by a beating with the wooden tray. Hours went by as he continued to threaten and bawl at me for humiliating him.

'The guys have got it all wrong; your training isnae finished.'

Grabbing me by the throat, Steve hissed in my face, 'If you ever try pulling a stunt like that again, you'll be picking up your teeth with broken fingers!'

His shove sent me staggering backwards. I clutched the back of the sofa and bent double to spew for the eighth time that day. The vomit splattered Steve's slip on shoes.

'You dirty cow!'

My head stayed down, as he kicked his shoes free. The smell of leather and puke smothered my face as he wiped his shoes clean by rubbing them from my cheeks to my chest.

'If you're no waiting in the kitchen with a hot meal ready tomorrow, then trust me, you'll be punished.' His stale beer breath made me gag. 'Understand?'

I sniffed back snot mixed with sick.

'Aye.'

'Look at me when ah'm talking tae you...'

I'd raised my eyes upwards and caught sight of Ben in the doorway, sooking at his ragged blankie before disappearing back up the stairs.

'Embarrass me in public again and you'll sleep on the floor at the back door, where untrained animals belong. Got it?'

Locked inside a Perspex sphere, Ben's hamster had more freedom to roll from room to room around the house. Before Ben had his fourth birthday, and his first outing to a Celtic match, my house was no longer my home. A place of comfort had become a place of torment. I kept a suitcase packed for Ben and me, ready to escape, and I hid it up in the loft. It never moved. It was only opened once or twice a year when I swapped Ben's clothes for a bigger size.

Finally, there was no need to run; I didn't need the suitcase anymore. Steve left me and Ben. He moved in with Kimberly and he took his abusive temper with him. No one should suffer like I did. No one deserved it, not even Kimberly. She was entitled to a luxury bouquet this Mother's Day. And, this time next year, I'd be celebrating motherhood too.

I leaned my elbows on the ancient patio table that Isobel had brought into work so we had somewhere to sit at on our breaks. I ran my finger along the hairline slash on the table's plastic surface. Rubbing at my eyes, I pulled the lids to the sides of my face in a vain attempt to ease the dull ache. The sandwiches I brought for lunch were untouched, I could barely think straight, never mind eat.

I flicked through one of Isobel's old copies of *Keep It Real*, until mid-way through the magazine a page made me stop - 'Ten Most Unusual Ways to Make Money'. This could provide the answers I was looking for...

Or maybe not.

Yes, I could sell advertising space on my car *if* I actually owned a car. Likewise, the idea of delivering takeaway orders also relied on the use of a vehicle. The next suggestion was to become a life model at art classes. Technically a possibility, I had all the necessary equipment for this one. And the students wouldn't expect a Kate Moss lookalike, would they? Perhaps a hand model for the jewellery industry would be closer to my comfort zone. I examined the back of my hand. The forty-two-year-old skin had the texture of crepe paper; modelling didn't appear to be an option either. Even more unlikely was the idea of me selling hair to be made into wigs. With my short bob, any extra hair would make pennies not pounds. The only person that had hair long enough to make any money would be Lynn's sister Julia. I couldn't imagine Julia ever needing to chop off her locks to fund anything, never mind to buy a baby.

None of the magazine's ideas would work. All of them required a lot of effort, and more importantly, a lot of time. Effort wasn't an issue, but time certainly was. And with my lunch break over, I was even closer to the end of another day without any guarantee for Dan that I could raise £10,000.

Tired as I was, this was the first time I'd read a true life magazine with fresh eyes. Tossing aside the tattered pages, I wondered how much time and money I'd wasted buying copies of trashy magazines? Elaine was right and it made me cringe. The stories of ordinary people in extraordinary situations had always interested me in the past, but recently I had paused to question whether it was fair to find other folks' heartbreak entertaining. My weekly fix of six or seven different magazines was a habit that had formed as easily as posting on Broken Cord, bidding on eBay and surfing the TV shopping channels.

Soon I wouldn't need to pass the time reading stupid features on 'real life' stories, fashion bargains and celebrity scandals. I would be too busy looking after my baby to bother with the headline stories and glossy covers that had lured me to dive into the loves and lives of folk I didn't know or care about. I would have my own front cover story. All I needed was the cash to make it happen. With my lunch break over, I needed to concentrate on flowers not the future. But when Isobel popped through to the back of the shop, she took one glance at me and told me to take a half day.

'Your eyes have more bags than Tesco. Go home, please, you'll frighten the customers!' Isobel joked, and I tried to find the energy to smile. I agreed to call it a day, it was quiet for a Saturday and Isobel would manage fine.

It was a good idea, except that I didn't want to be home alone with only Jinky to confide in. And although I answered for him, it wasn't exactly a balanced conversation. I needed to talk but the only person that I was allowed to discuss my problem with was the man himself.

Thirty minutes later, Dan sat opposite me in the window seat of Kath's Kafé and used his teaspoon to scoop the foam from the cappuccino I had ordered for him.

'Ah dinnae need tae wait until Sunday, ah've made up ma mind,' I stated, eyeballing him and trying my best to sound composed.

'You've made the right decision,' replied Dan, licking froth from his lips.

Was I so flustered that I'd no idea what I was saying? I was sure I hadn't actually told him my final decision. Dan carried on regardless and I accepted that faking being in control was pointless.

'So I take it you've got the money organised then?' asked Dan.

'No yet, ah might have a problem with the timescale...'

'I'm sorry Carol but I can't help you there. If you can't get the money sorted then let's just walk away from this today. It'd be a real shame though wouldn't it?' interrupted Dan, shaking his head.

'£10,000 is a lot of money. Ah just cannae magic it up overnight,' I pleaded. There was only an old dear in the café chewing on a bacon roll, but my whispered replies gave the impression I was doing a major drug deal.

'I know it's a problem,' said Dan, nodding his head. 'But let's look at solutions instead. There must be a way. Beg, steal, borrow- whatever it takes.' While I was freaking out inside, Dan seemed perfectly calm.

'That goes without saying. You know ah'll dae whatever it takes.' I surrendered myself to Dan's relaxed attitude and waited for his ideas. He stirred his coffee and sighed.

'Can't you just borrow it? From a bank, your family or friends? There must be someone that'd give you the cash.'

'No, ah'm already up tae ma eyes in debt and ah couldnae ask ma mum for money. She'd want tae know what it's for. And ah couldnae ask Elaine either. She doesnae have that kind of cash.'

'How about selling stuff? You must have something worth flogging? If it's not nailed down, sell it!' suggested Dan.

'I've got loads of designer handbags and shoes but they wouldn't raise £10,000.'

Dan sighed again, this time much louder and pushed his coffee cup to one side.

'Look I'm trying to help you here, but if I do my bit then it's down to you to do yours.'

'Ah'll get the money, ah just havenae worked oot how yet.'

'Well don't take too long. I need it by the end of the month or I'll be gone. This is your only chance.'

Dan tugged his jacket from the back of his chair and got up to leave. As he buttoned up his jacket, I was sure that I spotted Julia and Holly walk past the café on the other side of the road. On another day, at another time I would have waved over at them, not today.

'Keep in touch.' Dan said, patting me on the shoulder with a parting shot, 'Tick-tock...'

SUNDAY 13TH MARCH 2011

Dear Journal

Dan's texted me the phone number of a guy he says could lend me money. He didn't call him a loan shark, but what else could he be if he just hands out cash to anyone that's asking? I'm not sure this is my best option though, not yet anyway. I remember Isobel blethering about loan sharks and it sounded scary stuff. A single mum she knows borrowed money for

Christmas and she ended up paying back thousands more in interest at some ridiculous percentage rate. It's not the money that bothers me. It's that, according to Isobel, the loan shark was really intimidating. He turned up at a football match and threatened to break the legs of the woman's wee boy if she didn't settle her debt. I suppose I better keep the loan shark's phone number, just in case. But I've still got time to come up with a better idea.

After Elaine went home, I was busy taking photos of all my bags and shoes for eBay. I did a bit of research and the best end time for an auction is a Sunday night. So I've put everything on for 7 days and with the best of my stuff, I've put it on for a 'Buy It Now' price cos the sooner I start getting cash in my account the better. I'll never make £10,000 from the sales but I'm hoping that Dan will let me pay some of the money now and pay up the rest later, maybe during the pregnancy.

I've loved owning designer gear. It's a great buzz strutting about in killer heels when it's just me in the house. When I've had a wee drink, I put on a pair and walk round my bedroom till I'm dizzy. I've had my fun so it hasn't been too bad putting my collection up for sale. The worst bit was listing some of Ben's stuff on eBay. Elaine had come round to take Jinky out for a walk with me and I asked her if she could help me clear out Ben's room. I knew she would say yes cos she's mentioned it a few times that it wasn't a good idea to keep it like a shrine. Everything has been left like it was on the day of the accident. I've never been able to pack anything away or take down his Celtic posters. His football boots were sticking out of a sports bag still caked in mud, his schoolbag was dumped on his bed and a worn Celtic football top was thrown across a chair.

Charlotte has often suggested that clearing out Ben's room might help the grieving process, she said I'd become stuck in one of the stages of bereavement. She'd told me that it didn't mean that I needed to get rid of everything, I could keep a few treasured bits 'n' bobs and make a memory book. Charlotte kept saying that clearing out Ben's things didn't mean that I was removing all signs of him. She said it's a good idea to pass on your loved ones' possessions, so that others might benefit from them and I would get comfort from that.

That's why I decided to put some of his stuff on eBay. If his things can help me then surely that's a good idea. There's a TV, a computer, a Play Station and loads of games, DVDs and toys. I'll keep the clothes for now, but every wee bit towards the total will help and I know Ben wouldn't mind.

Charlotte will be chuffed with my progress when I see her at my next session. I won't tell her or Elaine that I sold them on eBay though. They wouldn't understand that bit. If they ask where the stuff went, I'll say that I put it all into the Red Cross shop. I hate lying to them. I've never been any good at keeping secrets either so this is tough. I'm trying to be strong; it'll all be worth it eventually. It wasn't easy uploading the photos on to eBay and writing a description of his things. All the memories of Christmas and birthday presents came flooding back. By the time I had finished, I could hardly see for tears. If Isobel thought I looked tired yesterday then she'd be shocked to see me now. My eyes are all puffy and red raw. Charlotte says it's good to cry. The tears started when Elaine was here and I said it was cos I was finally tidying out Ben's room. She wouldn't understand even if I could tell her about Dan. I know I'm doing the right thing and I'll have even better news for Charlotte and Elaine in a few months.

JULIA

I MET KIRSTY IN WALKABOUT, the place she'd suggested for a drink. I was clueless as to why my arty pal would want to hang out in an Australian themed bar-cum-club. The naff surfer style décor was in harmony with the cheesy DJ's choice of the 80s classic Down Under. Walkabout was packed with cloned girls from the council housing schemes, dressed in skimpy dresses and cheap stilettos, full of alcopops and desperate to sing along to a Kylie medley.

'Why are we in this dump? I'm scared to sit down in case I catch gonorrhoea,' I said, as we waited to be served a drink.

'I know it's not our scene but trust me, there's a reason for meeting here.' There was more material in Kirsty's batik silk scarf than any dress worn by the girls in Walkabout. If Kirsty had a beard she would look less out of place.

'Well it better be a bloody good one!'

We usually met in one of the bars on Byres Road that we've drank in since studying English at uni. But Kirsty had insisted on the city centre setting instead of the west end. She explained that meeting in Walkabout guaranteed that we wouldn't be spotted by the person she wanted to talk to me about - he was very style conscious and would never be seen in a tacky venue like this. She ordered a double G & T for me and advised me to take a large gulp before she would tell me about the man in question. By the time she'd filled me in on what she'd discovered about Chris, all I could do was repeat one word.

'Bastard!'

Once wasn't enough.

'Bastard!'

'Yeah, there's no other word for him. A complete and utter bastard,' agreed Kirsty.

'I just can't believe it. What a total bastard.' Like the Duracell bunny, I didn't tire, saying "bastard" over and over again, much to the satisfaction of Kirsty.

'That's why I kept calling you on Wednesday night. I'm as shocked as you,' said Kirsty.

'Come to think of it, I shouldn't be that shocked. Maggie hinted on Wednesday that Chris is always going out. And Lynn's been moaning a lot recently about him working late all the time and them never going out much anymore.'

'Bastard.' It was Kirsty's turn this time to use my favourite word of the night.

'Thank fuck I didn't know about this before I picked up Holly this afternoon. The scheming bastard said he was off to the car wash. For all Lynn knows he could have been off to meet the slapper for a quick shag.'

I knocked back my G & T in one gulp, hoping that alcohol would take the edge off my guilt. Should I have seen the signs and warned Lynn? Would my little sister have listened? Lynn would probably have dismissed it as me shit stirring. She would never believe that Chris, the darling hubby, was playing away from home, with no rugby involved. Maggie had obviously smelt something go off in the relationship but I hadn't picked up the scent at all.

'And with Lynn pregnant too…' sighed Kirsty.

'Yeah, dirty bastard.' The night was young and the word "bastard" was nowhere near worn out yet for me or Kirsty. There was plenty of mileage in it yet.

Kirsty explained that she'd been monitoring the situation on and off for weeks now. At first glance, Chris entering the west end bar with another woman could have been a perfectly legitimate out of hours business meeting. But Chris, and the blonde in the grey suit, were soon to become a regular sighting and their conduct was anything but business-like. Pawing at her with an intimacy not appropriate for public display, made it clear to Kirsty that this was beyond any sales technique that Chris employed to generate new orders. Customer care had limits.

'When I couldn't reach you I was going to take a photo of them and text it to you.' Kirsty paused. 'But then I thought it was better to tell you in person.'

'Thanks Kirsty.' I sighed under the weight of Kirsty's revelation.

'No worries, I thought you'd want to know,' said Kirsty. 'So what now?'

I shrugged. All I could attempt was a non-verbal answer; I had no idea what to do with the information Kirsty had shared. The only thing that was certain, was that I needed another drink. A large one. I tilted my empty glass and turned it slowly in a circular motion, hoping that Kirsty would take the hint.

'Well?' asked Kirsty.

There was still no response from me, I was stumped.

Eventually, Kirsty left the silence behind and squeezed her way through the crowd to buy us another round.

As I waited for Kirsty to return, a short-arsed guy lurked close by, eyeing up the available women, and it seemed that he'd targeted me. Like a puffed up pigeon, the guy straightened up to his full height of five foot four and launched his best charm offence.

'Canna buy ye a drink, gorgeous?' he drawled.

I looked him up and down, then extended my palm, holding it six inches above the tosser's head and calmly replied, 'You have to be this tall to go on this ride.'

Turning away from me, the wee man muttered under his breath, 'Stuck up cow'. I hadn't the energy or inclination to waste any more oxygen communicating with him. I had far more important things on my mind. On Kirsty's return, I was as distant as before, lost for words or a plan of action.

'Maybe I shouldn't have told you. Ignorance is bliss eh?' said Kirsty, using a plastic straw to swirl the ice cubes round in her drink.

'No you were right to tell me, I just don't know what to do now that's all.'

'How far on is Lynn's pregnancy?'

'Oh, its early days still, about ten weeks, why? What difference does it make to this shitty mess?'

'Well, call me a sick bitch if you like,' Kirsty didn't wait for a response. 'But it might not be too tragic in the long term if the pregnancy didn't go all the way.'

'No, you're wrong Kirsty. You know that Lynn's been trying for years since she had Holly. After three miscarriages she'd be devastated to lose another. Lynn's over the moon.'

'Yeah, I can understand that she'd be pleased. But who the hell would want to end up a single mother with two kids?' There was no need to answer Kirsty, the look on her face said it all. 'She's stuck with Holly already, but to have a newborn baby too would be a nightmare.'

I finished my drink, leaving Kirsty to nurse her half-finished gin, as I jostled for position at the bar. Ten minutes later, I slammed down two double G & Ts. Kirsty sipped at the fresh drink, as I struggled to come up with a strategy. Drinking in silence, Kirsty waited patiently.

'I can't tell her,' I said.

'Wouldn't you want to know?' asked Kirsty. 'What if I'd seen Andrew with someone when you were a couple, wouldn't you expect me to tell you? Or if you'd seen Nick with another woman, surely you would tell me?'

'Christ almighty, I don't know. My head's fucking pounding in here.'

Need You Tonight by INXS was the latest Australian chart hit served up by the DJ. I wondered if the time and effort selecting the themed music was wasted on the punters. Like me, the only thing they seemed interested in was the next drink. And, just like the Foster's advert, no one seemed to give a XXXX where the beer came from, as long as it kept coming. Stuff the crappy songs.

'Let's get out of this shit hole,' I said and with one final swig, I downed the gin as quickly as rancid cough medicine. My legs buckled like Bambi's, but I was determined to get through the crowds and escape. Kirsty dutifully followed me out into Renfield Street. We dodged a drunken girl with a pink '*Bride-to-be*' sash and her giggly pals, heading into Walkabout to join a squawk of hen parties. The gaggle of girls wore deely-boppers trimmed with black feathers and a jiggling *hen party* script inside a red warning triangle. Was there any need for the themed head boppers as a way to announce the hen night celebration? Surely the girls' cackles and screeches were warning enough. Anyone hoping for a quiet drink in town would keep well away, and socialise in another postcode.

'How about tapas at La Tasca?' suggested Kirsty. An intake of food seemed like a wise move and we swapped Australian pop for flamenco guitars piped through the PA. The tapas bar was buzzing and as packed as Walkabout. A couple were about to leave and I pounced on the free table, desperate for a bottle of chilled wine and a selection of Spanish flavours. Before long we were sharing tapas and the wine worked its magic.

'I know I've been busy with the book launch coming up and everything, but we really need to make a point of getting together more often,' commented Kirsty.

'Yeah, I hardly see you these days. Just lucky I'm not the sensitive type or I'd be well pissed off with you neglecting me for weeks,' I replied.

'Sorry'. Kirsty tucked into the dish of crispy patatas bravas.

'No worries, it's like I was telling Holly last night on the phone, you've got to be thick skinned to survive.' I chewed on a deep-fried ring of calamari. 'Life's a bitch and then you die!'

'That's a bit heavy for a seven-year-old.' said Kirsty.

'I was only trying to help. She needs to realise that life's not always fair. A girl in her class has invited all the girls, except Holly, to her birthday party in the church hall.'

'Ouch, that must have hurt,' sympathised Kirsty, dabbing her napkin at the tomato sauce dribbling down her chin.

'Yeah, she was in tears when she told me until I cheered her up. I told Holly the little cow is jealous of her, that's why she didn't get an invite. Beauty always threatens the ugly bugs. I said I'd take Holly and the other girls somewhere much better than the fusty church hall. That'll sicken the class bitch. Got any ideas where I could take them?'

'I'm not so sure that spoiling Holly and the other girls is a good idea,' cautioned Kirsty.

'Why not?'

'I wouldn't worry about Holly, she'll soon forget about not getting an invite. Kids are resilient. And anyway, soon she might have a lot more to be upset about than a party invite.'

'You're not still going on about Chris?'

The dish of paella between us was warm but the atmosphere had gone as cool as the wine in the ice bucket.

'Look Kirsty, you're not a hundred percent sure Chris is shagging that blonde bint and anyway even if he is, it's none of our business!'

'You need to confront him. I could take a photo of them if they're back in the bar again.'

'No Kirsty, I don't *need* to do anything. I've got my own problems.'

My appetite had abandoned me along with my tolerance.

'But your sister might end up being a single parent!'

'And what's so wrong with that?' I asked. 'If Chris is shagging about then she's well rid of him, and Holly and her will manage just fine.'

'And there's the new baby to think about. How...' began Kirsty.

'Not everyone needs a man around to cope with a baby,' I snapped. My knife and fork clattered as I shoved my plate to the side. 'Some of us might quite fancy motherhood minus the hassle of keeping a man happy too. Women are born to have babies. It's natural.'

Kirsty's snort sprayed garlic mayonnaise across the table. We had been close friends for almost twenty years, two of a kind. We had always aired our views on politics and passion, religion and rights, money and the meaning of life. No topic was taboo between us, and each of us kept secrets that had never been shared outside our tight-knit friendship.

'You have got to be pulling my tits this time! Are you seriously trying to tell me, as a mature, intelligent woman, that you would actually like to have a child for the hell of it?' Kirsty took a sharp intake of breath. 'Because if that's true, then you had a better grip on reality when you were nineteen!'

Her outburst caused a loved-up couple at the next table to stop and stare at us with upturned noses, as if we smelt as strong as their baked goat's cheese. Kirsty ignored the couple's distaste and carried on regardless, barely taking a breath mid-rant. I had sparked off one of Kirsty's all-time favourite discussions and she was not willing to let this opportunity pass her by.

'So let me get this straight, either you're suffering from a serious case of amnesia or you're more pissed than I thought. I mean, you should hear yourself, you've more or less claimed that women should have a baby because it's what we're meant to do.'

I took a large slug of wine. For once I wasn't sure where I was steering this conversation.

'And what's so wrong with that? Don't you want to keep your bloodline going?' I laid the challenge on the table. Kirsty seized it between gritted teeth, determined not to let go.

'My legacy will last forever in my writing. There are six billion people in the world already. I don't feel any pressure to add to the total.'

'That might be true for you. But deep down, if they're being honest, most women want to be a mother.'

'Motherhood isn't a woman's *only* role in life. It's not a design fault for a woman not to automatically want to reproduce.' Kirsty sighed. 'You don't have to have kids because you're a certain age! If you want something cute Julia, why don't you just buy a bloody kitten?'

'Don't be ridiculous.'

It was my turn to sound exasperated. Kirsty was deliberately trying to push my buttons.

'I'm being ridiculous? You need to take a look in the mirror!' Kirsty didn't pause with her tirade. 'Can't you just be happy in your own skin without the need to define yourself as a mother?'

'Christ almighty, Kirsty,' I sniggered. 'You sound like one of those militant hairy armpit feminists that we left behind in the Student Union.'

'And have you completely erased what happened in our second year at uni? *And* what you did about it? It wasn't like going to the dentist.' Kirsty shook her head and poured herself a glass of water. 'An abortion is a big deal.'

'I know that and you don't need to remind me. Don't patronise me.' I muttered through gritted teeth. 'You know I couldn't have coped with a baby back then. I wasn't ready. But I have the right to choose when having a baby's right for me. And I'm ready now.'

'You're sounding pathetic these days. What's happened to you?' asked Kirsty. 'Is *Project Baby* the latest must-have accessory you need to complete an outfit? Or are you still desperate not to let Lynn have one up on you?'

'You think you're so clever, don't you? Just 'cause you know a bit about me doesn't mean you know *everything* about me. Amateur psychologist now are we?'

'Well you wouldn't need to be a professional to see that all you're looking for is something to fill the gap that Andrew left. I'd never have thought you were so needy.'

'And I'd never have thought you'd be so self-righteous.' Kirsty's steely glare didn't cause me to waiver. 'How dare you sit there with your smug sneer and judge me. I don't need to justify myself to you - or anybody!'

Why had I started down a path that I'd been well warned not to stray on to? Dan had been very explicit in his instructions for confidentiality about the deal we had agreed. But if Dan's plan was successful, it wouldn't be a bad thing that I'd alerted Kirsty to my feelings. Then there would be no huge surprise if, one day, I appeared with a bump. I was simply paving the way for a future revelation. I carried on, more composed in my reasoning, despite the wine.

'I can see there's no point in going on with this conversation.' I crossed my arms. 'You just don't get it. I need a baby to complete me. My feelings are not only emotional, they're physical too and, unless you've experienced it first hand, trying to explain it is a waste of time.'

'You're damn right. And I don't need to sit here and listen to you insult me for daring to have an opinion. Can we have the bill please?' Kirsty asked the passing waiter. Already standing up to leave the restaurant, Kirsty grabbed her handbag and fished out two twenty pound notes. Slapping them on the table, she headed for the door, deserting me.

'What about your change?' I called after her.

'Keep it. Cashmere Babygros don't come cheap.'

The night was over and possibly our friendship too. Not a single 'mwah' or hug was exchanged. I consoled myself with the thought that, this time next year, everything would be different. I wouldn't need Kirsty's affection, as and when she could fit it in. We only managed get-togethers if Nick didn't mind, or when she was suffering from writer's block. I would have a daily source of kisses and cuddles, all for me, and me alone. "I love you mummy": the electric current of unconditional love that passes between mother and child. Something Kirsty clearly didn't comprehend.

The next day, I parked at the edge of the woodland trail and sat patiently waiting for Dan and Roxy to appear. I was too early, but I needed the time to run through everything I had to ask Dan about the terms and conditions of the deal. I'd toyed with the idea of referring to the notes I made after returning home from the restaurant the night before. Reading the notes, hungover, it looked like I had written them with my left hand whilst blindfolded. That's what double gins and white wine did for my calligraphy skills. The scrawl was barely legible, thankfully I didn't need to refer to notes. The confrontation between me and Kirsty had helped, not hindered. I was meant to be a mother and I didn't care if Kirsty's feminist principles were appalled at my stance. When I'd originally met Dan with Holly, I'd had no doubt that it was for a reason. It was my destiny, and I wasn't prepared to dispute it. I wasn't the only one to believe in fate, was I?

Yes, the money was a dilemma, but all I had to do was turn the problem into a challenge. I had proven my success in business and this was the same scenario: a transaction that satisfied the needs of both parties. And, as always, I would get what I wanted out of the deal.

Roxy's lithe body bounded into view, with Dan following behind. He had as much of a spring in his step as his frisky terrier. He waved. Anyone observing would assume that two friends or lovers had agreed to meet for a simple walk in the park and a chat. The walk would happen and so would the chat. No one would guess that sperm donation would be the only topic of conversation.

I zapped the key of *Gary's* locking system, joining Dan and Roxy on the woodland path. The little dog zigzagged in and out of the shrubbery, sniffing at every inch of greenery.

'You're looking a bit tired, are you feeling okay?' asked Dan.

'I'm amazed you would expect anything else. How could anyone sleep easy when they had to decide on whether to allow a practical stranger to father a child for them *and* come up with £10,000 in a matter of weeks?'

'I suppose you've got a point.' Dan agreed.

'Of course I look exhausted; my brain's melted with worry over all the questions that need answering. I don't know where to start.'

I'd woken up in a sweat worrying about HIV, STDs and a whole multitude of abbreviations that might be festering inside Dan. I spent hour after hour on the internet. Dr Google had thrown up alarming fears of using a sperm donor that would affect my physical and mental well-being, not to mention the impact on a child with unknown origins. But now that I had the chance to address my concerns, I was dumbstruck. The conversation was as lacking as the leaves on the trees. Dan took the lead.

'Look, I can understand why you're anxious, so how about you answer this question for me first? Have you noticed that all the branches in the park are black?' asked Dan.

I scanned the horizon of the woodland.

'Actually, I didn't and I don't know how I missed it,' I replied. 'But what the hell has blackened trees got to do with anything?'

'Because we don't always see what's right under our noses. I could tell you were meant to be a mum the minute I met you and Holly.'

Dan moved to sit on a wooden bench that was as black as the trees and motioned for me to join him.

'This is the Angel's Bench,' he declared.

'Eh? What're you on about now?' I asked, looking at Dan as if he'd developed a sudden mental illness.

'Do you see the distillery's warehouses next to the woodland?' Dan stood up to point to the west.

'Yeah.'

'A certain amount of the whisky that's stored in the barrel evaporates through the wood. It's called the *angel's share*, and it creates a black mould that covers things like trees - and this bench.'

Dan sounded like a Blue Peter presenter on an outside broadcast.

'Right, so that's why you call it your Angel's Bench?' I asked.

'No. It's because it's where I first spoke to you and Holly and I heard you call her Angel Face.'

I was here to talk business. Listening to this sentimental shit was like trying to swallow a clump of sticky candy floss. At any other time, I would have laughed in his face. Today I didn't have enough oomph in me.

'Talking of Holly, we saw you in Kath's Kafé yesterday. From a distance, it looked like you were with another woman.'

I had no idea why I blurted out the remark. Maybe it was the mention of Holly or some innate need to know about any other women Dan was involved with, other than me. Spotting him in the café had made me realise how little I really knew about the man sitting next to me.

Without a moment's hesitation and with sheer indifference, Dan replied, 'She's my cousin. That's one of the reasons I rented a flat in the area. Her name's Carol and she lives on the Woodlea Estate.'

'Carol Walker?'

'Yes. Do you know her?'

'Kind of, she's Lynn's neighbour. I'd no idea that you were related to her.'

'I didn't realise that you knew her too, so you must know about poor wee Ben,' said Dan.

'Yeah, I heard about his accident,' I looked away as if the sight of Roxy romping was the most fascinating spectacle I'd ever witnessed. Dan took my chin in his hand and gently turned it back to face him full on.

'If you know about Ben then it might not surprise you that Carol would sell her soul to have the chance of another child. Do you realise how lucky you are?'

Dan's fixed stare sliced through me, leaving me in pieces. How could I argue with him? Carol Walker's case history was tragic. Dan was right, a woman in Carol's situation wouldn't worry about finding the money if she could replace the baby she'd lost.

She'd be glad of the chance to buy a baby. But finance was still an issue for me, whether I had the same desperate need as Carol or not, I had to come up with cash I simply didn't have.

'So, this £10,000 payment, is it negotiable?' I asked. This time, I dug deep to find the self-confidence to match and meet his stare.

'No.'

One word.

One fact.

One requirement.

One prerequisite.

One baby.

Roxy lapped the bench impatiently as if she too wanted to move on.

'I haven't got that kind of money.'

'Not my problem. Yours.'

Both pairs of steadfast eyes locked in a fiery conflict. Glacier blue versus chocolate brown. Dan was not for melting and I couldn't defeat his glare.

'And anyway, there's more than a few issues I need to resolve before I go ahead,' I said. 'For starters, what if it doesn't work?'

'You pay your money; you take your chance. But I'm a good guy. We can give it a few goes.'

'That's not my biggest worry. I need assurances of your health and expectations of your role as the father.'

'Firstly, don't worry about underlying health issues. I'm happy to take any tests you want to organise. Secondly, my role as the father is only biological. When I leave the area at the end of the month, then I'm gone for good with no forwarding address. We can draw up a contract if it'll make you feel better.'

'Putting things down on paper won't make any difference,' I replied, holding my nerve. 'I'd still have concerns.'

I had spent hours looking into the various options. There was no denying that I was apprehensive about Dan's proposal, although the facts were in his favour. After all the internet research, I confirmed my initial fears that there was an extreme shortage of sperm donors. Due to the changes in the law, the right to anonymity for sperm donors had been removed. Surprise, surprise, there was a drastic fall in the number of willing men. Across the whole of Britain, there were fewer than four hundred sperm donors. The legal changes infuriated me, I couldn't accept the logic. Sperm is simply a cluster of cells, no different from a liver or a kidney. No one gets to know the identity of their lifesaving donor, and often they are dead, so why was there a need to have a different law for sperm? Regardless of the reasons, that was the status quo whether I agreed with it or not, and the way forward was to find a better alternative.

'Your only real concern is how to get the money. I don't see what your problem is,' said Dan.

'I don't know what kind of lifestyle you think I have but trust me, £10,000 is still a lot of money to me,' I protested.

'Spare me the sob story. A withdrawal from the sperm bank doesn't come free. And I'm sure your research shows this is a fair price. Or would you rather try IVF?' Dan paused. 'I think you'll find it'll set you back five grand plus per treatment. And let's not even try to put a price on the other hassles involved.'

'Yeah but…'

'Look, you drove here in a Mini Cooper. Sell it or do whatever it takes to get what you want. Carol would do anything to have another baby.' Dan turned to walk away. 'But maybe it doesn't matter as much to you. Maybe a baby isn't worth as much as your car.'

'It is! I really want…'

My phone's muffled ring interrupted us. I gripped the vibrating rectangle inside my pocket, not sure my voice was strong enough to speak. I stood upright and yet I felt dizzy.

'You'd better answer that,' instructed Dan.

I pulled out the phone. Maggie's number lit up the screen.

'Maggie, can I call you back? I'm in a business meeting right now.' As I pressed 'end call', I realised that I'd have to explain to Maggie why I was in a business meeting and couldn't talk. It didn't make sense on a Sunday afternoon although it wasn't a lie. This was a business transaction, only not one I could share the details of with Maggie. Practising the art of bullshit for Maggie's benefit was a minor problem compared to the dilemma Dan left me with.

'Speak soon. Tick-tock…,' said Dan.

Dan got up from the blackened bench and walked away from me, with Roxy scampering down the gravel pathway ahead of him. I wasn't sure whether to follow them or not. It wasn't as easy as Dan claimed. If his deadline was hard and fast, then I had to come up with the cash. Selling my beloved *Gary* wasn't the quickest and easiest means of raising the money. *Gary* hadn't come cheap, and neither had the loan repayments. Selling my car wasn't a quick fix and although I had spent sleepless nights trying to dream up £10,000, nothing had revealed itself as an easy solution. I'd considered all my options and every one of them felt like I had driven *Gary* down countless dead ends and hit a brick wall. There must be a way; I just had to figure it out.

CAROL

TEENAGE MUTANT NINJA TURTLES – TURTLES' LAIR PLAYSET.

THE SET IS COMPLETE WITH ACCESSORIES INCLUDING THE MISSILES AND WEAPONS THAT ORIGINALLY CAME WITH IT.

I HAVE LISTED THE ITEM AS USED BUT IT IS IN VERY GOOD CONDITION.

ANY QUESTIONS, PLEASE MESSAGE ME.

Ben had loved the Teenage Mutant Ninja Turtles comics and cartoons. My mum had given him the set of toy figures for Christmas one year, it was still in great nick and I reckoned that £30 for a 'Buy It Now' sale wasn't an unreasonable amount. Wouldn't there be loads of geeks out there that collected cult toys? It was worth a try. The playset was the last item to be photographed to go along with my written description. By the time I'd switched off the computer, my tears had finally dried up but I was left exhausted. My eyes nipped, my back ached and my neck moved like a rusty robot's. Time for bed.

Years before, I'd often have to coax Ben up to his bedroom, no more cartoons; it was time for a story. And if I tried really hard, I could still picture him in his wee Ninja Turtle pyjamas, yelling

Cowabunga at anyone who would listen. Which character did the PJs have on the front? Wasn't it Raphael with the red bandana? Although Michelangelo was Ben's favourite, wasn't he? I couldn't be sure, and there was no one left to ask.

But I did remember the *Turtle Power* stories, and their message that even Ninjas need their sleep. According to Ben's books, for a Ninja, sleep is a time of renewal, contemplation, and rejuvenation. And when a Ninja sleeps, it is a very deep sleep. Just what I needed. As a reward for the late night eBay selling session, I treated myself to a large glass of wine.

The alcohol usually worked in tipping me over the edge but I had a terrible night. I rocked in and out of disturbing dreams that robbed me of any hope of rest. It was Monday morning all too soon and the grating *beep! beep! beep!* of the alarm clock was a throbbing pulse inside my head. I hated that clock more than anything else on the planet.

A restless night left me knackered and my body screamed for more sleep. Groggy and grumpy, I prayed that a caffeine boost might give me the energy to face the day. Flicking on the kettle I turned to Jinky.

'Nae rest for the wicked, eh Jinky?'

'You can say that again.'

He stood patiently beside his empty bowl, and waited. Serving up the dog's breakfast was not at the top of my 'To Do' list.

I frantically checked my eBay account, only this time I was selling instead of buying. It was over five hours since I'd last looked at the *My eBay* details. Had there been some overnight action on any of my items?

Number of bids - zero. Was it really so stupid to think that anyone would be interested in buying stuff like the football programme from an old Celtic match? There must be thousands of copies in circulation out there I supposed. As it was the programme which Ben had treasured the most; I assumed that it must be valuable. The truth was that I had no idea if it had any worth; all I knew was that it was special to Ben. Maybe it was because it was the last time that Steve had taken him to a Celtic match and it was to honour their hero?

CELTIC

V

INVERNESS CALEDONIAN THISTLE

22nd March 2006

Jimmy Johnstone Tribute

I couldn't avoid the reflection of my creased face on the PC's screen; guilt had taken up residence in the ingrained lines etched around my eyes. Isobel claimed that crow's feet should be known as laughter lines. *"Live, love, laugh and get wrinkles, they're the sign of a life well lived."* This was no laughing matter. Thank God no one else knew that I was touting my dead son's prized possessions on eBay.

Even with bids on my designer bags and shoes, the assorted collection of Ben's books, games, toys and Celtic memorabilia, wouldn't raise as much as I needed. The sales might total a couple of hundred pounds maybe, if I was lucky, but not thousands.

I should have gone to the casino night with Elaine and her pals after all, at least then I might have been able to win some of the money. It was too late now. Elaine had invited me yesterday when she had been round to help clear Ben's room.

'A few of the girls fae the office went tae the Ladies' Night at the Riverboat last month and they had a great time. They're going back again this Sunday. Are you interested?' asked Elaine.

'Thanks but ah dinnae see me at a casino. And ah'm skint. Ah cannae afford a big night oot.'

'Well that's even mair reason tae come and try your luck. Listen, it's a brilliant deal. You get a free glass of bubbly on arrival, a three course meal and a shot on the roulette and blackjack tables.' Elaine paused for breath. 'Plus, the girls said the croupiers were dead handsome and really up for a bit of flirty banter. What's no tae like aboot that?'

'Ah'm sure you'll have a guid night but ah'm just no in the mood for it.'

'Ah well, it's your loss.'

It would take more than cheap fizz to lure me into a world I had no desire to enter. My only knowledge of gambling came from my dad's daily flutter at the bookies. Right up until the day he died of a heart attack, it was as much a part of my dad's routine as his morning cup of Tetley followed by two digestive biscuits, thick with Lurpak. If my mum knew that her husband was a regular at Ladbroke's betting shop, then she never acknowledged it, certainly not in front of her pals from church, or me.

'Mind, we never went anywhere near the bookies. Okey dokey?' my dad would always warn me gently.

'Okey smokey. My lips are sealed.'

I'd raise my chin up and my dad would run an invisible zip across my pinched mouth. It was our wee secret; I didn't need to tell my mum a fib or say anything at all. I learnt how to keep stum from an early age.

When we entered the balmy heat of the betting shop, my milk-bottle-thick glasses always steamed up. My dad would make his chubby pinky fingers into miniature window wipers to clear the mist away.

'Is ma darling nae a bonnie wee quine?' my dad asked his pal.

Even from behind the foggy shield of my glasses, I could see the man's eyebrows rise up as he took in the sight of a plain faced, speccy four eyes.

'Aye, she's gaun tae brakk heirts,' the old man replied.

I wasn't the only one who told lies at the bookies.

'As long as she's the one doing the heart breaking,' said my dad. I'd forced a smile and that was enough to please my dad when he winked at me. 'Because God help the man faaivver who ever hurts ma quinie!' declared my dad.

The bets my dad placed were in pennies rather than pounds. His trips to the bookies weren't about the money. With the backdrop of the one thirty at Chepstow, and in amongst the fug and the frantic commentary, that was when my dad looked most relaxed. If telling my mum meant that it would stop, then I was happy to keep a secret. I was good at keeping secrets. Being a wife to Steve had made me world class level. A gold champion keeper of undisclosed crimes. There was no dad to protect me now, my heart had been broken a long time ago and no one could fix it. Mending my heart was a DIY job.

If Ben had died before his grandad, it would have caused my dad more pain than his heart attack. Thankfully, my dad never lived to know about Ben's accident. I couldn't imagine how he would have reacted to the truth. Would he have sought revenge on behalf of his only grandson and daughter? Or would the agony of losing Ben be too much for his heart to bear? I missed my dad almost as much as Ben, but not having to witness how he would have dealt with his grief was a blessing.

My dad was even better than my mum in detecting any underlying upset. With a sense as keen as a bloodhound, he could instantly sniff out a secret. It was only because they lived so far away that my dad hadn't been able to penetrate the façade of my home life with Steve. He wouldn't have needed to see the cuts or bruises to be able to tell that I was hiding something.

Whenever we locked eyes, I became totally transparent. My dad could see right through to my soul and I would never have been able to keep the cause of the accident secret from my dad. It was for the best that my dad went first.

WEDNESDAY 16TH MARCH 2011

Dear Journal

I didn't go to yoga last night, it was pouring with rain and I forgot to ask Elaine on Sunday if she could give me a lift. It's too far to walk and I'd feel stupid standing at the bus stop with my yoga mat. I don't like to keep asking Elaine as if I'm just using her as a free taxi service. And I'd already got drookit when I took Jinky out for his walk so I didn't bother going. Anyway, I knew there was no way I could've relaxed enough to empty my mind like Jamelia tells us to. I'm all over the place right now. I even tried to use the TV remote control to phone mum! It was only when the channel changed that I noticed.

I don't know whether I'm coming or going. I was running late for my appointment with Charlotte today so I burst into the clinic and ran past the receptionist. I heard her call out: "Rushing?" and I shouted back, "No. Scottish!" I looked round and the rest of the folk in the waiting room were all sniggering. It was so humiliating. I was cut to the marrow.

Charlotte knows me well enough by now, so there was no point in trying to fake it at this afternoon's session. I couldn't have pulled it off even if I tried. Once we'd gone through the usual warm up chat about the weather, work, blah blah blah, she went straight in for, "How's Dan? You haven't mentioned him for weeks. Have you seen him again?" I must say I was taken aback, I thought she'd forgotten that I'd told her about meeting him. Mind you, I suppose it's her job to remember what I say every week. I'd been so excited when I told her that she probably wrote about it in her notes after our session. I must have looked a bit freaked out when she said Dan's name, cos she asked me if everything was alright between us. My head's so full of stuff that I didn't see the question coming and just mumbled something about us emailing each other back and forth, that was enough to fob her off and keep her happy.

Isobel must have noticed that I was distracted too cos she made a comment today that "the light was on but no one was home." I tried to laugh it off and said that she should know by now that I'm a professional daydreamer. It's kind of true though cos my mind has always had a tendency to wander, to daydream and fret about the future, to reminisce and stew over the past.

There was no chance that I'd be able to focus on breathing techniques at yoga while I was wondering how the bidding was going on eBay, so I did something more productive than trying to stretch my spine into the shape of a cat. I phoned mum and asked for a loan. I'd been thinking about asking her ever since Dan told me I needed to get my mitts on £10,000, but I couldn't come up with a reason for the money without lying to her. Then, last night when I couldn't go to the yoga cos I didn't have a car, the idea came to me! Mum knows how much I miss having a car so I said that if I had one, it would mean that I could visit her more often. I knew she wouldn't mind helping me to buy one. I told her that I'd got the chance of a great deal and it was a one-off opportunity. I kidded on that I'd been given the first refusal on the car, so I needed the money soon or I'd lose it. I said that Isobel knew a customer who was emigrating to Canada so they're selling a brilliant wee car. The customer had a buyer lined up but the sale fell through and if I wanted it, I needed to have the money by the end of the month. Mum seemed to understand that I didn't have long enough to organise a bank loan. She told me not to worry, she'd say a prayer to Saint Matthew, as he was once a tax collector and is the patron saint of financial matters. Anything's worth trying. I might start praying too.

I hate lying to her but what else can I do? I'm already stressed about my visit back home for Mother's Day. I'll need to have a car and pretend it's mine. At first, I thought of hiring one, then I realised that it would probably have company logos all over it. So maybe I could ask Elaine to borrow her Corsa for the weekend? I'll work something out. I'm getting better at problem solving.

Anyway, mum said she'll do what she can to help and that she would have a think about how much cash she could give me. I felt rotten telling her a lie. Although I will probably need a car, once I have the bairn, so it's not really a black lie. I've never told her an actual black lie. Dad always told me that there were white lies and black lies and that your biggest problem is if you don't know the difference. I'm not concerned, cos surely this is just a white lie?

I'll worry about getting more money for my own car after the bairn's born. Mum'll be happy she helped me when I visit with her new grandchild. I keep looking at the keepsake card that Charlotte gave me saying, '*One step at a time- this is enough*' and that's exactly what I'm doing. Explaining the real need for a car to mum is not at the top of my priority list right now. Dan's already texted me to say that it's all or nothing: £10,000 upfront or he'll walk away - taking my hopes of having a bairn with him.

My mum was back on the phone later. 'It's an affa siller fir jist ae thing,' she said.

'Ah know it's a lot of money mum.' I agreed. 'But it's a braw wee motor and it'd mean it would be easier tae visit you if ah had a car again.'

'Aye, it would be gweed tae see ye mare aften. Ah ken ah try and keep busy but ah still get lonely athoot ye here.'

'Ah'd be up the road in jig time if ah took the chance of the car.' I let the sense of my suggestion sink in. 'That's if you can lend me the money.'

'Ah'm feart tae tell ye. Ah ken ye said the car was £5000 but ah cannae manage the hale lot. Ah'm really sorry Carol but aw ah can give ye is £3500. It's aw ma savings. Ye ken ah'd gie ye the shirt aff ma back but...' said my mum, her voice breaking off in shards.

'Dinnae worry mum. If you're sure you can afford tae lend me £3500 then that's mair than enough for a deposit on the car and it'll give me time tae get the rest fae the bank.'

The thick words congealed in my throat, lumpy and awkward. I tried my best to sound as chuffed as my mum would expect at the offer of half the money I'd asked for, but it was hard to hide my utter disappointment. My face flushed with fear; my performance was more effective on the phone than in the flesh.

I wasn't surprised to hear that my mum didn't have a massive savings account bubbling under the surface of her thrifty lifestyle. My mum and dad were just ordinary folk that had worked all their days, for not much more than the minimum wage. Before retiring, my dad had worked in a timber yard and my mum took a job as a dinner lady at the local secondary when I started primary school. It was no wonder that my mum had made such a big deal about it being a lot of money to spend on a car, only *one* thing. My mum and dad had never had a car so it was even harder to justify. It left me wishing I could have told my mum the truth, instead of feeling guilty for lying to her. A devious and dishonest daughter, it wasn't a badge I wanted to wear.

If only I could explain to my mum that the "just *one* thing" I was actually buying was priceless. My mum would surely understand. She would appreciate the value of a child, and my dad would have recognised the logic of placing a bet on a sure thing. You have to make your own luck.

When a bird crapped on me the next day, it was a good luck sign from above. The putrid splatter was fate and I wasn't about to ignore it. Two old women at the bus stop had witnessed my encounter with the bird. One of them choked back her laughter, while the skinny one rummaged in her handbag.

'Dae you need a hankie?' asked the twig-thin woman.

'No you're fine thanks,' I replied. 'And anyway, it's good luck.'

'Aye for your dry cleaner,' cackled her pal, as her chops wobbled up and down.

'Just a pity it was a single magpie, eh hen?' sympathised the scrawny spectator.

One for sorrow, two for joy, three for a girl, four for a boy...

The woman was right; it was a shame that it was a magpie flying solo. But that didn't cancel out the good luck from the bird shitting on my shoulder. Did it? One magpie or not, the bird's dirty deposit was the same as reading my horoscope. The trick was being smart enough to interpret the signs, and to know which ones count, like when I met Dan.

I stopped outside the window of Ladbrokes on Shawbriggs Main Street. As I paused to wipe the stain on my cagoule, there was a poster advertising the betting odds on the Scottish Cup. It was another sign.

CELTIC V INVERNESS CALEDONIAN THISTLE
3/1

My dad had never sat me down and taught me about betting odds but, like osmosis, the lingo of Ladbroke's had soaked through my skin. Along with a win on 3/1 odds, I worked out that I would also receive my £3500 'stake' back if I won the bet. That would give me a total return of £14,000!

Wouldn't my dad have been proud of his bonnie quine?

Wouldn't Ben have been proud of his clever mum?

I'd seen the signs and been sharp enough to read them. The only intelligent thing to do was to bet the £3500 on Celtic beating Inverness Caledonian Thistle. Ben's team had won 2-1 at the Jimmy Johnstone tribute night, they'd win again. It made perfect sense.

'Thank you Saint Matthew,' I mouthed silently. Maybe my mum's prayers were working after all? The bird shit was the silent, slimy answer to my mum's prayers. I was wise enough to look beyond my soiled shoulder to see a clean path forward. My head tilted heavenward and I gave Saint Matthew a smile. Ben and my dad wouldn't be the only ones proud of my decision.

My mum will be proud too, and I can't wait to see her face light up when I arrive in my new car. Although that would be nothing compared to the first time my mum held her new grandchild in her arms. And all that joy would come from the £14,000 that I was sure to win.

It was meant to be.

Who could argue when common sense and superstition combined?

SATURDAY 19TH MARCH 2011

Dear Journal

I'm writing this before I go to work. I had to do something to distract myself cos I've been awake since half five this morning and I've finished reading all my magazines and checked my eBay sales umpteen times.

Yesterday lunchtime, I put a bet on Celtic beating Inverness Caledonian Thistle and I NEED to win!!! Before I went out, Isobel could sense I had a lot on my mind, cos I was quieter than usual and hardly spoke all morning. We're total opposites. If she's stressed then she's like a budgie and blethers constantly. She can get a bit hyper when we're busy with a big wedding or funeral order. She asked me if I was okay cos I'd stayed in the back shop since I'd come in that morning. I told her that I wasn't keen to take any Mother's Day orders for next week. I knew that she wouldn't push it, and it worked. It's hard keeping all this worry over the money a secret. I wish I could talk to Isobel or Elaine, even Charlotte or mum. But Dan said I can't tell anyone about our plan and none of them would think that betting £3500 is a good idea, so I've got to try and keep my mouth shut.

I'm not daft though. I remember that my dad always lost more than he ever won. His motto was, *"Don't bet more than you can lose".* And I CAN'T lose this money. Even if I could tell someone else, I know it wouldn't make sense to them, but I truly believe that I'll win. I know it. It feels right, in the same way as when I met Dan and I knew that he was going to be good for me. I mean, why else would I have bumped into him with Jinky or have the bird crapping on me outside the bookies? You can't fight fate, there's no point. And I'm long overdue a win!

When I was clearing out Ben's room, I read a poem he'd copied down in his old school jotter. His handwriting made it hard to read at first. The letters were all joined up along the lined paper and the teacher had used her red pen to write, *"Remember to keep a finger space between each word!"* Ben's words were all squashed but I was able to understand every line. His handwriting might not be perfect, but the poem he gave me was. I read it over and over until I knew it off by heart. The poem is called '*Thinking*' by Walter D. Wintle. It sounds like the kind of poem my dad could've made up, although it's not as if I can imagine him writing poetry on his break at the timber yard. I can almost hear my dad read it out though. Anyway, it goes like this:

> If you think you are beaten, you are;
> If you think you dare not, you don't!
> If you'd like to win, but think you can't,
> It's almost a cinch that you won't.
>
> If you think you'll lose, you're lost
> For out in the world we find
> Success begins with a fellow's will;
> It's all in the state of mind!
>
> If you think you're outclassed, you are;
> You've got to think high to rise.
> You've got to be sure of yourself
> Before you can win the prize.
>
> Life's battles don't always go
> To the strongest or fastest man;
> But sooner or later the man who wins
> Is the man who thinks he can!

JULIA

Kirsty's launch invitation sat on my mantelpiece. The photo on the front was mainly in sepia tones, except for the green leaves and white flowers of the snowdrops, poking through the rubble of a derelict gothic mansion. Inside the fancy font announced details of Kirsty's latest book launch:

At this year's 'Aye Write' festival,
featuring Scotland's award-winning crime writer,
Antonine Publishing is delighted to invite you and a guest to the
launch of
Kirsty Anderson's brilliant new novel
Snowdrops in June
Thursday 17th March
7:30pm
The Mitchell
North Street, Glasgow G3 7DN
RSVP to rosie@antoninepublishing.co.uk
Please arrive between 7:00 & 7:15pm for a complimentary drink

How long had my name been on the publisher's guest list? If Kirsty had updated it recently, would I still feature, or was it compiled long before our last get-together? I couldn't answer the question or decide whether or not to attend. Would I receive a warm welcome by my closest friend? Or would I feel that my loyalty was no longer needed or appreciated?

If I didn't go to the event, the snub could damage our friendship for good. If I wanted to keep my best pal, then this was the best, and possibly only, opportunity to draw a line under our recent fallout. This wasn't the time to take a high and mighty huff. Minutes later I'd responded by email that I would be delighted to attend the book launch. All I needed now was a *guest* to go with me at short notice, preferably someone I could depend on for unconditional moral support. It was obvious who I should take with me to the book festival. I was lucky enough to have one person who gave me unreserved backing when I needed it most. That's what mothers are for, aren't they?

The spontaneous email reply had drained my emotional energy levels. A ciggie first, phone call to Maggie second. I strode into the bedroom to find my handbag. It was a gorgeous limited edition Mulberry Abagail in coral croc-print suede. It had been reduced from £600 to a mere £160. Two years ago, Andrew had agreed to camp overnight outside the House of Fraser store to guarantee that we were the first in the queue when the doors opened for the end of season sale. Dressed in a thermal suit and tucked inside his sleeping bag, a devoted Andrew had spent the whole night awake, fending off rowdy Friday night drunks staggering up and down Buchanan Street.

'Hey mate, it's Friday night. Dae ye ken what that means?' shouted a passer-by.

Andrew told me later that, as he'd no idea if the guy was a friend or foe, it was safer to play along.

'No, what does that mean?' asked Andrew, making sure he avoided eye contact.

'Wednesday was two days ago!'

Happy to laugh at his own pathetic joke, the tanked-up guy stumbled off towards St Enoch's station leaving Andrew in peace. Andrew's tales of that night had made me smile. He was my hero. Rachel and all the girls at work had been so jealous of my bag *and* my man. At the time, I had it all and yet, in the end, I had nothing that actually mattered.

Scrambling around inside the bag for my pack of Marlboros, I still couldn't grasp why Andrew had had no problem in understanding that I desperately wanted a handbag - but he couldn't understand my desperate need for a child. He went from hero to zero.

I turned the bag upside down on to the bed, leaving its delicate silky innards exposed. This was serious. The cigarette packet was empty, with only a grey knob of chewing gum inside.

'Shit!' I yelled, hurling the empty fag packet across the room. Other women, with layers of fat, (like Dan's cousin Carol) clearly relied on sugar to keep them sane but I had never been one of them. There were no sticky cakes or creamy pastries in my flat's kitchen cupboards. If I didn't buy them, then I couldn't eat them. I had no desire to find that the only thing that fitted me in the Princes Square boutiques was the jewellery. I liked being slim more than I liked chocolate. It was all about control. Of course I enjoyed a weekly nibble on the chemical pink icing of one of Holly's sugar mice, but that was it, a once a week guilty pleasure. Since secondary school, I'd chosen to take a draw on a fag, rather than a dip in the biscuit tin to relieve tension.

There was no other way round easing my stress, I needed a cigarette. Immediately. Pacing past my desk, I was wound up tighter than the ball of elastic bands that I'd added to over the years. It was now as big as a cricket ball and just as hard and unforgiving. Nicotine had to be purchased. Now. I reckoned that rather than phoning Maggie and inviting her to Kirsty's book launch, I might as well visit her if I had to go out anyway.

Within half an hour, I'd been to the shops and sucked the life out of three Marlboros before walking up the path to Maggie's front door. I loved the heady surge of nicotine. The rapid release of adrenaline was just what I needed to also ask Maggie for £10,000. But I had to remember: softly, softly, catchee monkey…

'Wouldn't you prefer to go with Lynn?' asked Maggie.

'Oh no, I'd rather go with you. And we haven't been out together for ages. So let's make a night of it. We could go for a nice meal and drinks after the launch. Sound good to you?'

'Yes, quality time, it would be lovely to have a whole night, just you and me.' Maggie looked as pleased as I'd hoped.

'Brilliant.'

'So what's the dress code for the launch?' asked Maggie, as she fetched me a glass of water.

'Maggie, you're always immaculately dressed, wear whatever you're comfortable in.'

Maggie wouldn't have ventured to Tesco without first considering what she was going to wear. Her default setting was to overdress rather than underdress.

Even over the kitchen's background music of Radio Two's easy listening tunes, I heard the ping of a text message and I couldn't resist a peek.

Money shouldn't be the reason 4 u not being a mum.
How u getting on finding £10k?
D x

'It's okay, don't mind me, you'd better reply to it,' suggested

Maggie.

'No, it's fine, it's only work,' I replied.

'Well, it's nice to hear that you know when to switch off once in a while.'

'Don't worry Maggie. I know that I've got to get the balance right.'

I slipped my phone back inside my bag.

'Hallelujah! Finally, at thirty-eight years old you realise that work isn't everything!'

I silently began to count to ten; I only got to three before Maggie continued.

'So, how's the love life going now?' asked Maggie. 'You haven't mentioned anyone else since that guy Peter.'

The only thing worse than a born again Christian was a reformed smoker. I wished Maggie still smoked, then maybe I'd be allowed to light up in the kitchen. But it would take more than nicotine to take the edge off Dan's text. Maggie's mention of Paedo Pete was the nudge I needed to dangle my toe in the murky waters of family finances.

'There's nothing to tell but there is something I need to talk to you about...'

I barely took a breath as I described a fantastic investment opportunity that I had to respond to within a matter of weeks, if I could get financial help from Maggie.

'It's an amazing chance. Energy is the future. It's where we could make big money.' I fired facts and figures of the fluctuating price of oil barrels at Maggie. 'All my connections through *Business Scot* tell me that years from now we'll be looking at substantially higher prices for oil and gas...'

Maggie was suitably bamboozled.

She was speechless and simply nodded obediently as I continued, 'While growth in Asia continues to steam ahead, especially China, the US dollar's decline is a major reason why oil and gas companies will once again become excellent long-term investments. But it also means that it's the right time to consider alternative energy sources such as wind and wave power...'

I paused for effect before prattling on with a detailed outline of the deal on offer. Would Maggie want to invest £10,000 in a wind power company? Or would the proposal blow Maggie's plans for a trip abroad way off course? I waited patiently for a reaction. Maggie was dumbstruck and I could almost hear the cogs in my mother's brain whir.

'I know I've sprung this on you but it really is a one off opportunity. Truthfully, you only get a chance like this once in a lifetime.'

Still not a peep from Maggie, her eyes swept the kitchen floor tiles like a searchlight scanning a prison yard.

'If you could lend me the money, quickly, then I'll pay you back with interest as soon as I can,' I pleaded.

A loan for a fake investment was the best option, and the only option that I had, to try and raise the cash at short notice.

'I know you were planning to go off on your travels but I'll pay you back.' I was well beyond the age of using cute puppy dog eyes on Maggie, but anything was worth a try.

Still not a cheep or a chirp from Maggie.

'You're retired; you can go your trip anytime. There's no hurry.'

The silence was infuriating. Jack had been a shrewd old bugger and I was certain that Maggie hadn't been left with a lack of money. Even Maggie had joked that she often wondered if Jack's wallet was sewn shut, though there was little doubt in my mind that surplus money was available. Surely Maggie wouldn't have planned a trip that would cost thousands if she was strapped for cash, so what was the problem? Maggie wouldn't spend *all* her savings on a jolly jaunt round the world, would she? There was bound to be enough money left over to lend to me. Finally, Maggie looked up to meet my penetrating gaze.

'Honest-to-God, this is a lot to think about, especially with your dad not here. Can I let you know on Thursday?' asked Maggie.

My silent answer of, '*Well I don't have much fucking choice, do I?*' remained unspoken.

'Of course you need to think it through. Maggie, I hate to put you under pressure like this, but I wouldn't ask if I could get the money anywhere else.'

'Can't you get a bank loan? I mean you work hard. Surely they'd lend you the money if it's such a great investment?' suggested Maggie.

This wasn't going to be as easy as I'd hoped. Even without Jack holding her back, Maggie wasn't prepared to dive straight in and throw me a lifebelt.

'I would get a business loan if I'd time. The deal is a now or never chance. I can't wait for weeks on the bank processing all the paperwork involved.'

'Oh dear,' was all Maggie could muster.

'Yeah, it's impossible to pull off without *you* backing me.' I sniffed. 'But I suppose Thursday will be fine to let me know if you can help me out or not.'

The emotional plea sailed through the air with the subtlety of a brick being hurled through the kitchen window, yet it provoked no response from Maggie.

Again I had to fill the silence.

'I'll pick you up at a quarter to seven for the book launch, okay?'

I made a move towards the door.

'Oh, is that you going away already?'

It would appear that even Maggie thought cute puppy dog

eyes were worth a try too.

'Yeah, I'll leave you in peace. You've got a lot to think about.'

Two days later at Kirsty's launch, Nick was sucking up the buzz that bounced off the oak panelled walls of the Burns Room at The Mitchell. Instead of trying to destroy a parasite, Kirsty wrapped her arms round Nick as if he'd flown across the globe to be there with her.

Spotting me and Maggie, Nick waved at us, whispering at a passing teenage waitress to scuttle across the wooden floor and offer us a drink. In my four-inch Jimmy Choo heels, I click-clacked my way towards the smoochy pair but was beaten by the P.R. from Antonine Publishing who guided Kirsty up on stage.

A classic horror movie soundtrack filled the hall, creating the desired eerie atmosphere. The crowd dispersed and dutifully shimmied along the crimson velvet seats. Nick clapped his hands theatrically to announce that his *'significant other'* was ready to begin her performance. It was show time, and Kirsty was ready to treat her guests to a taste of her novel.

'Sounds a bit too gory for me. I'll stick with my Mills and Boon. You know where you are with a good romance,' whispered Maggie.

'Yeah, we all like a happy ending.'

More comfortable with the *Business Scot* functional language of facts and figures, I struggled to tune into the purple prose that my friend spouted.

Thankfully, it wasn't long before Kirsty was ready for questions from the audience. There was always the usual guff when someone asked about the author's writing routine, but now and again there was a little gem unearthed from beneath the trash. Then the real entertainment could begin. But after the first question, my optimism sank as fast as the Titanic.

'Kirsty, does your working day have a distinct routine? Or do you wait for inspiration before you can write?' asked a loyal fan, aka Susie the Stalker. Nick strained his sinewy neck to see who'd asked the question. He rolled his eyes at me in recognition of Susan, a fully paid-up roadie on Kirsty's book tours.

'Thanks Susan and it's good to see you again,' said Kirsty.

Hearing her name, Susan looked like she would melt into her chair with pride.

'I always admire authors who can work from nine till five. I wish I was disciplined enough to keep office hours. But the truth is, hours, even days can go by without a single sentence occurring to me. If that happens I go for a walk with Nick, have a large glass of wine, I read and I wait.'

This was the same answer that Susan had heard Kirsty trot out on numerous occasions, although this time, she added part two of her usual query, 'Does that not worry you? You know, having writers' block?'

Kirsty gave Susan a serene smile.

'Sometimes, when inspiration fails to strike, I must admit that I do become a little anxious. And then suddenly a sort of unlocking occurs. I don't know how it happens but I can write, in a kind of trance like state, for say eight hours at a stretch. So no, I always get there in the end.'

Satisfied that her literary idol would never be lost for words, Susan's shoulders relaxed and she generously nodded in the direction of the only other hand being casually waved in the air. Seconds later, the roving microphone hovered in front of a man sporting a beard that looked like a 70s porn star's bush. His bowling ball belly was ready to pop out of a t-shirt with the slogan 'SUITS SUCK'. This was a man who did not follow the dress code from Maggie's school of decorum.

'*Ms* Anderson, do you feel that you need a 'Y' chromosome to be taken seriously as a crime writer?'

Nick's Adam's apple bulged; Susan had never dared to ask such a bold question. Stalling for time, Kirsty reached slowly for the jug of mineral water. Only the gurgling of the liquid could be heard reverberating around the wooden panels.

Kirsty was no longer looking at Nick. Her eyes were now firmly fixed on the man with the microphone and I could feel the intensity of her steely glare. It was easy to imagine Kirsty, a ruthless sniper, projecting a little red dot onto her target. All Kirsty had to do was squeeze the trigger and the shot would impact where the red dot was aimed, right between the eyes of Mr 'SUITS SUCK'.

'I have never felt the need to define myself as a female crime writer. I am a crime writer, there's no need to clarify that further with a gender statement. Women writers are often advised to use only their initials - or to pick an androgynous pseudonym - to avoid putting off male readers. J.K. Rowling is credited with getting young boys reading again. Would it have happened if she had referred to herself as Joanne? But I've never subscribed to being promoted as 'K' Anderson. My name's Kirsty and I'm very pleased to see it in bold Copperplate Gothic font on my book covers.'

Taking a long, slow sip of water, Kirsty continued, except this time she ignored the 'SUITS SUCK' man; her sights were now trained on me. The red spot was on my forehead, ready to wound and maim.

'Books are about people and the choices they make, about the social and political setting of the characters. I believe that what women bring to the crime novel is a sensitivity to the everyday, and to the state of the victim. Since, in a certain sense, they are victims as well. Women are the victims of society's expectations that we must conform to certain stereotypes.'

Casting her eyes round the room for further effect, she settled them again on me, ready to fire the final fatal shot.

'I mean, who in this room doesn't know a single, thirty-something woman who feels the need to have a child, just because she's been made to believe that if she doesn't, she's incomplete somehow? Forget fictional crime, that's a real life victim!'

I felt a sharp prod from Maggie, 'Honest-to-God, I've no idea what all that was about. You'll need to translate it for me later over dinner.'

'I wouldn't know where to start,' I replied, without ever losing eye contact with Kirsty.

There were no further questions from the audience and the action moved on to the performance art of Kirsty and Nick swanning amidst the swooning fans. Busy flourishing her enamelled fountain pen, Kirsty got down to the business of signing copies of her novel. She never noticed me guide Maggie out the door and back out on to Granville Street.

'I thought you'd want to speak to Kirsty and get a signed copy,' commented Maggie as we walked towards Sauchiehall Street.

'No, she's too busy and I've arranged to meet up with her tomorrow after work anyway.'

Lying to Maggie was as easy as being drunk and falling off a bar stool.

Soon we were settled in Café Antipasti with a bottle of house rosé as we both scanned the Italian menu, anxious to fritter away more time before dealing with the money lending issue.

Maggie took a long, deliberate gulp of her wine as she studied the grain on the table's woodwork, before launching into her speech.

'Julia, I know that you need £10,000 and I really want to help you out…'

'Fantastic. I know you'd do anything for me and Lynn,' I said.

'That's true, but your dad budgeted for our retirement and had it all worked out. He always liked to have an extra buffer for an emergency, but I was going to take a chance for once and use it for my trip.'

I gripped the edge of the table and remembered to breathe. Was Maggie giving me the cash or not?

'The trip would cost £6,000 so that's all I feel I can give you, without upsetting your dad's plans,' explained Maggie.

How could Maggie still be an emotional prisoner confined within the walls of married life, unable to break free? Even though Jack was dead, his power wasn't. The old miser could still take command of Maggie's finances, even from the grave. Irritation flooded my cheeks with a furious blush. Maggie's mind-set was inexplicable. Nonetheless, £6,000 was still £6,000 and worth the effort of bouncing to my feet and embracing Maggie tightly.

Our embrace was followed by an awkward pause, neither of us knowing what to say or do next.

'Thanks Maggie, that's brilliant. Are you're sure about this?' I asked.

Wasn't that the sort of thing I was supposed to say? I couldn't just snatch the cash right out of my mother's hand. The generous mother/grateful daughter performance required to be acted out in its entirety.

'I'm absolutely sure, honest-to-God, I'm sorry it's not the full amount. It's just I know your dad would be so angry if…' and for the first time since we'd sat opposite each other, Maggie met my bug-eyed gawp.

My dad, the eternal dictator. I cursed inwardly. At least with him gone, I'd gotten most of the money from Maggie. What was the point of letting Maggie be the richest woman in the graveyard? It didn't make sense, but then neither was my mother's willingness to part with cash without any questions.

It had been easy after all. It was too easy. And yet I had to ask, I knew how much the idea of an adventure meant to Maggie.

'But what about your trip?'

'There are no buts, I've forgotten about it already,' Maggie's attempt at a casual throwaway comment was feeble. Instead of clearing the air, it caused a toxic fog of tension to swirl around the table, choking us.

'Can't you still afford to go on your trip?' I asked, hoping to defuse the polluted atmosphere.

'No, not comfortably. And anyway, you thought it was a mad idea, the couch surfing and everything. You're probably right and I trust you...'

'But I thought you really wanted to travel and had it all worked out?' I asked.

'I did. But if your child asks for help, whatever it is, you give it to them. Believe me, when you become a mum, you become number two. And anyway, call it a mother's intuition but I think Lynn'll need me here for her during this pregnancy. Oh, that reminds me...'

Maggie ducked below the table to delve inside her handbag. Seconds later she slid a grainy black and white ultrasound scan photo across the table with a scribbled note attached.

'Lynn asked me to give you this.'

Here's the scan for 'Angel Face No 2' at 10wks and 5 days. He/she measures 3.34cm!! Baby waved its arms and kicked its legs loads, so daddy is sure it's a rugby player, whatever sex it is!!! Chris was crying all the way through the scan!

It was easily one of the most exciting moments of our lives.

'I'm not surprised he was in tears,' I blurted out.

'Lynn said she'd never seen him so emotional,' said Maggie.

'Hmm, I bet he was,' I said.

A shiny waiter clutching his notepad lingered patiently, but no orders from either us were forthcoming. Pouting his lips, the waiter twirled his pen like a majorette's baton, between his long fingers. The candlelight gave out just enough light for me to make out 'Dino' embroidered in silver thread on the young guy's black polo shirt.

'Are you ready to order?' asked Dino, in a phoney Italian accent. He was more likely to come from Nitshill than Naples.

The seconds turned to minutes. Our menus had been abandoned in favour of staring at the scan photo and its message. The piece of paper lay between mother and daughter.

Both of us had lost our appetite.

CAROL

According to my horoscope, "*More is lost with indecision than making the wrong decision*". Maybe it was time to stop reading them. Looking at the shredded scraps of the betting slip on the floor, I could still make out the words:

Celtic to win

The ballpoint scribble was all that was legible on the strips of paper that littered the laminate flooring. My chance to raise the cash in a quick hit at the bookies was gone, and so was the £3500 that my mum had lent me.

Sobbing and seething, I hugged the cushion tightly, rocking myself back and forth. Even with my head buried in its padding, a howl-at-the-moon cry escaped. The foam of the cushion failed to muffle my misery and the velour cover was soon damp with salty tears and snot. Finally, my wailing was reduced to the mew of a kitten and I threw the soggy cushion at the floor, sending Jinky running for cover.

'Aye, you better run if you know what's good for you.'

'Nae danger. Ah'm oot of here.'

Lying next to the paper debris was a Barbie-pink tax disc

holder. The novelty car accessory was shaped to look like a handbag and it had a clashing acid green Post-It Note attached.

For your new car! God bless. Love mum x

The tax disc holder had come along with a note, saying that my mum had transferred the money into my account and that, *"now that you've got a car to run, this will be the only new 'handbag' you'll get for a while! HA HA!"*

'Funny, ha ha!' I roared, causing Jinky to bolt up from underneath the coffee table. The dog's glassy eyes reflected my panic.

'Great joke, eh Jinky?'

'Ah'm no splitting ma sides laughing.'

He slunk back down, trying hard to dissolve into the shagpile rug.

This wasn't funny in any shape or form. Giggles had abandoned me along with hope that luck was on my side. Even if I sold every handbag I owned on eBay, I could never make the £10,000 needed for Dan.

There was no question that the eBay sales had been a minor success. My designer bits 'n' pieces and the contents of Ben's bedroom had made more than a thousand pounds. It was a good result, but not good enough. The money was being paid into my account in dribs and drabs. But Dan was not willing to accept a few hundred here and there, he'd made it as clear as Highland air.

"All or nothing" said his text.

There was no room for doubt.

My dream of motherhood was over. Selling stuff for money hadn't been enough. Borrowing money and then gambling it away hadn't been successful, and Dan's suggestion of a doorstep lender wasn't for me. I'd deleted the loan shark's number a few days after Dan had texted me it, in case in a moment of madness I made the call. Yes, I could easily get the money, but at what cost? I was desperate, not daft. I couldn't handle the hugely inflated interest rates and the menacing stories about what happened if you missed a payment. I'd watched pitiful folk cry their eyes out on *The Jeremy Kyle Show*, always looking over their shoulders. No, I'd rather sell my soul than pay one of those thugs extra cash back.

The image of me holding a newborn child was as tattered as the slivers of paper that I scrunched up into a tight ball of despair. Tossing it into the wicker wastepaper bin, I scored a blinder of a goal from the centre half of the living room.

'Goal for Celtic! Did you see that Jinky? Funny, ha ha, eh?'

'Aye, they'll be dancing in the streets at Parkhead.'

I squealed, before realising that the dog had already retreated to the kitchen, leaving me alone with my hollow victory.

When my doorbell rang, I froze. Could I be heard at the other side of the front door? Squinting through the Venetian blinds there was no mistaking the roly-poly figure of Elaine, who was now bending as best as she could to keek through the letterbox.

'Coo-ee!' Elaine's high-pitched call made my stomach churn. I'd lost track of time and had completely forgotten that Elaine was due to pop in for a visit. Only Jinky seemed pleased to hear Elaine's dulcet tones as he bounded down the hall, ending in a mad circuit of chasing his tail.

There was no hiding place. Elaine knew that Jinky wouldn't be running loose up and down the hall if no one was home, which left me with only one option.

'Ah thought you were never gonnae let me in and it's pissing it doon ootside!' Elaine had already dumped her wet umbrella on the floor, unzipped her puffa jacket and waddled through to the living room, before I had closed the front door.

'So, how're things?' asked Elaine.

'Fine...'

'By the way, ah'm sorry.' Elaine settled herself in her favourite armchair. 'Ah meant tae text you tae see if you needed a lift tae yoga but ah totally forgot. So much for elephants never forget, eh?'

Funny, ha ha.

'Nae worries, ah got the bus.' I replied, without giving Elaine eye contact. A lie was the easiest answer.

'Ah'm glad tae hear you're still keeping it up cos ah've got a wee pressie for you.'

Elaine heaved herself back out of the armchair to rummage in her handbag, before chucking a small plastic tub at me. I failed to catch it and the tub dropped to the floor allowing Jinky the first sniff at the suspect package. Picking it up, I read out the label,

'J.L. Bragg Charcoal Capsules 50 pack. Why's this a gift for *me*?'

'Duh, they'll stop you farting in yoga!' snorted Elaine.

Had someone in Shawbriggs told Elaine about my embarrassing incident at the first yoga class? Was everyone laughing at me? Fresh tears threatened to well up and spill over.

'Where's your sense of humour?' asked Elaine.

'Aye, well ah'm a bit tired. And ah've been busy...'

'Ah can see that, studying hard were you?' asked Elaine, eyeballing the scattered magazines covering the sofa.

'Eh? What are you on aboot?'

'Studying for your master's degree in gossip magazines,' explained Elaine.

All these jokes, it was a pity that I found none of them funny.

'Although ah thought that noo you have *new* friends, like your posh pal Lynn, you'd be oot mair and wouldnae be reading these night and day. And what aboot the charming Dan, have you been on another date with him?'

Elaine's laser beam stare penetrated right through me.

'It's no like that; we're only dog walking pals.'

'Hmm, well that explains why your living room's still full of mags. Nae wonder you're skint.'

Wedged into the armchair, Elaine fanned through the glossy pile. Her rant wasn't over, 'Listen to this!', her finger jabbed at the article's headline.

10 meals to make with walnuts

'What a load of absolute guff! The only time ah'm interested in eating walnuts is when they're covered in chocolate in a Walnut Whip.'

Another article caught her eye.

Celeb hairstyles we love

'Huh, it takes mair than asking the hairdresser for a 'Rachel' tae make you look like Jennifer Aniston!'

Elaine continued flicking through the pages at random searching for articles, laughing at her own wit and ready to pounce on a headline like a hungry hyena.

7 tricks to lose 7 pounds

'Who are they trying tae kid? Even ah know that there are only two tricks- eat less, exercise mair - duh!'

Normally I would have been able to manage a giggle at Elaine's outburst, but not today. Elaine didn't seem to need encouragement as she was far from finished reading out the cheesy headlines.

How to live in the moment

'Noo this is the only feature that actually sounds worth reading.'

I couldn't listen anymore.

'Fancy a cuppa?'

'Thought you'd never ask. Have you been tae Asda yet?'

'Dinnae worry, the biscuit barrel is well stocked.'

On my way to the kitchen, I stashed the tax disc holder away. I was leaving no chance for Elaine to interrogate me on the meaning of my mum's Post-It Note about getting a new car. There was no need to add another lie to the load that was pressing down on my chest like a sleeping toddler.

As Elaine munched, it was obvious that Kit Kat biscuits weren't fit for purpose. So much for, *"Have a break... have a Kit Kat"*. It hadn't worked on Elaine, even the four finger bar wasn't up to the job. She was still reading out headlines from the mags, after devouring a chocolate feast.

'This is ma favourite, wait till you hear this one...,' the dramatic pause failed to get a reaction from me.

My husband destroyed my self confidence

Elaine's cackle startled Jinky and he fled to the kitchen.

'Huh, ah could use one word tae sum up that instead of six - 'marriage'. That story's hardly unusual, is it?' Elaine slapped her thigh.

'Aye, you're right aboot that and ah should know better than most.'

At last, Elaine was silenced.

'Sorry, ah didnae mean tae...' began Elaine.

'It's okay.' My eyes scanned the ceiling, searching for invisible clues to deal with painful memories.

'It's no okay though is it? Ah dinnae know how you can read all this stuff when your story is bigger than anything in here. How can you enjoy it?'

'Ah dinnae *enjoy* the stories, ah understand them.'

After half an hour of strained chit chat, Elaine had to admit defeat. Gossip and banter were wasted on me; nothing was going to lift my mood. We talked about everything and yet we said nothing.

'Ah think ah'll head up the road. Unless you want tae take Jinky oot for a walk,' offered Elaine.

'No, ah'll take him oot later.'

'Okay.' Elaine stood up. 'If ah dinnae see you through the week, ah'll see you through the windae!'

Elaine said her goodbyes, leaving me as the only guest at my exclusive pity party. I wasn't completely alone though, I still had the company of my journal. Charlotte had asked me to think of someone real, that I could imagine writing a letter to, instead of starting my entries with *Dear Journal*. She had explained that the benefit of creating a pen pal was that it made the journal entries more personal. It would give me a sense that I was talking, telling something -*everything*- to a pal or a sister. With time, this would become like my best friend, my silent confessor and witness.

Portcullen was twinned with Saint-Cloud, a French suburb to the west of Paris. At primary school, I'd had a pen pal called Nadine from the wealthy, hilltop town. My journal entries couldn't be written to Nadine. I needed to be free to completely unburden my emotions, and I didn't want to attach a person's identity to my journal. My childhood letters to Nadine were from my past, not connected to my future. I used to dream about visiting Nadine one day, but my mum and dad had never taken foreign holidays.

'There's a beach on yer doorstep. You can get sand and sea here athoot needin tae spend a penny.'

My mum had been quick to snap back when I moaned that Elaine's family were going to Corfu.

'Aye, and they dinnae aw ken foo how tae speak English ower there,' added my dad.

Elaine scoffed at folk like my mum and dad, who had chosen to stay put on the Moray coast and never travelled abroad. My parents weren't small-minded people who had no desire to stretch up and grow any taller. They were just people who loved a sense of community and were rooted to where they belonged. I understood that now.

My mum had been heartbroken at the thought of her only child living a hundred and thirty miles away. She couldn't understand why I agreed to leave with Elaine to try city life. My dad had eventually convinced my mum that me and Elaine would be fine, and that I would return to the nest, after I'd tested my wings.

The 'Helping Hand' packages became a feature of my mum's long distance mothering and, although I missed home, nothing lured me back to Portcullen. And yet when my mum used Doric words and phrases it pulled at my heart strings. It was tempting to return home after Ben died- to be wrapped in my mum's arms, rather than her sending her love in a brown paper parcel. Living up north again was an attractive idea, but the draw of being closest to my memories of Ben had kept me living in Shawbriggs. The *Angel's Bench* was my special spot and I didn't want to leave it behind.

SUNDAY 20TH MARCH 2011

Dear Journal

When I started writing my thoughts and feelings down it was cos Charlotte had suggested that keeping a journal would be therapeutic and help me express myself. She was right. It does help and it was a nice change from talking to Elaine or even mum or Isobel. But now, with all this stuff going on with Dan, I've no other option than getting it all out on paper. There's no one else but you - so thanks - you're the only one I can be truly honest with these days. Charlotte insisted that it was important for me not to censor myself and that's what I enjoy most about writing in my journal. I don't have to hold back on what I really think, even if it makes me sound vicious and horrible. I could never write these things down if I'd tried to start my entries with 'Dear Nadine' like Charlotte suggested, cos anybody that knows me at all would be shocked at the thoughts that run through my head. I don't swear, but today, inside my head, I was screaming, "I hope that bloody bitch Kimberly and her unborn bairn get knocked down and wiped out!" What would anybody think about me if they knew that I'd said that, even to myself? Steve's the only one walking the planet who would know why I have these bitter feelings. No one else would understand cos no one else knows why I'm disgusted at Steve getting another chance at being a parent. I tried to rise above the situation and I thought I could cope with the idea of Kimberly having a baby. I was wrong; I can't bring myself to feel happy for them.

You see, I was really angry for a long time after the accident. Recently though, the rage inside had calmed down a lot and it no longer felt as if my stomach was in knots all day. I was much better at work too and was starting to enjoy meeting the customers again, I'd been to the yoga class and I'd met Dan. Things were definitely getting better. Everyone had noticed the difference in me. Isobel had said she was happy to see that I seemed to have, *"turned a corner"*.

I was glad cos I don't want to have rage inside me all the time again, but I can't help it. It's back. Charlotte will be disappointed if I tell her, although it's no wonder I'm so upset. I saw Kimberly yesterday at lunchtime AND I saw another poster for Steve's latest charity night. The poster was in the hairdresser's window advertising a 'Murder Mystery Night' in aid of 'Broken Cord'. Mystery? There is no mystery about who killed Ben! It makes me SO angry!!!! Elaine says that he's got balls of steel to be known as one of 'Shawbrigg's Stars' after all he's put me through, and that folk should know the real story behind Ben's death.

Kimberly's just as bad, flaunting herself around town. I walked past Chop and Change and she was standing at the front desk with her hairdresser pal patting her belly. It makes me want to puke when I see her strutting about Shawbriggs, showing off her bump. Maybe I should think about moving back to Portcullen and then I'd never have to see her again? But why should I get driven away? I silently willed her to step out of the hairdresser's and fall underneath an HGV. It would be even better if Steve was with her at the time. He deserves it more than her. A sick thought isn't it? But I lost my bairn, so why should Steve get another chance when I can't? It was Steve that killed Ben.

HE killed his own son. Not the guy behind the wheel.

There, I've written it down. It's a fact. I've only ever said it out loud once to Elaine, no one else knows. Especially not Kimberly, or the folk at Broken Cord. But Steve and I know that it was never EVER an accident!

I would never be able to erase memories of the accident. When Ben disappeared under the wheels of the estate car, I screamed as my heart was ripped apart and I fell backwards into hell.

Something else screamed too. The wailing came from the other side of the road. It sounded like starving gulls swooping down on the remains of a poke of chips. A teenage Goth girl stood at the bus stop, hands covering her mouth and yet her cries still escaped and sliced through the air.

I wanted to scream blue murder. There was no need for the 'POLICE ACCIDENT SLOW DOWN' sign that was placed further up the road minutes later. There had been no accident; it really was a case of murder.

'It wasn't my fault.'

The elderly car driver was shaken to the core and was gently ushered away, as he told the police over and over that he wasn't to blame. Still to this day, I can't forget his quivering voice repeating the words, 'It wasn't my fault', like a prayer to any god that would answer him, and make the horror go away.

That day, no god listened to me either when I'd cried out, 'Please God no, dinnae take ma baby!'

My plea went unanswered and the driver's conscience wasn't eased. I found out later that the man's name was Ian Roberts. I never referred to him by his name. He was always 'the driver'. It was the term I was most comfortable with. To call him Ian or Mr Roberts would have made him an actual person, with a family, friends and a life. Something Ben no longer had. Thinking of the driver as Ian Roberts would have made the tragic event real. There would be no chance of denial. I still struggled to believe that it was true, that I would never hold Ben in my arms again.

Ian Roberts was right to protest his innocence. He deserved forgiveness, and, if he was anything like me, he'd lie awake for hours each night, replaying the 'what ifs' of that day.

What if, what if, what if…

I was willing to bet that Ian Roberts spent countless nights of tossing and turning, tangled up with the possibilities. It was easy to imagine us. Two different people, lying in bed in two different towns. Both tormented each night until our bed sheets wrapped round us and clung to our body, clammy with sweat and damp with tears.

Now in his late seventies, I wondered if Ian Roberts should still be driving? Did his eyesight need checking? Endless questions. But he had told the police the truth. There was nothing he could do. He could never have braked in time. Ben hadn't stopped, looked or listened before he had run headlong into the oncoming traffic. It wasn't the fault of Ian Roberts, and it wasn't Ben's fault either.

Steve had collected Ben earlier on that fatal Saturday for his weekly access visit. It was the first time that I had agreed to allow Ben to go to the flat Steve shared with Kimberly on the outskirts of the town centre. The plan was that Steve and Ben would watch a DVD, while Kimberly was at work at Street Beach. It had seemed like a reasonable idea, until I heard the football results on the bus driver's radio on my way back from Asda.

'*Rangers-2, Celtic-1*', the sports reporter had announced with a casual tone, completely unaware of what a result like that meant for the wives and girlfriends of the losing team. There would be female passengers sitting alongside me who would be wise to stay on the circular bus route. Until Monday.

My bitter experience was that when Celtic got beaten, so did I. When we had been married, I had been the wife of a die-hard football fan and I was the one who suffered for the final score. As I sat on the bus that day, I wondered if Kimberly had taken my place in that respect too. Except that, on that particular afternoon, Steve wouldn't have a handy punch bag. Or did he? Without me or Kimberly within a fist's reach of Steve, I couldn't assume that he wouldn't attack Ben instead. And yet I would have sworn on my mother's life that Steve would never ever hit Ben, wasn't that a given? But once the question was lodged in my brain, I couldn't erase it. Without the facts, I couldn't answer with absolute certainty.

Steve had solemnly promised that he wouldn't drink when

he had Ben in his care, but asking him to watch a match without alcohol, was like expecting a fish to go without water. There would be no regrets that I hadn't intervened to save my son from the disastrous combo of whisky and Steve. Without hesitation, I jumped off the bus at the next stop.

It was over half a mile to Steve's flat, but I reckoned that I'd be quicker running through the back streets, than following the winding bus route. The carrier bags cut into my palms and I cursed the fact that I had no car to get there quicker. But I would have been more dangerous behind the wheel, than on foot. Speeding along, I could have just as easily killed a child running out on to the road in front of me, if I'd been driving.

Ian Roberts hadn't been speeding though, he didn't kill Ben. Steve did.

Panting and panic-stricken, when I arrived at Steve's flat to pick up Ben, he wouldn't answer the front door. I'd battered it harder and harder until my knuckles stung and turned livid red. I'd prized opened the slit of brushes that sealed the letterbox and bawled Ben's name between difficult breaths.

'Steve, answer the door!'

No response.

'Ben, let mum in right now!'

No response.

'PLEASE!'

No response.

'Ben!'

Still nothing.

I'd yelled Ben's name again and again until finally, Steve hissed, 'Shush, ignore her!' Nothing else met me at the door except the *The Fields of Athenry* ballad playing in the background. Hearing the patriotic anthem was all the proof I needed that I had to get Ben out of the flat. The melancholy tune of the rowdy Irish folk song chilled me. The music was all part of Steve's routine following his team's defeat. In high spirits, Steve would bounce along like Tigger to the tempo of football chants until he dive-bombed into a darker mood with CDs of Irish rebel songs for company. Except that today was different, along with the Celtic music and his simmering temper, he was able to wallow with his son while his rage was brought to boiling point.

I pressed my face up to the letterbox. Like a nightclub stripper, Steve began his performance by teasing me with the burgundy bottle top that appeared gradually from behind the living room door. Inch by seductive inch, his bony arm extended to reveal the near empty bottle of Bell's whisky, slowly swinging back and forth in time to the music that Steve had commanded Ben to crank up.

The second that I kicked the door, I knew I'd made a big mistake. I should have remembered that when I lashed out with frustration, I scored an own goal. This was exactly the result Steve had hoped for and it only encouraged him to up his game even more. His next move was to stand in the doorway, with Ben in a tight bear-hug pose, Celtic scarves draped over the shoulders of father and son. With a sharp dunt to my boy's back, Ben nervously mouthed the words along with Steve singing,

'Hail Hail, The Celts are here,
What the hell do we care,
What the hell do we care,
Hail Hail, The Celts are here,
What the hell do we care now

For it's a grand old team to play for,
For its a grand old team to see,
And if you know the history,
It's enough to make your heart go,
Nine-in-a-row...'

His team had lost but Steve was winning this battle. For once, I was determined to be the final victor. I would protect Ben from any danger.

'Ah'll call the police if you dinnae answer the door!'

My next kick at the door was the red cape taunt that made Steve respond. He released Ben and charged down the hall like a wounded bull. Throwing back the door, Steve's hand lunged forward to grab me by the throat, making sure his other hand hit his target full on. The stinging skelp echoed down the hallway. My yelp sent a signal from Ben's brain to his feet, to run - past his mum, past his dad and to keep on running.

He took off, as if the gingerbread man was urging him on. *Run, run, run as fast as you can...* Ben knew many nursery rhymes by heart. I'd also taught him to *stop, look and listen.* Pure fear wiped out the road safety message I'd drummed into him.

I'd never see my Ben grow from boy to man.

JULIA

Leaning against the balcony's railing, I took a drag from my cigarette. A powerboat sped up the middle of the river Clyde carrying a family group. They were kitted out in fluorescent life jackets aboard the Clyde Ride powerboat, hurtling towards my waterfront home. The shoulder length hair of the mum thrashed around in the wind; she gripped the metal bar in front of her as if her life was in danger. The wind smudged the words but I could still make out the speed boat's driver, shouting backwards to his passengers, 'Scream if you wanna go faster!'

'Faster, faster!' all three of the children urged, with squeals that could make ears bleed. The bow lifted and the boat surged forward.

'Faster!' the dad cried out too.

The boat bounced up and down as it steered into the south-westerly wind and met the waves it created head on. Again and again, the bow cut through the waves, turning the slate-grey waters into a frenzy of white wake.

The mum stayed mute, while the dad pointed up at me and encouraged the children to wave at the woman standing alone outside her glass fronted box. My hands grabbed the stainless steel railing as tightly as the woman in the power boat. Watching the family at play on a Saturday afternoon was a white knuckle ride for me too, and I couldn't bring myself to respond to the children's excited waves. Instead, I gawped blankly as the family disappeared from view, leaving only the foamy wash as a trace of their thrill ride.

Even though I needed to get going for my meeting with Dan, I didn't move until my cigarette had burned right down between my fingers. The ash tower toppled to sprinkle its death dust on to the decking. My spirit was as spent as the fag butt I tossed down and kicked off the balcony.

I retreated into the flat, pushing the glass door back in place with the satisfying click of the lock, secure in the knowledge that the smug outside world could no longer reach me. Through in the kitchen, the dishwasher's beep signalled the end of the cycle and I realised that, if I had any chance of meeting Dan on time, then I had to move fast. Already feeling flustered, my plan of waiting calmly for him to arrive at the Angel's Bench was unlikely now. Just this once, in front of him, I'd hoped to seem in control. It pissed me off no end that although in business I could skilfully be in command, with Dan I'd never mastered the dominant role.

The weekend meant the traffic was much lighter and I needn't have worried about being late. I parked *Gary* while torrential rain tattooed patterns on the mini's windscreen. Flipping up my fur trimmed hood against the downpour, I set off for the blackened bench and made it with minutes to spare; Dan was nowhere to be seen.

Scanning the horizon, I noticed a robin on a nearby branch, thrusting its orange-red breast out as if it was a perma-tanned page three model. Maggie didn't like robins. When we were children, she told Lynn and me that they weren't the cute Christmas card birds that everyone believed them to be. A robin is aggressive, it fights with its own kind and attacks other birds. Maggie had witnessed a robin pin its rival to the ground, raining blows down on the other bird's head until its opponent was undeniably dead. At the time, I'd listened to Maggie share her dislike of robins, although I refused to judge the little bird. Survival of the fittest was nature's way, so wasn't that a good reason to respect the robin? And anyway, it was probably just guarding its territory or a simple case of self-defence. So who could blame the little bird for protecting itself?

The robin hopped down into the shrubs and disappeared from view. But I could still hear it making a series of sharp, highly pitched *tick* sounds. Despite the heavy rain and my black mood, I couldn't help smiling. Waiting for Dan, the most appropriate noise was the robin's *tick, tick, tick...* Even a bird-sized brain knew that the clock was against me.

I paced up and down, and studied a pock-marked puddle at the side of the path; this wasn't a day to be sitting on a wet park bench. Was Dan playing games with me? It was now ten past four, he'd never been late before and hadn't texted me to say that he would be. All I was certain of was that the biblical rain threatened to seep right through my skin, just like my paranoia.

I returned to the deserted car park to take refuge in my beloved Mini. Dan was now almost twenty minutes late and I had to fight my instinctive urge to give him a call. Could I hold off until at least half past four? That wouldn't smack of desperation, would it? As I practised aloud my closest attempt at a casual tone, a set of knuckles rapped against the car window.

'For fuck's sake!' I jumped, and my head almost hit the car's ceiling. Sniggering, Dan opened the car door and patted me on the shoulder like I was Roxy.

'Sorry, I didn't mean to give you a fright. I thought you'd see me coming in your rear view mirror.'

'You're late.' I was sphincter tight but I resisted the temptation to add anything more aggressive. I might have been the one who'd asked to meet, but I was well aware of who called the shots. The only suggestion I dared to give Dan was to join me inside the car.

'Sorry, I was just about to leave the house when my cousin Carol called and I couldn't get her off the phone,' said Dan.

'Couldn't you say you were on the way out the door? Haven't you noticed that it's pissing down? I looked like a weirdo hanging around that bench.'

'It's lucky then that there's no one about to see you,' said Dan with a smirk creeping across his face.

'It's not funny.' I nudged Dan's shoulder. 'My jacket's ruined.'

'Only dogs can hear you now.'

'What're you on about?' I asked.

'I'll tell you what's not funny, how about this? Carol's upset that it's Mother's Day next weekend and that she'll not get a card from her wee boy. Ever. Carol was really low; did you want me to cut her off as she cried so you wouldn't get wet?' asked Dan, his eyes drilling through me.

I turned away from his glare, droplets of rain raced each other down the windscreen. I had no answer for him. Dan watched and waited too. The silence was deafening.

If he was trying to prove that he really wasn't a completely unfeeling bastard, then surely he'd come and go a bit on the £10,000 fee? Maybe then I could celebrate Mother's Day one day too. It wasn't as if Carol had *never* experienced motherhood. Of course I was sorry for Carol's short-lived relationship with her child, but at least she had actually had a child. Carol had held her own baby in her arms. She'd taught the boy nursery rhymes and rocked him to sleep. Carol had had her chance to do all of these things and more. Unlike me. What was so fair about that?

'I know you'll not negotiate the fee but would you consider an extension of a couple of weeks to let me raise the rest of the £10,000?' I pleaded.

'Julia, I can't go into the details but I *really* need the cash. And I need the full amount by the end of the month.'

'Can't you even give me a few extra days?' I begged.

'You're not listening! It's not an option. You really don't want to know why but just trust me; I can't budge on the timescale or the amount.'

'But what difference would two or three days make?'

'If I say it's a matter of life and death it'll sound like I'm on Oprah, but it's true.' Dan leaned in closer. 'And you *really* don't want to know the details.'

'Are you trying to scare me?'

'Think whatever you want.' Dan closed his eyes for a second and took a breath. 'The fact is, I'm in serious shit if I don't have that money on time.'

'But couldn't you ask to extend your deadline?'

'Do you actually know the true meaning of the phrase deadline? I'll tell you. It's a boundary around a military prison beyond which a prisoner can't cross without risk of being shot by the guards. Does that help you understand?'

Dan bent his head into his hands and rubbed fiercely at his temples, an angry vein twitched.

'Honestly, if I could, I would. Please believe me; it's not up for debate. If you can't get the money on time then let's just forget it, but I need to know now. Well?'

The expression on Dan's face said it all; there was no chance of a reduction or an extension. His hand slowly reached out for the car door handle.

'Here's an idea.' Dan's face lit up with a lightbulb moment. 'Why don't you spend the six grand you've already got and book a ticket to Croatia? Make a holiday of it and visit a sperm clinic while you're there?'

'I don't want to be a fertility tourist!' I cried.

'Yeah, but if you did, I guarantee you'd still be filling out forms this time next year, especially with you not being married. Do you know that the legit clinics are only taking on couples these days? Even if you got one that'd take you on, who knows whose sperm you'll be given. You're a clever woman; you must have read the reports of all the mistakes. Is a mixed race baby trendy in the west end?'

I knew exactly what he was getting at, and he was correct. I'd done my research and had seen the story of a mixed race baby being born to a white couple, after the woman's eggs were fertilised with the wrong man's sperm. It wasn't an isolated case. It only took minutes on the internet to reveal that there were plenty of other reports detailing a catalogue of blunders at IVF clinics visited by fertility tourists. The mishaps included staff dropping embryos, eggs and sperm found on the floor or samples being mistakenly thrown out with the rubbish. I was well travelled, but this kind of trip abroad scared the shit out of me.

'But if you can't get the £10,000...' continued Dan.

The car door opened and Dan stretched one foot outside, before I hauled him back inside.

'No! Don't worry. I'll get the rest of the money. The full ten grand.'

I hastily raked around in my handbag for my diary, my hands trembled and I hoped that Dan didn't notice. I was desperate for a cigarette but I couldn't chance stalling to stop and think too long. After a quick calculation, I looked up and smiled across at Dan. The end of the month was perfect. Give or take a few days, next weekend I'd be ovulating. Right on schedule. For once, the clock was ticking in my favour.

The deal was sealed and, by the time I drove off in *Gary*, we'd agreed to meet next Sunday and exchange hard cash for bodily fluids.

Gary was well used to my erratic braking and crunching of gears, except that today was even more of an endurance test as I jerked to a halt at the traffic lights on Springburn Road. It was hard to distinguish between fear and excitement at the prospect of going through with the arrangement I'd made with Dan. Not to mention the fact that I still had to come up with another £4,000 within seven days. I had to get home as quickly as possible and work out what my options were.

I was already a week late in submitting this month's articles for *Business Scot* and I hadn't got round to tendering for work as a contributor to their new corporate website. Both jobs were big commissions that I couldn't afford to lose, and neither could I afford to lose the opportunity to dictate my destiny. I couldn't waste time on work right now. There would be other jobs. But there might not be another chance like this. My priority was to get the money as promised; this was one deadline that I had to meet.

It was a good deal. Dan was a smart, handsome white guy, and the main bonus was that there was no need for any emotional payback in this relationship. No tempers and tantrums like I had with Andrew to get what I wanted. Dan obviously needed the cash as much as I needed a child. This was an honest, clean business agreement where we both got what we needed most.

The traffic lights seemed stuck on red. Revving *Gary's* accelerator to make him throb didn't make the signals change any quicker. The rain stopped and finally I got the chance to enjoy a cigarette and, little by little, I blew the tension out the car window. I tapped the ash out the window and spotted the reason I had to brake at the pedestrian crossing.

Without waiting for the green man to appear, a young mother had already edged out a screaming toddler in a nylon baby buggy on to the road. The junkie-thin woman was barely out of her teenage years and walked like a recently beaten dog. Her hair looked fried, dried and petrified into a vulgar shade of nicotine blonde. And what was the bet that the sportswear the mother wore had never seen the inside of a gym?

'Stop yer fuckin' greetin' or ah'll skelp yer arse!' the woman's Parliamo Glesga accent was so thick you could cut it with a knife and fork. I was grateful to be safely shielded inside my metal cocoon.

The traffic lights changed as I clamped the steering wheel, instantly losing any ounce of calm I gained from my Marlboro. I crunched into third gear. In the rear view mirror I could see that the mum had left the toddler in his buggy outside a Spar. The child was packaged up and good-to-go, if anyone passing fancied a simple case of abduction. No wonder children got snatched in broad daylight. Taking a chance with stranger danger, the little boy couldn't fare any worse. It made me want to ram *Gary* into reverse, jump out of the car, grab the child and run.

Although, the more I thought about the prospect, the less I was convinced that the Nature versus Nuture debate would work in my favour. Adopted babies came with baggage. A whiff of 'eau de worthiness' could make anyone high on the powerful fumes of righteousness. Whenever I'd flirted with the idea of adoption, I'd come up gasping for fresh air. None of these babies came free from the stench of deprivation. Would I ever be able to get rid of such a rancid smell? Odours as strong as despair were sure to cling and choke me.

The mother and child scene made me wonder why scum like that got the chance to have a child? If you're not fit to look after a baby, then it was selfish to have one. Women like that don't deserve children. They don't have the right to be mothers.

If I hadn't heard the little boy's cries, I would have assumed that the buggy contained a pile of dirty washing. The child's nose was crusted in snot, and a plastic dummy dangled from a grubby piece of string tied round his neck. How could a mum threaten a child with violence and ignore the tear-stained face? Who would pay no attention to the distressing howls and fail to recognise the danger of the boy strangling himself with his own comforter?

The street scene was all wrong. Topsy-turvy. The woman was an imposter. The real part of the caring mum should have rightfully been given to me.

My only consolation was that soon, I would get to play the role that I deserved. All I had to do now was get back to the flat, fire up my computer and get busy problem solving. No one I knew would be able to lend me any more money, not that kind of amount, and not that quickly. But I was sure that there had to be opportunities to access a quick loan via the internet. There were umpteen ways to be a better mum than the one I'd witnessed in the street. But I struggled to come up with even one way to find the remaining four thousand pounds within days.

Settling down in front of the computer, I needed to send an email to *Business Scot* before I started my search for quick cash. I wondered if Kirsty was the only one that was gifted at creative writing, as I reread my account of the fictional case of food poisoning, that had prevented me from meeting the work deadline. I was so convincing, in my tale of a rampant fever, non-stop vomiting and stomach cramps so bad that I couldn't stand up, that I almost felt sorry for myself at having to suffer such an ordeal.

There were three unread emails in my personal inbox account. The first one's subject heading was, *Spring Bloom* and had been sent from LK Bennett, one of my favourite online shops. The attached photo didn't improve my mood at all.

"Orchid is a sleeveless shift dress in a classic wool and silk mix. Such a bright and feminine dress, combining a bold Indian flower print with a classic shift style. Team this colourful piece with the Lotus cardigan for a day outfit that works hard but is easy to wear. Embrace your softer side this Spring with blossoming floral prints," urged the blurb.

'I'd be happy to, if I could afford the £195 for the dress and the £75 for the bloody cardi!' I growled at the screen, sliding the latest overdue credit card statement under a sheaf of business magazines.

Message deleted.

Next message.

From: kanderson@yahoo.co.uk
Sent: 18 March 22.07
Subject: Delia's Way

Hi Julia,

In case you missed this list of "Delia-isms" doing the rounds on Facebook.

Delia's Way Stuff a miniature marshmallow in the bottom of a sugar cone to prevent ice-cream drips.

The Real Woman's Way Just suck the ice cream out of the bottom of the cone, for fuck's sake. You are probably lying on the couch with your feet up eating it anyway.

Delia's Way To keep potatoes from budding, place an apple in the bag with the potatoes.

The Real Woman's Way Buy Smash and keep it in the cupboard for up to a year.

Delia's Way If you accidentally over-salt a dish while it's still cooking, drop in a slice of potato.

The Real Woman's Way If you over salt a dish while you are cooking, that's tough shit. Please recite with me the Real Woman's motto: *'I made it and you will eat it and I don't care how bad it tastes.'*

Delia's Way Wrap celery in aluminium foil when putting in the refrigerator and it will keep for weeks.

The Real Woman's Way It could keep forever. Who eats it?

Delia's Way Cure for headaches: Take a lime, cut it in half and rub it on your forehead. The throbbing will go away.

The Real Woman's Way Cure for headaches: Take a lime, cut it in half and drop it in 8 ounces of vodka. Drink the vodka. You might still have the headache, but you won't give a shit.

Delia's Way If you have a problem opening jars, try using latex dishwashing gloves. They give a non-slip grip that makes opening jars easy...

The Real Woman's Way Why do I have a man?

Finally, the most important tip... I LIKE THIS ONE BEST.

Delia's Way Freeze leftover wine into ice cubes for future use in casseroles.

The Real Woman's Way Left over wine???? Helllloooo...

Kirsty x

On a different day, in a different frame of mind I might have found Kirsty's email funny. The email was meant to achieve much more than just make me laugh. After sharing a flat together for three years at university, not to mention sharing secrets and a friendship spanning almost twenty years, I was well aware that passing on a joke was the closest Kirsty would get to apologising for her behaviour at the book launch. If I replied 'lol', with a few quick taps on the keyboard, everything between us would be back on track. One click was all Kirsty was worth right now.

Message deleted.

Next message.

From:enquiries@gazette.com
Sent: 18 March 10.35
Subject: Is there anybody out there?

Hiya Julia!

Long time no hear??? Thought you were gonna keep in touch with your old pals at the Gazette?

We haven't seen you since Neolithic times!!! What're you up to these days? Bet you're spending your freelance money faster than you can earn it! Same as ever, eh?

Short notice I know, but Becky on Features - remember her? (When the pubs are closed the only thing still open are her legs? We called her Basil behind her back? A ginger in denial but we all know she must have a red bush) Well, anyway, she's leaving to go to work for the Daily Record (how low can you go?) and there's a night out organised for this Saturday in town. We're meeting up at the Corinthian at 7.30pm - hope to see ya there and get to catch up, get pished and flex our bitch muscles! Like old times, eh?

Rachel x

Again, on a different day, I might have been in the mood. I was too busy trying to find a way forward to waste time with ex-colleagues and indulge in the pretence that *"old times"* were all fun and games.

Message deleted.

As I binned the invite, a *bloop* signalled that I had new mail in my 'play' inbox.

From: petergwhittaker@btinternet.com
Sent: 19 March 15:54
Subject: Missed me?

Missed me? For fuck's sake. Paedo Pete had a bloody cheek, although his arrogance didn't surprise me. This was a man that I'd assumed was highly intelligent, and yet, he'd failed to take the hint that I wasn't interested in seeing him again. Ever. The fact that I hadn't made any contact with him since our last date obviously hadn't made a dent in his massive ego. I'd even gone to great lengths to simulate a crude bout of diarrhea in an attempt to sicken him. The man was invincible.

But I was unable to resist opening the email, and my flabber was well and truly gasted at his message. His conceit was breathtaking.

Dear Julia,

I thought I'd better touch base with you, as you must have been wondering why I haven't contacted you. Let me put you out of your misery; I've been in good ol' London town on company business. Tedious meetings every day, won't bore you with the details, then networking most nights at the city's best restaurants over a bottle or two (well, you know that all work and no play makes Peter a dull boy, eh?) of Chateau Latour (an amazing 1952 vintage that I might treat you to one day- if you're a good girl!).

Anyway, I'm back in Auld Reekie now and I knew you'd love to hear about my new toy (another treat for you to enjoy - I know, I spoil you!). I've attached a pic for you to drool over, but you need to see her to really appreciate her beauty. I've called her 'Ecsta-Sea', like it? I'll give you her full spec when we're at the marina in Inverkip, my second home now (ha ha).

Up for a sail down the west coast soon? Maybe we could stop off at Millport one weekend? We could even take your wee niece on the trip too. Sounds like a first-rate plan????

Ciao, for now,

Peter xxx

P.S. There's Cristal chilling in *Ecsta-Sea's* fridge with your name on it...

My memory of our last date when I'd spent most of the time in the toilet must have faded for him. Or perhaps no other women on *Men2Be's* site wanted to be treated to Peter's unique style of charisma?

I was so absorbed with the audacity of Peter's email, I barely registered that someone was buzzing my apartment's intercom.

'It's Holly and granny. Can we come up Auntie Julia?'

'Sure Angel Face.'

I pressed the entry buzzer and ran back to my computer to minimise my *Play* inbox. Long before I opened my front door, the tension poured through my letterbox like an acidic liquid. Waiting on the other side, I was confronted by Maggie's frosty glare and Holly's excited babble.

Holly raced to grab the binoculars on the nest of tables, beside the patio doors to the balcony, whilst Maggie hustled me into the kitchen.

'So you forgot about tonight?' asked Maggie in a clipped tone. I took a deep breath, with six thousand hassle free pounds already transferred into my bank account, it would seem unwise to antagonise my mother with a cry of, 'Well what does it look like? Of course I fucking well forgot about Holly!'

226

Maggie had called earlier in the week and asked if I would be able to baby sit for Holly on Saturday, as she hadn't been able to help Lynn out herself. The most annoying part was that I was barely back in the door after meeting Dan. If I'd remembered, then I could have picked Holly up less than an hour ago.

Instead, Maggie fumed that she'd had to drop Holly off before she got ready for her big night out. Every year, the Prince and Princess of Wales Hospice held a Black Tie and Diamond Ball. It was a champagne reception and four course meal at the Marriott - it was the highlight of Maggie's social calendar. Maggie's hair had to be coiffured, her outfit and accessories had to be carefully chosen, and nothing would stand in Maggie's way to dazzle in front of her charity shop colleagues. Holly's granny could baby-sit almost every weekend, except this one.

Chris had won a sales target bonus of vouchers for a romantic overnight stay in Cameron House, on the shores of Loch Lomond. Maggie had insisted that she'd sort it out so that they'd get away together. And she did. I had said it would be no problem to have Holly overnight, and I would take her shopping for holiday clothes for Disneyland the next day. Two facts that had completely slipped my mind.

'When you never showed up, Holly was near to tears you know. Honest-to-God, if she knew you'd forgotten about her she'd have been howling. I told her you had to work today so I'd take her over to yours. It's bad enough that she's heard her mum and dad talking about the BA air strikes.' Maggie sighed. 'If she doesn't get to Disneyland, she'll be gutted. Never mind all the other carry on.'

'What other carry on?' I asked, in hushed tones. Holly was out on the balcony, busy scanning the Clydeside horizon with the binoculars and I instinctively lowered my voice.

'Oh, it might be something or nothing, but I get the feeling things are not too good between Lynn and Chris right now.'

'What makes you say that?' I asked, curious to find out where Maggie's anxieties were rooted.

'Oh, it's just that Chris seems to be working late all the time these days and Holly let slip that they've been arguing a lot,' sighed Maggie. 'That's why I was so keen to make sure they had some time alone together.'

'Do you think having this baby was only Lynn's idea?'

'Lynn did admit to me that she *forgot* to take the pill', replied Maggie. 'I just pray it's not her way of trying to mend her marriage. A baby will only add to any problems. Here's hoping I'm wrong...'

I was fit to burst with Kirsty's revelations and her offer to capture a photo of what Chris gets up to when he was 'working late'. It would be a priceless image. A highly valued commodity. If Chris was having an affair, a photo of his indiscretion would be worth a fortune to him, to conceal his betrayal. But what would it cost Lynn and Holly?

I took a moment. For once I pressed the 'pause' button on my brain before my mouth let me down.

It would be so easy to share with Maggie the snippets of guesswork that Kirsty had passed on to me. And to tell her about Chris's after hours meetings in west end bars.

Would Maggie want to hear my gut feeling that Chris saw marriage as a tedious, bourgeois convention that he'd grown tired of? In Chris's executive sales world, fidelity was like a pair of cosy tweed slippers: comfortable to wear but utterly boring. I was sure that Chris had lost his enthusiasm for monogamy and saw it as monotonous. And I would be willing to bet that my brother-in-law was seeking instant gratification from more than a thrill ride at Disneyland. But who was I to interfere? I only had the right to play God in my own life.

I didn't get too long to mull it over. Holly bounced back inside and tipped out the contents of her overnight bag. Maggie said her goodbyes as Holly and I planned our girly night in. High up on our agenda was a pampering session and it always started with bath time.

I kept a stash of bath time goodies exclusively for when Holly came for a sleepover. Delving inside a willow basket under the sink, I produced a purple bath bomb and plopped it into the depths of the warm water. Instantly, the bomb discharged iridescent glitter, making the bath water fizz and release bubbles that bobbed up and down in time with Holly's delighted squeals and splashes.

Since Holly was a toddler, part of our bath time routine was that my childhood dolly joined her in the bath. I was given the newborn baby doll, which I had named Tina, for my third birthday. Tina no longer sat on my bed as she did all through my childhood, these days my precious dolly was safely swaddled in a pram blanket at the bottom of my wardrobe. And Holly loved 'adopting' Tina whenever she came to mine for a sleepover. I wondered how long it would be before Holly was too grown up to want to carefully undress the doll and soap up Tina's plastic body. The doll's sapphire blue eyes blinked as if Tina anticipated the shampoo was heading her way.

The other toiletry kept for Holly's sole use was more of a treat for me than my niece. The apple scented shampoo had a fragrance that was so fresh, like the sweet juicy smell you get when you bite into a Granny Smith. It made me want to nibble at Holly's neck. Delicious. While I was busy shampooing Holly's hair, inhaling the intoxicating aroma, she forgot about Tina and jutted her chin out, to stretch her mouth wide enough to show me her wiggly tooth.

'Mum says it could be like that for weeks, but what if it falls out when I'm here, or when we're at Disneyland? Will the tooth fairy know I'm having a sleepover at your house or if I'm in Florida?' asked Holly, clearly troubled at the thought of losing out on a pound coin, or a dollar.

I was momentarily floored for an answer. Did seven-year-olds still believe in the tooth fairy? Holly had written to Santa last Christmas so I supposed that, along with the Easter bunny, the tooth fairy was another harmless mythical character that my niece believed existed. What was I supposed to say? I couldn't destroy Holly's childhood fantasies and reply, 'You know there's no such thing as...' and if anyone else tried it, I would happily nail their hands to the floor.

'Don't worry, if it falls out tonight, the tooth fairy will know you're here *and* she'll know when you're away to see Minnie Mouse.'

'Really? Are you sure?'

'Cross my heart and hope to die, stick a needle in my eye.'

I drew an invisible 'X' from corner to corner over my heart, otherwise the promise didn't count.

'Hey, did you know that in South Africa, children leave their teeth in a slipper under their bed?'

I'd no idea how I knew this fact, or whether it was even true, but it seemed to impress Holly. That was the beauty of kids; you could tell them anything if they trusted you.

'Bit smelly for the poor fairy, eh?' I added.

I pinched my nostrils and made a series of gagging noises. Holly giggled so hard, a cheeky little fart popped out and caused a bubble to break the surface of the bath water. The bottom burp made us both hysterical, but once we'd calmed down, my niece's petted lip appeared.

'What's up Angel Face?' I asked, gently rubbing a cotton flannel over Holly's wet back.

'I heard dad telling mum that the plane might not be going to Disneyland. Is that true Auntie Julia?'

'Listen, there's no way you'll not get to the Magic Kingdom.' I patted Holly's hand. 'Don't worry, your mum and dad'll find a plane that's going. Now c'mon, time to get you dried off before *Dancing on Ice* starts.'

Glued to the TV, Holly wolfed down a bowl of Vienetta, leaving me free to respond to the magnetic pull of my computer. Peter's email was still minimised, but instead of deleting it, I reread it several times. None of the bragging surprised me at all; I'd sat through two dates where he'd bored me witless with tales of how he liked to flash the cash. When we'd left the Rogano, Peter took me for a drink in 29, a private members club in Royal Exchange Square. The bartender recognised him instantly as the guy who'd put two thousand pounds behind the bar for drinks, when he'd been out with the Glasgow office of his firm of lawyers. Peter boasted that he liked to attend charity events so that he could publicly bid for novelty paraphernalia, all in the name of a good cause. Maggie would have loved our relationship to have worked out. He would have been the ideal invite to one of her hospice fundraising events.

And then it dawned on me. I didn't need SatNav to find my way to the money. The route ahead was obvious.

Peter's email was the first signpost to send me off in the right direction, bringing me within touching distance of the £4,000 shortfall. That kind of sum was nothing to him. Peter had bid more for a hot air balloon ride a Cancer Research auction.

And me asking him for money to buy a baby wouldn't be charity. It would be a hand up, not a hand out. All I needed was a good reason for Peter to lend me the cash, which should be easy for a clever woman like me. As Holly would say, it was *easy peasy, lemon squeezy*.

CAROL

THERE WAS NO WINE LEFT and I'd run out of teabags, poor planning for a Sunday night. And I couldn't face Monday morning without a cup of Tetley. The only option was to venture out in the dreich weather to the late night Esso garage at the outer edge of the estate. I needed to take Jinky out for a walk anyway; he'd sulked all day as he hadn't had his Sunday stretch around the woodland trail.

'Nae need tae look so scunnered, ah'm taking you oot.'

'Aboot bloody time.'

The rustle of my cagoule being tugged off the hall cupboard peg was enough to send Jinky into an excited spin, claws skidding across the laminate floor. Wrestling the lead around Jinky's neck, he towed me out of the door and along the path. A thick fog covered the street in a heavy blanket of damp air and I pulled up my hood to shield me from the drizzle.

We were both on a mission: Jinky's was to sniff the street scents that clung to every lamp post, and mine was to get home and into my PJs as quickly as possible. Up and out of the estate, I soon found myself on the main road and followed the beacon of neon light that led to the petrol station.

Jinky pulled me across the deserted forecourt and reluctantly stood still while I tethered his lead to the newspaper stand. Alongside the last remaining copies of the Sunday papers, was the *Shawbriggs Herald*, reminding me that Elaine hadn't left her copy of this week's edition as usual in exchange for my magazines. Once I had my emergency supply of Tetley teabags and a bottle of wine, I couldn't help but wonder if Elaine had deliberately forgotten to give me the newspaper. Had she once again tried to play God and protect me from whatever scandal lurked inside the *Shawbriggs Herald*'s pages? Or was I being paranoid?

Back home, I settled at the kitchen table, opened the paper and topped up my wine glass. The 'Family Notices' on Page two meant that it didn't take me long to find out why Elaine had conveniently failed to hand over her copy. Under 'Engagements', was the announcement Elaine had hoped I'd miss I read it over and over again.

Walker-McKechnie

On March 12th, Steve, youngest son of Alastair and Pauline proposed to Kimberly, eldest daughter of Jim and Linda, at her 30th birthday party. She said YES!! Both families are delighted to announce the engagement and send congratulations and love to the happy couple. X

Fat tears blurred the words but the details remained in sharp focus. It made no difference, reading it repeatedly still didn't make it sound true. Or stop it hurting. There seemed no end to the media coverage of Steve's new life - fiancé, father-to-be and all round good guy.

I swiped the newspaper up and hurled it across the living room. The newspaper knocked the pile of magazines off the arm of the chair, leaving a scattered mess of lives laid bare on glossy paper.

Mid saunter, Jinky paused and looked blankly at me before delicately padding around the debris. The dog had a quick sniff at the splayed pages before retreating into the kitchen, leaving me to snatch up the magazines. I ripped each page out and shredded the shiny paper into strips that fell to the floor with my tears.

Ripping paper was almost as therapeutic as a trip to the bottle bank, except that I missed the noise of the glass smashing against metal. The sound of the pages tearing wasn't quite as satisfying and sometimes a clump of paper wouldn't rip easily. I tore a bundle of pages free from their staples, and then stopped, mid shred.

'Yessssssss!'

The magazine advert I was about to tear up was the answer. Who needed Saint Matthew's help when you had *Natter*?

All night on the internet, I clicked in and out of the online world of 'real life' magazines, checking whether any similar stories had ever been featured in the past. Love and betrayal, loss and sin were common themes but I was relieved to find that none of the magazines' sites had anything like my story.

Apart from the tap-tap-tapping of my computer keyboard, the only other sounds were Jinky's wheezy snoring and the clock in the hall tick-tick-ticking. Thank God I'd restocked the teabags, on the fourth cup of tea that night, it was all that kept me going. Each time I'd entered the darkness of the kitchen, to switch on the kettle and feel the chill from the floor tiles crawl up my legs, I made myself promise to go to bed after my drink. But as I moved towards the glow from the computer screen, I was a moth to a flame, drawn once more to the websites, full of people opening up their lives to strangers under feature headings like, "*You*

Confess…" and *"It happened to me…"*

It wasn't uncommon for me to sit up all night on the computer, but tonight's marathon cyber session was taking its toll. I was so tired. I toyed with hunting out the sleeping pills that had been prescribed to me when Ben had died. The capsules still lurked somewhere at the back of a drawer in my bedside cabinet, a safe place for secrets. And yet every time I considered shutting down the websites, the real life stories pulled me in to tell yet another moving story that lured my zombie eyes back to the screen.

The online search had taken me longer than I'd expected. My research uncovered that this was a crowded market place with at least a dozen different magazine titles reaching over seven million gossip hungry readers each week. *Natter* claimed to have over one million devoted readers, all eager to greedily gobble up the latest extraordinary tales involving ordinary people. The magazine websites invited their readers to submit their true-life stories. Each magazine claimed that it was their job to help readers tell their story sensitively. It was what they did best. And of course, they all promised that they'd also pay the most money for it too. If I felt lonely, depressed, wanted revenge or I was seeking closure, the magazines' websites could help me. Sharing my suffering with the general public was the only sensible thing to do. A win-win situation.

My story fitted into one of the magazines' most loved features. According to the internet, it was known in the business as a *"womb trembler"*, where anything emotional that involved mothers and babies was always popular. From my own love of the magazines, if a story contained a triumph over tragedy angle, then it would be a good read. Exposing the success of Steve's award winning fundraising when all along he'd caused Ben's accident would have huge appeal to *Natter*'s readers. It was only a matter of finding the strength to share my story. Could I allow my soul to be ground down to dust so that the readers could snort it up their nostrils and get their weekly fix?

Throughout that sleep deprived Sunday night, I found myself wondering whether I would be able to sell my story for cash. Would it be the uplifting, therapeutic experience that I hoped for? Or would I regret airing my grief in public?

I had to face up to the fact that there would be a far-reaching ripple effect caused by selling my secret. Once the heavy stone of truth had been dropped, it would plummet and demolish any notion of calm. The powerful surge caused by the printed magazine story would not only wreck Steve and Kimberly's world, and both sets of their parents, the effects would also reach my mum in the North East, Isobel, Elaine and all my extended family, friends and neighbours.

Would it really be in everyone's best interests to tell tales for cash? Would the magazine article deliver shame or satisfaction to my mum's door? Anytime these doubts floated to the surface, I was quick to push the negative thoughts back down, until they sunk out of sight.

With the prospect of daylight leaking through the bedroom curtains, I plumped my pillows, lay flat out, did a slow starfish stretch, and screwed my eyes tightly shut. I concentrated hard, willing my brain to magic up a favourite image that I'd created over the years. It had started as a simple vision of me flopping down softly inside cotton wool clouds and drifting gently to sleep. But over time, I had added more details and now the feathery clouds lined a silver chariot that dashed across the night sky, pulled by a galloping moon-white unicorn, to transport me safely to the land of Nod. It never worked. It hadn't worked for a long time. I stepped aboard the fantasy carriage and prayed that for once, I would reach my destination.

My alarm clock ruined the silence of the bedroom peace, squawking that it was already seven o'clock. I lunged at it with a swift tap on the 'snooze' button and turned my back on the alarm's neon numerals to hide under the duvet. I lay there, engulfed in the fug of warm body and stale air; the nearest thing to being back in the womb.

I'd waited patiently for the clock to turn its digits into a reasonable time for me to text Dan. Was seven thirty too early? It didn't seem a ridiculous time to send a text and, after a sleepless night, I couldn't hold off a minute longer. I had to get in touch and let him know the news. I'd found a way to raise the rest of the £10,000.

MONDAY 21ST MARCH 2011

Dear Journal

I'm absolutely knackered with the nervous energy that's kept me awake all night with ideas. Steve's taken the next step in reinventing himself by proposing to Kimberly, no doubt wanting to make sure that it looks better that they're at least engaged when she has their bairn. It really hurt too. It feels like the past never existed, the way his mum and dad joined in with Kimberly's to wish them all the best. It's no surprise really. The Walkers were always stuck-up snobs. My dad never took to them, he said they were all show and no substance. Me, Ben, and his previous life, have been conveniently wiped out. That's what gave me the idea. Well I suppose, to be fair, it was really Elaine that got me thinking about "sell and tell" when she was laughing at the stories in my magazines.

I've worked out a way to get the £10,000! I might even be able to sell the story for more than that and pay off some of my debts before my bairn comes!

The announcement in the paper was so typical of Steve and his family wanting to make sure that the 'Shawbriggs Star' was doing the right thing by marrying his pregnant girlfriend. It's thanks to them though that I've come up with a plan. It's so simple too! Wouldn't everyone want to hear the REAL story about the town's best loved charity fundraiser? Just the kind of thing that Natter would love, but even better if it is the TRUE story! The magazines that I tore up were practically shouting out the answer to me. I should have thought about it ages ago and saved myself the worry. And it's quick cash. I've already started the ball rolling!

I've spent most of the night on the real life magazine websites researching my idea and it's a winner! I've reread this week's edition and it was full of regular sections, where my story would fit in perfectly. I circled the '24 Hours that Changed my Life' feature as one of the most obvious places for my story, but I'm sure the magazine people will know best. It's the best idea I've ever had. My story is worth a fortune!

I've emailed Natter with my contact details and told them that my story makes a much more interesting read than Steve's version of events. Wait till Natter hear that Broken Cord's award winning fundraiser and respected hotel manager used to batter his first wife AND that his violent abuse caused his son to run out on to the road and get killed? Worth reading, don't you think so? This could be Natter's best story yet!

I never thought for one minute that I'd ever want anyone to know about the accident but Elaine's right; people should get the chance to read the true story about the 'Shine On' winner and his affair with a teenage babysitter. Just cos it was a while ago and they're getting married now doesn't make it okay. I can't bring Ben back, but I can get justice. Why should they strut about the town with their heads held high and I'm stuck at home alone? I've done nothing to be ashamed of, ever! I can't just sit back and wait to see them push a pram around Shawbriggs.

When Ben died I felt like a leper. Loads of folk that I'd known for years practically ran across the street to avoid talking to me, cos they didn't know what to say. A snub from people I thought were friends and neighbours felt terrible, but when they were nice to me, dishing out sugary sympathy, it was even worse. It's horrible watching folk steer clear and I know it'll be the same feeling again. When the magazine buys my story, people that I don't even know will look at my photograph and make comments about what they think of me and how I look. There's no point in kidding myself. I know they will cos Elaine always does it when she reads the stories. I'll not like people gossiping about me when the story gets printed, but I've been through that before. When Ben died, a report of his accident was in the *Shawbriggs Herald*. I survived my tragedy being public knowledge and I'm starting to deal with things better these days. The only difference is that this time at least there'll be something good comes out of it. All the bitching behind my back will be worth a baby.

It's hard to describe how I feel; it's a weird mixture of fear and satisfaction. I'm a bit hyper except that, for the first time since meeting Dan, I actually feel in control. I can only admit it to you, but I'm quite excited at the thought of Steve getting what he deserves. AND it's even better that, when I sell my secret, I'll get what I deserve too! I've waited a long time for this. Like

Isobel keeps telling me, "*Every dog has his day.*"

Sitting at the kitchen table that morning, time seemed to stand still. Rather than constantly stare at the clock, I focussed on the twinkling specks of dust, rising to dance and twirl up into the shaft of sunlight. It was now ten minutes past eight and there had been no reply from Dan. The trouble with not knowing his day-to-day routine was that I had no idea when Dan usually got up and, as he worked from home, he might not even work regular office hours. When I tried to visualise Dan's daily timetable, I had to admit that I couldn't picture him at home. He'd never actually given me his address, never mind taken me to his house. He was a man of mystery.

A flicker of concern swept over me that I didn't actually know very much about him at all. Wasn't it best that I didn't have too much information? That way I didn't have the fear of discovering things that I might be better off not knowing. Look what happened to the curious cat. Isobel had trained me well.

Every week in the Daisy Chain, Isobel carefully smoothed out the nylon tabard over her hefty bust, wrapped her meaty arms round her middle as if her jelly belly ached, and sighed slowly with a sorry shake of her head.

Only when she was good and ready, would Isobel treat me to comments like, "*ignorance is bliss*" or for a bit of variety, "*what you don't know can't hurt you*". A perfect example of Isobel at the top of her game was when Mrs Stewart, a regular customer, arrived to buy a fresh bunch of whatever was on special offer. Every Friday morning Mrs Stewart moaned to us that she had to buy her own flowers, as there was no hope of her husband *ever* buying her a bouquet. And yet, *every* Friday, minutes before closing time, we had a visit from Mr Stewart, to collect his standing order of a deluxe hand-tied bouquet on his way home.

'Remember, we're only in the business of selling flowers, nothing else.' Isobel would often say when Mrs Stewart appeared at the door each Friday morning.

In my early days at the Daisy Chain, I had once asked Isobel if we should drop a hint to Mrs Stewart that her husband came into the shop on a weekly basis. Isobel grew pale at the very idea of revealing any customer confidences. Without a word, she took me gently by the hand, led me through to the back shop and pointed up at a plaque mounted on the wall. Up above the door frame, three monkeys sat in a row, each one with its eyes, ears or mouth covered. The motto underneath said, "*see no evil, hear no evil, speak no evil*".

'There's a lot more to this business than how to arrange flowers. But don't worry doll, I'll train you well.'

An hour later, Isobel commented on a customer's order for funeral flowers.

'That one's got a bloody nerve. She's got more faces than the town hall clock. She comes in here all: "My poor mother, I'll miss her dearly" when I know for a fact that she never visited her mammy from one month to the next. The old woman died a lonely wee soul. Only had her cat for company. *And* she lay dead for days behind her front door. Her neighbours said the stink would've knocked you on your back. It's a disgrace.'

'That's terrible. But I thought we weren't supposed to blether behind the customers' backs?'

'Oh no, us chatting together doesn't count. What gets said in the shop, stays in the shop. Between me, you and the flowers,' said Isobel as she tapped the side of her nose.

From that day on, I accepted Isobel's advice about not getting involved in our customers' lives without argument. We had no right to dig and dabble. There was no doubt in my mind that I didn't need or want to know too much about Dan. If I asked too many questions, I might not like the answers. I couldn't comment for Mrs Stewart, but in my own situation, I believed that Isobel was as wise as the monkeys.

It was nearly half twelve before Isobel finally gave me the nod that I could nip home to let Jinky out for a pee. When I arrived home, there was a postcard lying on the door mat. A package required a signature and couldn't be delivered that morning. I walked through to the kitchen, letting Jinky bolt out the back door. I wondered what would be waiting for me at the Post Office when I collected the parcel. It would probably be from my mum, the latest 'Helping Hand' package.

With my head fit to burst, I still had room to wish I lived nearer to my mum. Although we were close, I could never have discussed Dan, never mind the deal we'd struck. But being able to see, hear and touch my mum, someone in this world that gave me unconditional love, would have helped me steer my way through difficult decisions. No one, not even the Farrells next door, could hear me scream in Shawbriggs.

Whilst Jinky sprayed his way round the patch of scorched grass, burnt with his acidic urine, my fingers trembled as I opened up my email account. *Natter*'s website boasted that their team responded to every query within a maximum of twenty-four hours from receipt. I only hoped they lived up to their own hype.

No new electronic mail, the only snail mail for me was waiting at the Post Office and when I collected the parcel, inside there was a note from my mum.

Me and the girls from the bowling club went on a day out to Fochabers. Mrs MacWatt heard that it was a great day out and we weren't disappointed. The minibus dropped us off and we went on a tour to hear all about the history of the Baxter's soup story. The factory was originally opened by George Baxter in 1868. It was absolutely fascinating. The tearoom is lovely with clean toilets and the scones were delicious. When you come up to visit with your new car, maybe we could go a wee run? I remembered seeing a 'Chicken Soup for the Soul' book once on your bedside cabinet on one of my last visits. It reminded me that you've always loved chicken soup so I've sent you a couple of tins of Baxters Chicken Broth. I just wish you were still up here to enjoy my own home-made soup. I hate to brag, but the tinned stuff is nowhere near as good as my Cream of Chicken but at least it'll keep you going until I see you. Will you be coming home soon?

God bless,

Love mum. x

Finally, I finished my shift at the Daisy Chain and could get back home to check my emails again. Home? Where was home these days? When I had moved south, I had no idea how much I valued a sense of belonging. Wouldn't having my own family root me to a spot that I could call home? And would a job, a few friends and a house in Shawbriggs be enough? Not anymore. Home equalled family and without Ben here, Shawbriggs would never feel like home. The only family I had now was my mum.

Looking round the living room, I longed for my mum's cottage and cooking. The open fire was the thing I missed most. There was no fireplace in my modern villa, it was an energy efficient house but it had no inner warmth; it had no soul. My semi in the Woodlea estate no longer gave me comfort. I lived in a house, not a home. My mum's cottage had a beating heart, and although it had been damaged when I left, it could always be repaired to full health.

Click, click, click and there it was in my inbox, straddled between an eBay alert for sellers and a junk email offering me a discounted supply of Viagra.

Click. Just one click revealed that my personal heartbreak was worth no more than £500! *Natter* was certainly interested in my story, as long as I could provide photos of Ben and Steve, and then they *may* be able to offer me as much as five hundred pounds. Five hundred pounds. I read the email again, slowly. Yes, it was definitely five hundred, not five thousand. That's what a soul stripped of all its secrets was worth to *Natter*. Good value for money.

I could have this tiny amount of cash in exchange for ripping my heart wide open to let it bleed all over their glossy pages. *Natter's* readers could suck up the juicy details like greedy vampires and dine on my tragic story. A whole belly-full for a 90p magazine.

JULIA

As part of our girly pampering session, I asked Holly to get my makeup from my Mulberry handbag. Snooping was one of Holly's favourite hobbies, she loved to rake amongst the grown-up glamour that lurked inside my treasure trove.

I didn't need to see through walls to know that by now, Holly would be trying on my *pop star sunglasses*, spitting out my extra strong *nippy* chewing gum and squirting my *sexy* perfume. I remembered too late, that along with a spare set of false nails, I also had enough tampons in my bag to stock a branch of Lloyds Pharmacy.

'What are these?' asked Holly, clutching a handful of tampons.

'Eh, they're called lady sticks. Your mum'll tell you all about them when you're a big girl. Now, never mind those, what's that in your other hand?'

Holly's rummaging had also unearthed the ultrasound scan print of her brother or sister, aka *The Bump*, which had been nesting inside an inner panel of the calfskin leather bag.

I was now the proud curator of an exclusive and very limited collection of three black and white ultrasound scan photos of babies in their womb hammocks. The oldest one was very grainy, it had been taken more than seven years ago and showed Holly sucking her thumb, a habit that still resurfaced when she was world weary. The newest, crease free picture was of 'Angel Face No 2', showing a pair of cartoon feet. The other photo in my collection was a much tattier print of its unborn cousin.

'Have you got a scan picture of me too?' asked Holly.

'Of course I have. It's more precious than anything else I own.'

'So you keep it somewhere safe then?'

'Under lock and key. It's so special I just can't leave it lying around.'

I might've guessed that wasn't enough to satisfy Holly's curiosity.

'So can I see it? Can I go and find it Auntie Julia?'

'The thing is, Angel Face, it's so valuable, that I have to keep it in a safe place, a secret place, so hidden, that I can't even tell you where I keep it.'

'Oh, please Auntie Julia. I just want a wee look and then you can lock it away again.'

'Okay, but you need to promise, no peeking while I go and get it. Cross your heart?'

'Yep. You know I can keep a secret,' Holly said, as she crossed her arms across her chest. 'Cross my heart and hope to die, stick a needle in my eye'.

'Excellent. Being able to keep a secret is very *very* important. Will you remember that?'

'Easy peasy lemon squeezy.'

'Good girl. Now, keep those peepers shut!'

The hyped up secrecy bought me enough time to retrieve the scan from a ragged buff envelope, stashed under the musk scented drawer liner of my bedside table.

I hadn't told Holly any fibs that the scan of her was lovingly kept in a secret location. I often slipped the print out of its protective cover to lay it out on my bed and tenderly run my finger round the curved baby blobs. I did the same with the other ultrasound scan that snuggled inside the worn envelope.

I had a strict routine; I liked to caress each scan image in chronological order of when they were conceived. Lynn and Chris had created the first heartbeat that, nine months later, became Holly. The other black and white image in the envelope was of the little cousin that Holly never got the chance to meet.

The second print was now over four years old. The scan had been taken when I had swithered over the reality of another abortion. I called the baby shape *The Bean*. During my hospital appointment, The Bean had wriggled and jerked like it was a fan of rave music. I had often wondered if the foetal movements had anything to do with its frantic conception. Andrew and I had danced until the early hours in Amnesia, and I would never forget staggering back to our hotel, hammered and happy. Our wild, boozy binge in Ibiza resulted in me puking repeatedly the next day, spewing up the remains of a dodgy late-night hamburger. Partying hard and keeping the Pill down was a dangerous combo.

Andrew never knew about the pregnancy, and it was so early on in our relationship that I hadn't dared to tell him about the abortion either. When I later found out that he had no desire to be a father, I was satisfied that I'd done the right thing on both counts.

The Bean would not have been Holly's only cousin. The eldest of Holly's unborn cousins would have been nearly twenty years old by now.

Only Kirsty knew about my first abortion, the one that I had in my second year at university. My best friend had suggested that I should discuss my choices with the father. A reasonable idea, but as I wasn't entirely sure which one of the three possibilities could have made me pregnant, it wasn't an option. I made do with debating the pros and cons of motherhood with Kirsty. Together, we sprawled across my bed and scribbled on an A4 page of an Oxford pad. The lined paper could barely cope with the cons list; it filled both sides and could easily have spilled out on to a second sheet. There were no pros.

'You do the maths,' was my only comment to Kirsty.

Not once did I ever regret my decision. But although there wasn't a photographic memory of my first pregnancy, thoughts of my two ghost children were never far away. Cosy and snuggled up beside the image of their cousin Holly, my 'wasn't meant to be' baby slept soundly.

I gave in, and let Holly pin the scan photos of her and The Bump up on my kitchen memo board to show her mum when she collected her the next day.

'It's just for a wee while and then you can lock them away again when I go home.'

'Okay, as long as you guard them with your life.'

'No problemo!' Holly said, with a satisfied smile.

When she arrived on the Sunday morning, Lynn immediately noticed the two ultrasound photos on display. She ran her slim fingers over both of them affectionately, looking as if she could actually feel the velvety softness of their unblemished newborn skin.

'I see mum remembered to give you the scan of The Bump.' Lynn leaned against the breakfast bar. 'At least she's got something to look forward to now her trip's cancelled.

I resisted the temptation to retaliate; I simply busied myself with the espresso machine and ignored her. The weight of Lynn's disapproving silence collapsed as I deliberately slurped my coffee. Having had no visit from the Tooth Fairy, Holly was still crashed out in my spare bedroom, the only female at peace in the flat.

Lynn was the first to crack.

'You know, I honestly can't believe you've taken mum's money. You've no shame.'

'You make it sound like I robbed her at gun point; she offered the cash to me willingly.'

'Yeah, whatever you say,' muttered Lynn.

'What's that supposed to mean?'

'Whatever you want it to mean. It's always about what you want. A once-in-a-lifetime investment opportunity, huh! What about mum's once-in-a-lifetime chance to travel? But what do you care about that? As long as *you* get what *you* want, that's the main thing.'

I wanted to spit out the facts and rub them into Lynn's self-righteous face. Maggie was a healthy, active sixty-three-year-old woman, hardly decrepit by anyone's standards, so what was Lynn's problem? By the time I paid back the £6,000, Maggie would still be fit and able to gallivant to wherever took her fancy. In her early sixties, Maggie's dream could be easily postponed. But for me heading into to my forties, it would be mad to postpone my dream. If Lynn knew about the dilemma I faced, then she surely wouldn't expect me to stall on the option of having a child. If I was able to explain my situation to Lynn, then maybe she would understand that Maggie could wait, I could not.

Blah, blah, blah. Lynn was stuck on repeat mode and failed to notice that I had tuned out completely. I made no attempt to respond to her protests that Maggie might never get another chance to fulfill her dream, I had cloth ears.

'Yeah, tell me about it,' I mumbled under my breath as I flicked through yesterday's copy of *The Guardian*.

Lynn was preaching to the converted, I completely understood the concept of grabbing a unique opportunity. I had been pregnant twice before, without even trying. But this was most likely to be my *only* possibility to satisfy my dream of motherhood on my terms. I knew all about dreams and, now that I was so close to achieving my goal of becoming a mum, there was no chance that I was willing to walk away now.

'You obviously don't know how much this trip meant to her,' huffed Lynn.

'It's between me and mum. Nothing to do with you', I snapped.

A bleary-eyed Holly stumbled into the kitchen, instantly ending our head-to-head confrontation with a simple stretch.

'Let's get you home and give Auntie Julia a bit of space; she's got a lot of thinking to do.'

'What about?' asked Holly.

'Doing the right thing.' Lynn's comment bounced off me like a rubber bullet. 'Right, c'mon, time to get dressed and get going Holly.'

As much as I had enjoyed having Holly to stay overnight, I did need time to organise my plan. Lynn's catty comments gave me the final confirmation that my idea was a clever one.

If travelling to places that she'd only imagined meant everything to Maggie, then it was the perfect reason to ask Peter for £4,000. What decent guy with money to burn wouldn't help a lover's mother to fulfill her dream holiday? And if he was led to believe that my mum had been diagnosed with cancer, wouldn't that seal the deal? All I had to do was play the game. If I was forced to take on the role of lover, even to a seedy guy like Peter, then so be it. I would soon have the cash I needed for Dan.

I'd sent my reply email to Peter inviting him for an intimate dinner, long before Lynn had arrived to collect Holly. I had cast my net, and I didn't have to wait long for him to bite. It took less than three hours for Peter to take the bait and accept my offer of a romantic dinner for two at my flat.

From: petergwhittaker@btinternet.com
Sent: 20 March 12:32
Subject: Dinner chez Julia

Dear Julia,

Many thanks for getting in touch and for your kind invite to dine at your place. I should appreciate that not everyone feels at ease in the Rogano, so I understand that you feel more comfortable eating at home (particularly after the unfortunate incident the last time we met, however there's no need for you to worry, I'm renowned in business and pleasure as a soul of discretion).

So yes, of course, I'll come over to Glasgow and sample your culinary skills (I do hope that deep fried Mars bars don't feature on your menu - I'm not that adventurous!)

I don't need to tell you that I'm a very busy man but there is a window in my diary this Tuesday, before I head back down to London to meet one of my high profile clients.

Ciao, for now,

Peter xxx

P.S. Probably safer if I select the wine – so please let me know the menu in advance.

Peter hadn't disappointed, it was exactly the reply I was hoping for, and all I had to do now was to reel him in.

Tuesday dragged by as slowly as a dial-up modem while I prepared for Peter's visit. The bathroom sparkled, the kitchen was stocked with everything needed for a meal worthy of the best west end restaurants and, most importantly, the Egyptian cotton 1000 thread count sheets in my bedroom were clean and crisp.

Much as it made my stomach churn, I had to consider the opportunity of a free sperm donation from Peter, there was no denying that it would be much cheaper than paying Dan. But on his last disastrous visit to my flat, Peter had been at pains to reassure me that he would never be stupid enough to have unprotected sex. He'd boasted that no matter how drunk he was, he always remembered to practise, *"no glove, no love"*. I squirmed at the memory of his cheesy comment.

Even if I could have fooled him into riding me bare back or sabotaged his condom, I wasn't prepared to conceive and be connected to Peter for the rest of my life. But if being screwed by Peter made him keener to lend me the £4,000, then that was all I wanted from him.

When the flat's entry system finally announced Peter's arrival, I was relieved that my plan would soon be executed. It wasn't long before Peter was sitting at my dining table and oozing a relaxed vibe.

'Nothing can beat the Rogano's pheasant but I've got to hand it to you Julia, your pigeon is delicious and really complements the delightful Beaujolais I brought.'

'I'm flattered. I know you've got such high standards.' I replied.

I had taken great care to dispose of the packaging that was now hidden at the bottom of the kitchen bin. The skinless breasts of wood pigeon poached in a red wine and thyme jus were very acceptable to Peter's love of locally sourced seasonal produce considering that the entire meal had been delivered directly to my door, by a local caterer.

Peter's thick tongue emerged, a fat slug, probing for the sticky red sauce that had trickled down his chin. I seized my chance and lurched across the table with my linen napkin, poised to tenderly dab away the dribble.

Peter's eyes slid down the valley of my low cut velvet bustier, he was hooked, and then he gently pushed my napkin away.

'It's kind of you to be so attentive but it would be a waste to wipe it away. I do love the sweet juice of a fresh young breast.' His slimy tongue reappeared from its damp hiding place to slowly lick away the burgundy sap.

Watching him perform, I gagged involuntarily into my napkin, muffling the sound of my disgust. If I was actually going to go through with shagging Peter, then I would have to get it over with quickly.

In my four years at university, a one-night stand was no big deal, in the same way as drinking a pint of cheap cider and smoking a joint of hash. In pubs on Byres Road, with Nick wrapped round my best friend like a suffocating scarf, Kirsty had often lectured me about my promiscuity. It made no difference, her disapproval didn't make a dent in my 'up yours' attitude which I wore like a badge of honour, pinned to my BAN THE BOMB t-shirt.

I was used to finding my skimpy knickers where I'd stepped out of them in the bedroom of my student flat. But my self-confidence had never been on the floor too. Wasn't waking up to a raging hang-over, on crusty sheets with an unknown male's rank Kebab-breath on my face, all part of growing up? I had no teenage excuses these days, a date with Peter was premeditated and I was supposed to be older and wiser after all these years.

Whilst Peter chomped his way through the meal, I chewed on the question of whether it would be better to ask for the loan before, or after, sex. Either way, once inside the bedroom, I'd have to use all my best tricks to secure £4,000. To swap the dining table for my king-size bed, it was essential to gulp down a few more glasses of wine, but not too much, I needed to negotiate the transaction semi-sober.

His rodent cheeks were jammed full of dauphinoise potatoes,

yet Peter decided it was the perfect time to describe the luxury spec of his new sailing yacht, *Ecsta-Sea*. Every now and then, I picked up phrases like, *2006 Grand Soleil 43*, *racing lead keel*, *Volvo Penta 55HP Engine*, as Peter reported the yacht's many features. Did I look as fascinated as he'd hoped?

'So are you up for it?' asked Peter.

'Oh, sorry, you lost me a bit there with all the hi-tech stuff. But yeah, I'm always up for it.'

I leaned forward to give him another eyeful of my cleavage to go along with my cheeky wink.

'No need to apologise, I have to admit, I do get a teeny bit carried away with all the technical data. As I was saying, are you up for a trip on *Ecsta-Sea* to Millport with your niece?'

I was struck dumb. Peter had mentioned the invite in his email, but I hadn't prepared a reply. He moved out of his chair and over to the console table behind my sofa. Peter picked up the photo frame, bringing it closer to his face. His eyes penetrated the glass with his intent stare. Peter was no longer with me in the flat, he was now on the beach at Millport. He was within touching distance of Holly, a topless toddler, in her Minnie Mouse pants.

'Holly, isn't that your niece's name?' he asked.

At the mention of Holly's name, my resolve dropped through the floor. My heart beat as loud as a kettle drum, Holly was not supposed to be part of tonight's script. This was between me and him. Why did Peter have to refer to or involve Holly in any way?

'How about we take her out over the Easter holidays?' He didn't wait for an answer; it was more of a statement than a suggestion. Peter wasn't the type to expect his authority to be challenged, if he had a plan of action then that was it. Sorted.

'She'll love it!' he continued, barely taking a breath. 'Imagine her telling all her school friends that she'd been sailing on a luxury yacht? I'll treat her like a little princess and it'd give her mum and dad a break too. Peter barely paused for breath. 'I could take her out on the rowing boat to Castle Isle. I believe it's uninhabited and quite picturesque. It should be perfect to pose for some new photos.'

He wittered on about beach picnics and going fishing but there was very little reference to me being part of the picture. Was I ever going to be able to set the romance of the evening back on course?

And then there was a sudden realisation, my light bulb moment. There was every danger that I might choke on the words, I took another gulp of wine and swallowed hard. Change of tactic. There was no need to use the excuse that I wanted to borrow money to send a cancer riddled mother on a well-deserved, no expenses spared trip. This idea was even better. This proposal made much more sense. My gut feeling had been correct all along. Paedo Pete would be far more interested in helping little girls, than little old ladies.

'Peter, that's really great of you offering to take us sailing because it looks like my sister's original holiday plans have fallen through…'

I paused for effect; he hung on my every word. I took another gulp of wine.

'You see, Lynn and Chris were supposed to take Holly to Florida for the Easter holidays, but they've going to have to cancel. It's a bloody shame and I only wish I could help. The wee darling is heartbroken.'

He listened intently whilst a gush of lies spilled effortlessly from my mouth. I emptied my glass of wine.

'My brother-in-law's been made redundant and with my sister being pregnant, they just can't justify spending the money.'

'Oh, how awful.' His face creased in concern.

'Yeah, the whole family's gutted. It was Holly's dream to visit

Disneyland. They can't afford the £4,000 to take her anymore and they'll lose their deposit.'

Paedo Pete hadn't let go of the photo of Holly in her Minnie Mouse pants. Was it simply the red wine that made his cheeks glow?

'I'd give them the money in a flash,' I sighed. 'But the problem is they need it right away to pay the balance. And I can't juggle my finances that quickly,' I added.

Would it help to elaborate the tale by adding an extreme illness? I had already spent hours creating a variety of heart wrenching scenarios of Maggie going for chemotherapy. It seemed a shame not to use the same upsetting descriptions to exaggerate Holly's situation.

'Poor little mite,' he sighed.

It was tempting to pile on the guilt for sheer impact, but it was a step too far, even for me. Paedo Pete's pained expression meant it wasn't necessary to strike Holly down with a phantom case of leukaemia. The word 'problem' offered him the chance to play the role of the knight in shining armour.

'I can help. It's not up for discussion. I'll give you the money,' he stated firmly. 'No question about it.'

At that moment, I would have killed for the satisfaction of a long deep draw on a Marlboro, if only Paedo Pete wasn't anti-smoking. I was in my own flat, my own personal space and yet right now Paedo Pete possessed the oxygen I breathed. All I could do was try to avoid suffocation and slowly inhale the rancid air of dishonesty and obligation. The fraud had been simple, but that didn't make it any easier to swallow.

Like a Viennese Waltz, Paedo Pete and I danced round the details of him lending me the money; it was exhausting.

'I insist that there is no interest paid back on the loan.' Paedo Pete slapped his hand down, a done deal.

'I can't expect you not to make any profit,' I said.

'A gentleman would never make money from a little girl's happiness.'

I had effectively secured the money I needed to pay Dan. So why wasn't I experiencing the elation that I had anticipated? The terms of the deal weren't what I had wanted at all. Paedo Pete and I both worked in the same worlds of finance and business and I understood only too well that, for a man as successful as him, he always got a substantial return on his money. It couldn't possibly be that straightforward. So what would Paedo Pete want, instead of money, as a satisfactory payback? A single shagging session would scarcely be enough to repay him. How many times would I have to spread my legs? Would he want me to dine on his dick tonight?

Paedo Pete's plans for the rest of the evening came quicker than I expected, there was no time to mull it over. He left me in no doubt that he was not interested in sex being the fifth course on my menu. No sooner had he finished his espresso, he asked if I could get his jacket.

'It'd be an after dinner delight to knock back a few cognacs with you, but unfortunately I have to travel down to London for the rest of the week on the red-eye, so I really must dash.'

'But I was hoping you might stay a bit longer. You could always leave for the airport from here in the morning,' I suggested, running my hands through my hair.

'It's an attractive offer sweetheart, but the flight leaves Edinburgh at six twenty. So I should go now, while I can still resist temptation.'

The bustier I had on was tighter than a gastric band. Not to mention the irritation I'd suffered all night from the pearl-encrusted micro thong, that only a Rio Carnival queen could cheerfully endure. All this effort had been wasted; there would be no need to bite on my pillow tonight. It left me confused. What did he want in return for his investment in bailing my family out of a financial crisis?

I handed Peter his corduroy sports jacket and had to accept his intention to leave. This week, I would be denied any chance to satisfy Peter. He didn't appear to want anything from me and promised to post me a cheque first thing tomorrow. It was too easy. There were no strings attached. Had I been too hasty in my character assassination? Was it fair to con the guy? I was trapped inside a bubble of guilt.

He paused briefly at the console table on his way, hovering beside my cluster of framed family photos.

Then the bubble burst.

'Listen sweetheart, I could tell that you're not entirely comfortable with simply taking the money from me without offering me anything in return.' Paedo Pete patted me on the arm. 'I totally respect that. I'd feel the same.'

My guilt was already starting to seep away.

'Look, if it makes you feel better, how about as a token gesture, you give me this adorable photo of little Holly in Millport? It'd be a great start for my collection of West coast scenes to decorate the interior of *Ecsta-Sea*?'

Was I being totally paranoid? It was an innocent scene of a cute child on a beach. That's all it was. It was hardly kiddie porn. Or did I only imagine that his eyes became saucer wide when he seemed to fixate on Holly's nipples, erect with the chill of the sea breeze?

'Wouldn't you prefer something a bit artier? It's just a holiday snap,' I pleaded.

'I have to disagree. I told you, I dabble in photography and trust me, there's nothing more artistic than the purity of childhood. I'd love to take more photos of Holly posing with different backdrops, there's something really special about her. Is it a deal?' he asked.

I said nothing.

Paedo Pete's sweaty hand held the image of a semi-naked fresh-faced tot, smudging the glass that encased the pink panties. His other hand was firmly extended towards me, ready and eager to complete the transaction with a swift handshake.

CAROL

I was running on empty. Dan had agreed to meet me to discuss my options and it was a relief to know that there was someone who would listen, understand and might even be able to help. We took our usual route around the woodland trail and when he spoke at last, the inner pressure slowly oozed out of me.

'You've missed a trick Carol. Selling the story to *Natter* wasn't the easiest way to get you the most money.'

He threw the grubby tennis ball for Roxy and Jinky so that it disappeared into the dense undergrowth. It bought us enough time to pause and take a seat at the *Angel's Bench*.

'I know who would pay more than £500 for your story. A lot more,' stated Dan.

'But ah've done loads of research into the magazines…'

'Forget magazines. That's not where you'll get the money you need,' said Dan.

Who would pay anything close to £10,000 if *Natter* only offered £500? His confident tone reassured me that I'd done the right thing by admitting that I still didn't have the money.

'I'm surprised a clever woman like you never worked it out for yourself. But maybe you're too close to it all to see how obvious the solution is. Think about it.' Dan paused. 'My idea is much the same. Your story is valuable, but not only to a trashy magazine,' said Dan.

'Ah'm sorry Dan, ah still cannae work it oot.'

'There's someone out there who would definitely be prepared to shell out a substantial amount to make sure that the story never sees the light of day.'

'Who?'

Dan had to spell it out to me.

'Steve.' It took a few seconds for the realisation to sink in. 'Who else would pay £10,000 to stop you supplying *Natter* with a juicy story that would make his life crash and burn?'

'You mean blackmail him?'

'That's a dirty word, but call it that if you like. In my opinion, from what you've told me, I'd describe it more as...' Dan paused and held my gaze, '...revenge,' the word rolled off his tongue as slowly as syrup.

The thought of blackmail left me speechless. Almost daily, Isobel shared scandalous stories with me. But threatening to reveal shameful, incriminating facts in exchange for money was in an entirely different league. Blackmail was the kind of thing I watched on TV, in soap operas and gangster films; it didn't ever feature in the real world of Shawbriggs.

'Ah'm no sure ah can get ma head roond blackmailing Steve. Ah dinnae think ah could dae it.'

'So you don't think Ben deserves justice? You don't think Steve should pay in some way for what he took from you?'

'Aye, of course ah've fantasised aboot getting ma own back for Ben and me but this is scary stuff.'

'It is, but it makes sense. Think about it. You get the money we both need, and he gets to keep his reputation intact. And if you can't do it for yourself,' Dan leaned forward and took my hand.

'Do it for Ben.'

Dan was right, his logic did make sense. Cash *and* comeuppance. Who could argue with that?

WEDNESDAY 23RD MARCH 2011

Dear Journal

I was due to go to my session with Charlotte today but Dan advised me to phone in sick and cancel it. It's not really a lie cos I am sick with worry. I did feel guilty cancelling the appointment, but Dan said that I couldn't risk seeing Charlotte. He knows best. If Charlotte said the wrong thing, then I'd probably burst into tears and maybe end up telling her all about our plans. I did miss talking to her this week, but Dan's right; we're too close to take the chance of spoiling everything now. I can't be trusted not to let any of my emotions leak out. Dan said to remember that people like Charlotte can't think outside the box, so it's safer to stay away from her.

Instead of going to the clinic, I met Dan again today at my Angel's Bench to talk over his idea. He's even better than Charlotte at giving me self-belief and, from the minute I sat on the bench, he could see right away that I was anxious. Now that I know the full plan that Dan has set up, after Friday, it'll probably be the last time that I ever visit my Angel's Bench.

Without me even saying a word to him, (although he knows who I think about when I sit on that bench), he told me that it'll all be worth it cos Ben is always watching over me. Dan said there's no doubt that Ben will send down a new angel for me to love as much as I adored him. It was the nicest thing he could have said to me. Dan is the only person that really understands this is not just about making me happy, he knows that if I have a new bairn; it would let Ben rest in peace.

Just as Dan had promised on the phone, he'd come up with a way to get the money I need. He even thinks that I could get more than £10,000 but I don't want to be too greedy. He's worked it all out for me and says it's a fool-proof plan. All I have to do is to ask Steve for the money to stop me from selling the story to Natter. Dan says I've to tell Steve that the magazine is prepared to pay the full amount anyway, but that I'm willing to give Steve the chance to stop me from going public with the true story if he pays up instead. Dan's planned exactly what I need to say to Steve and he's even thought about what I should do after Friday. To be honest, I hadn't thought that far ahead. Dan's worked out all the details about organising the sperm donations and I agreed with him that I need to leave Shawbriggs right after we do the deal with Steve. I know he's thought this whole thing through for me, so that makes me a bit more confident. I trust him.

I know that Dan's right about Steve getting what he deserves, although I wasn't sure about the whole thing at first. It isn't that I feel bad at all about taking the money from Steve; it's cos I couldn't see myself being brave enough to face him and pull it off. When I said all this to Dan, he'd already guessed that I'd be too nervous to go through with meeting up with Steve, so he'd worked out the best way to set it all up.

Dan is really very smart. He's going to make up a mock version of how the story would look if it went into Natter. The false headline will be something like, 'MY HUSBAND MURDERED MY SON' and I've to give him photos of Ben and Steve to go with the words. He's even got glossy paper to print it on so that it'll look like a real magazine page. The best bit though is that I don't even need to confront Steve, all I have to do is to drop the fake pages through his letterbox, along with a note. The note makes it clear to Steve that, unless he pays me £10,000 by the end of the week, the real article will be published in the next copy of Natter. Dan says not to keep thinking of it as blackmail cos it's a straightforward business deal where both folk involved get what they want.

Trying to put on a brave face at work wasn't easy, although keeping busy was better than phoning in sick. I didn't fancy having to amuse myself at home until Friday night, when Steve was expected to arrive with the cash.

Do u fancy cinema on fri?
John won't go cos it's a chick flick
I want 2 c
X

For once I had alternative plans when Elaine's invite appeared on my phone.

Sorry going 2 c my mum
this weekend
xxx

My excuse was true; I would be visiting my mum at the weekend, after doing a bit of business first. It would be a nice surprise for her, but explaining an unexpected visit and the lack of a car was way down on my list of worries at the moment.

There had been no response from Steve at all since I had delivered the envelope on Wednesday. Dan was confident that this was a good sign and repeatedly reassured me that everything would work out as planned. Dan reckoned that if Steve had instantly dismissed the idea of paying up, then he would have immediately let me know that he wasn't prepared to enter into the arrangement. Dan assured me that Steve was playing games and was simply unwilling to show his hand. And yet, none of Dan's texts or calls helped me to relax. Steve had access to large amounts of cash and contacts at the hotel he managed, but I wasn't convinced that he would be willing or able to raise £10,000 in less than forty-eight hours. Was the silence from Steve definitely in my favour?

There were so many things for me to worry about. Would I be able to follow the script in the performance that Dan was directing behind the scenes? The reality of both mine and Steve's roles being played out exactly as Dan had stage managed caused panic to simmer inside. My fears were ready to boil over at any time. Talking to, and for, Jinky hadn't helped me air my nerves; the dog must be demented listening to me go through all the pros and cons.

I spent hours wondering whether Steve would call my bluff and if Friday night would come and go without a visit from him. Despite Dan's claims that he had worked out every eventuality, I was still nervous that it was a high risk strategy. Dan's plan could end my dream and instantly create a fresh nightmare. Not only would I be faced with the threat of violence from Steve, the chance of becoming pregnant again would disappear along with Dan.

On Mother's Day, Isobel always opened up especially for those customers frantically seeking a last minute order. It was one of our busiest days of the year, though Isobel never asked me to work the extra shift. It would be too painful to deal with the sentimental messages that we needed to attach to the flowers. Isobel's concern was unnecessary; I would be nowhere near Shawbriggs on Sunday.

The only upside of Mother's Day this year was that Friday was very busy at the Daisy Chain. I could hide away for most of the morning in the back room, getting orders organised. Being out of sight didn't stop Isobel noticing my failure to eat or my frequent trips to the toilet, trying to literally get rid of the feelings of dread.

'Have you had another takeaway from Shish Happens?'

'Eh?'

'You've been up and down like a yo-yo to the toilet. I'm getting dizzy just watching you.'

'No, ah'll never touch their doner kebabs again after the last time ah had the runs.'

'Well whatever's up with you, I think you'd be better off at home doll.'

'Thanks but ah'll be fine. And ah'd rather keep busy here than be at home.'

'Well, if you're sure, 'cause I need to get out with the deliveries.'

With Isobel out in the van, I was left alone with my thoughts. There was only the brass olde-worlde doorbell to break the silence. I reluctantly emerged from the back shop to find Lynn hovering around the buckets of blossoms.

Lynn immediately moulded her lips into a smile but her eyes were as sad as a spaniel's and didn't match her mouth's feeble attempt at appearing cheery. Where was the sparkle that had lit up the room when Lynn had hosted the swishing party and announced her pregnancy? Was it the tiredness, common in the first trimester, that was hitting Lynn hard? The bloom of pregnancy was nowhere to be seen on my neighbour.

'Can I order some Mother's Day flowers? I'd like to get my

mum something extra special this year.'

Despite Isobel's strict instructions that they should never pry into our customer's private lives, I dared to ask about Maggie. As Lynn was my neighbour, and I'd met Maggie, that meant it cancelled out the need to maintain a professional distance.

'Ah hope you dinnae think ah'm being nosy Lynn, but is everything all right with your mum? Ah'd hate tae hear she was ill.'

'No, my mum's as fit as a fiddle. The deluxe bouquet is cos she's had a big disappointment recently and I'm hoping the flowers will cheer her up,' explained Lynn.

'Ah'm sorry tae hear that, ah hope it's nothing too serious,' I sympathised.

'Do you remember her telling everyone at my party about her plans to go travelling?' asked Lynn.

'Aye, she was really excited and looking forward tae it. Ah thought she was really adventurous.'

'Yeah, me too. It's a long story but she's not able to go now. She's putting on a brave face but I know she's devastated not to be going.'

'That's a real shame she's missing her trip. It must be terrible no being able tae follow your dream.'

'Hmm, yeah, life doesn't often work out the way you want it, eh?'

What had happened to Lynn? My neighbour was always an upbeat Boden clad queen, swinging her silky pony tail, hand-in-hand with Princess Holly. It wasn't just that Lynn's hair had lost its bounce, it seemed as if there was something upsetting Lynn a lot more than just her mother's cancelled trip.

I couldn't dwell on Lynn's visit to the shop for very long. Before I knew where the day had gone, my shift was finished and I was back at home.

'It's only me Jinky.'

'Who else would it be?'

I fed Jinky but I couldn't face dinner. Steve had been instructed to be at my house at seven o'clock. Eventually the deadline approached, whether I was ready to actually cope with Dan's plan or not.

Jinky was scunnered by my relentless pacing. Each time I reached the hall cupboard where his lead was stored, he leapt towards me in the hope that his evening walk was finally going to happen.

'Content yourself, you're going nowhere tonight.'

'Might as well watch *EastEnders* then.'

All sense of Jinky's routine had been abandoned tonight, and tomorrow would never be the same for me or the dog. A car parking outside made me stop in my tracks. I dared to peek through the living room blinds and allow a slice of light to creep into the room.

Buooooop. Buooooop. The alarm on Steve's car signalled his arrival, he activated the remote and swaggered up the concrete slabs to my front door.

Steve's eyes darted back and forth, was he searching for Jeremy Beadle to pop up from behind the hedge? If this was a practical joke, no one would ever find it funny. Steve was early; he still had ten minutes until the game was up. Was he willing to play by my rules for once?

I peered through the slats of the blinds to inspect the man I'd once loved as the father of my child. It was hard to imagine that I'd been connected to Steve in such an intimate way. How could love and hate be so easily interchangeable? It didn't make sense. One year, I would wake up to feel the heat from his body caress and wrap around my own. Then the next year, the same person could punch and kick me in the stomach until I curled up and begged him to stop. It was as warped and distorted as the idea of blackmail.

There was no time to think about the bizarre circumstances I found myself in, as Jinky barked an agitated greeting at Steve's firm chap at the door. My heart palpitations were as loud as the knocking. It was tempting to conduct our business though the letterbox. Steve continued with a, *I-know-you're-in-there* knock and I had to accept that there was no hiding place.

I shook like a horse in a cloud of midges, but there was no going back now. My hand felt clammy against the metal door handle and after one massive deep breath, trembling inside and out, I slowly eased the door open, no more than the security door chain allowed.

I had rehearsed my lines over and over in my head all day, but now that I was standing only feet away from Steve, I struggled to find my voice. Dan's ghostly presence was willing me on to deliver the dialogue that he'd so carefully invented. My mind went blank. The script that I had worked so hard to memorise was gone. I'd been right all along; this was never going to work. I didn't have the inner strength to challenge Steve.

'For fuck's sake, what's this all aboot? You drag me here on a Friday night just tae stare at me through a gap in your door.' He puffed out disgust before he continued his rant. 'You're a fuckin' loony!' snarled Steve.

I turned my head towards the tiny cloakroom toilet at the end of the hallway, my stomach heaved and I feared that I would mess myself. An image came back to me, as if it had happened only yesterday, instead of years ago when we'd been married for only a couple of months.

Steve had come home late from work and was showing signs of being drunk, the start of a routine that became the norm. When I had presented him with his dinner of a Thai green curry, he'd bawled at me that he didn't eat anything that his granny didn't class as a meal. As punishment for forgetting his dislike of foreign food, he'd barricaded me in our bedroom for the rest of the night. Listening to his taunts through the bedroom door, I'd ended up shitting my pants.

His sneer through the slit of light in the doorway had created an almighty flashback. It was exactly the same feeling from years before. Waves of sweat rolled over me and my sphincter muscles pulsed. The only difference was that I was the one with the most power tonight. A surge of resolve propelled me forwards to release the door chain and I swung the door wide open. My bold move momentarily surprised Steve but he seized the opportunity to enter the house. I remained silent and merely stood aside to allow Steve to move inside to the living room.

The instant that I crossed the threshold of my living room, Steve spun round to smack me across the face. He delivered the blow with the rolled up pages from the fake article that Dan had designed as an example of the type of feature that *Natter* would print.

'What the fuck dae you think you're playing at?' Steve unfurled the glossy pages and waved them in front of my flushed beet-red face.

'Think you're clever?' Not expecting a reply, he continued with his outburst. 'Mind you, ah've got tae give you ten out of ten for effort. Ah didnae think you were that talented, but this is where this shit belongs.' Steve marched across the room, crunched up the pages into a ball and launched it into the wicker bin.

My voice was barely audible, but I summed up enough strength to deliver my lines. Dan would be proud.

'Pay up or watch your reputation end up ruined,' I uttered. My clunky words dropped with a thud to the floor and I wondered if it was too late to snatch them up and cram them back into my mouth. One glance at Steve's repulsive sneer was my answer. He was going nowhere until he was satisfied. There was no other option; the prospect of civility was long gone. It was my edge-of-the-cliff moment. I stood defiantly in front of Steve with my feet wide and my arms tightly crossed.

For such a skinny man, Steve's booming laugh had a depth to it, except it lacked any real heartiness. The hideous sound made me want to take flight, but I stood firm. Repeating my demand would help him understand that I was deadly serious.

'Are you having a fuckin' laugh? Or are you actually attempting tae blackmail me?' snorted Steve, spraying spittle into my face.

'Call it whatever you like, but ah mean what ah say,' my rapid breathing gave away any pretence of calm.

'And you think that ah'll just hand over ten grand because you made up a story for a shitty wee magazine?'

'There's nothing made up aboot any of it and you know it! It's a fact. You caused Ben's death!' My voice was louder now but not any stronger, it quivered, a wounded animal trapped and facing its predator. I only hoped that I could hold back the tears that threatened to spoil my performance.

'That's a very big accusation tae make withoot any proof,' countered Steve, taking a step nearer to me. 'And who's going tae listen tae *you* anyway? Everyone knows you're neurotic!' Steve's finger jabbed at my face.

'Ah told you, *Natter* has already agreed tae pay the money.' I tried my best to sound assured, backing nearer the kitchen door, keeping him more than a fist's reach away.

'So why ask me for the cash if you can get it anyway?' he was determined to box me into the corner, close enough now for me to smell his stale beer breath.

'Listen, ah dinnae want tae see the story printed either but ah need the money.' As an untrained actress, surely Dan would be pleased that I'd barely strayed from the script?

'You stupid bitch, ah thought you did nothing but watch telly these days? So you should know that blackmail is illegal? Go fuck yourself!' Steve's roaring laugh filled the room.

Jinky sprang up from under the coffee table to growl with as much bravery as he could manage. Barking wildly, he put one set of paws forward. Steve advanced too and gave the dog a brutal kick in the ribs. Jinky scuttled across the laminate floor, yelping and shrinking to make himself as small and invisible as possible, I knew that trick well.

'Noo, it's your turn. You silly cow.'

Steve lurched forward and grabbed me firmly by the throat. It was his favoured technique, swipe, seize and squeeze. The next 'S' was always smack, that was the routine.

As his grip tightened, my eyes bulged as if I was blinded by a spotlight used to illuminate the drama of this evening's production. Only this time the audience watching Steve's attempt to throttle me wouldn't be Ben. Just as planned, from stage left, the leading man of the final act burst through the kitchen door. Right on cue.

Dan had his camcorder ready at a perfect angle to capture the full scale of the action.

'Smile for the camera Steve!' he taunted. It was the line of the grand finale that would achieve our goal. Dan couldn't resist looking down and grinning into Steve's scrawny phizog, despite the fact that I was still being choked and was hysterical.

'You brainless prick! Don't you know that domestic abuse is illegal? Don't *you* watch telly?' smirked Dan.

Steve's hand immediately transformed from a clamped vice into a boxing glove. I stumbled backwards, rubbing at my neck as Steve made a frenzied swing at Dan. Just as in our planned script, Dan swiftly passed the camcorder to me to record Steve's sideways blow to my accomplice's shoulder. Dan's bulky frame was immediately on top of his ill-matched opponent. With a skilful punch to the guts, Steve fell to the floor like a Thunderbird after its strings had been cut.

With Dan straddling Steve's weedy frame, I handed him the gaffer tape that we'd stashed earlier. Steve was trussed up; a Christmas turkey ready to be carved. Steve's feeble jerking movements made me want to laugh. The scene terrified me and yet my ex-husband looked so ridiculous that I feared I might break into nervous giggles. Steve spat out a thick blob of phlegm at my feet.

'Where's your manners?' asked Dan. 'Just remember that you're our guest tonight. And speaking of which, Carol, don't you think Steve here should have shaved before his visit?' Dan didn't even try to hide his enjoyment as he produced an open razor from the pocket of his jeans.

'Ever had a *tashir* before Steve? Know what it is?' Dan asked.

'Fuck you!' The words were fired out along with more frothy slobber, whilst Steve persisted in writhing around the floor, underneath the cool glint of the blade that Dan was swishing Zorro-like in the air.

'I've warned you already about your manners but I'll give you one last chance and ignore that rude reply. A *tashir* is a Turkish shave and I think you could do with a *proper* shave. Trouble is though, I'm not Turkish. But hey,' Dan laughed. 'I'll try anything once.'

Dan had never mentioned the razor to me when we'd talked through our parts in securing the money. Was this ad-libbing just bravado? This was never meant to be a horror show.

The sharp razor gently grazed Steve's neck stubble as Dan continued with his speech.

'Don't worry about my shaving technique though, cos I was

good at wood carving at school, particularly initials. Mind you, I admit, 'S' is too hard even for me, so how about I do a 'K'?'

'You bastard!' Steve's reply was rewarded by a strip of gaffer tape to his mouth and the first cut to his neck. A round ruby bead, the first jewel of a necklace of blood.

I was mesmerised as Dan used the cut-throat razor to make a series of tiny nicks over Steve's flesh. It felt as if I was witnessing an operation, like something I'd watch on *Casualty*. It was repulsive and riveting at the same time.

'The straight lines of a 'K' are easier than an 'S' and it makes more sense, eh?' Dan hissed like a pantomime baddie into Steve's ashen face. "K' for killer cos that's what everyone will call you after the magazine prints the story.'

'Enough!' I squealed. There was no remote control to switch off the live action; this wasn't a TV drama. I had no wish to watch the rest of Dan's performance and I had to do something fast.

Seeing a sadistic side of Dan that had never been shown before, reminded me of how little I really knew about him. Although the fact of the matter was that Dan was only providing a service, and it didn't mean that I had to like the supplier to be satisfied with the product. It wasn't as if I was in a relationship with Dan and once our business was over, we would never see each other again. We had an agreement and if Dan judged it necessary to threaten Steve to achieve success on his part of the deal, then I had to be prepared to accept it.

Dan seemed a little miffed that his performance would be cut short. With my insistence, he only delivered the occasional scratch across Steve's bulging Adam's apple to finalise the full details of the transaction. There were no more stunts from Steve; he accepted his part in tonight's show. When the curtain went up, the only place Steve could go from here was somewhere to source the money. This wasn't show business, this was real.

The bizarre play acted out in my suburban living room had reached its natural conclusion. I sat back in the wings, an audience of one, trembling, but still capable of admiring Dan's stage management and his starring role. If I'd been bold enough to clap his performance, I felt sure that he'd have happily taken a bow to my cries of *Bravo!*

Dan's script was a success and he gave a BAFTA-worthy performance. I didn't want applause for my part as the Best Supporting Actress. I simply wanted my original role back: Mum.

JULIA

D<small>RIVING THROUGH THE</small> W<small>OODLEA ESTATE</small>, I noticed that the For Sale sign had been plastered over with an Under Offer sticker. Had Lynn gathered any fresh snippets of gossip on the whereabouts of Carol Walker since she was last seen more than six months ago? The neighbourhood speculation on Carol's moonlight flit was the most exciting topic the estate residents had had to gossip about in ages.

Usually the biggest drama Lynn relayed to me was about kids and parents caught up in the crossfire of arguments over petty garden disputes and the occasional late night blast of music. It was a change for the estate chit-chat to be a bit juicier; surely someone knew where Carol had gone? Lynn's most likely explanation was that she'd moved back up north, but if it was as simple as that, then why wouldn't she have told anyone? And why had there been such a rushed departure?

'I see Carol's house is under offer now. Anymore goss?' I asked, as I slipped off my woollen cape to reveal a loose tunic top covering a pair of stretchy leggings.

'Jeez, wait till I tell you the latest!' cried Lynn.

My sister positively beamed with the thrill of having some

scandal to share; Lynn really did need to get out of the house more. It was a sad fact that the Woodlea estate had become the centre of Lynn's universe. I made a mental note that if I ever got that hyper over neighbourly gossip, I would seek immediate treatment.

'Well...' Lynn paused. I hauled myself on to a stool at the breakfast bar, this better be worth the build-up.

'Annie told me that Kimberly's had her baby now, she's Carol's ex-husband's partner, by the way,' explained Lynn, almost breathless now. '*And* they called the baby Paris, how tacky is that?'

I could picture Lynn with her stuck up pal, Annie the Fanny, spitting out crumbs of hand-baked biscuits into their espressos as they ridiculed the naff name of Kimberly's newborn.

'So, I don't know if Carol's left Shawbriggs to avoid Kimberly and baby Paris,' she paused for a quick snigger, 'but I bumped into Moira Farrell yesterday, you know, Carol's neighbour?' she paused again to take another theatrical breath, 'Well she heard from Isobel at the Daisy Chain, you know the florist?'

I didn't know or care who the fuck Isobel or Moira Farrell were, but Lynn seemed content to carry on without an affirmative. My only concern now was that the tale didn't get any more complicated with extra random names, or I would lose the will to live.

'Well, apparently Carol has gone back up north to stay with her mum in some back of beyond fishing town. Moira Farrell said that Carol disappeared the day after her ex-husband and a big tall guy came round to her house and there was a lot of shouting and screaming,' stated Lynn, taking *another* deep breath.

'And, that's not all... Moira Farrell saw Carol came back to the estate really late one night a few weeks ago to collect some stuff from the house.'

Moira Farrell doesn't miss much. I was truly grateful that I seemed to be able to come and go anonymously at my flat.

'Is that it?' I asked, beginning to wish I'd never mentioned the 'For Sale' sign. When did the rot set in to turn my sister into a Stepford wife? It was agonising to watch the transformation.

'Oh no, listen to this, when I called Annie to tell her the full story, she was absolutely gob-smacked!'

'And? The full story?' I asked, eager now for the climax and to finally be put out of my misery.

'Well, Mrs Farrell couldn't help but notice that Carol had a definite baby bump when she came back that night! But who's the daddy? That's what we're trying to work out. So, what do you make of all that?' asked Lynn, who was now happy to lean back and enjoy the satisfaction of her cliff-hanger.

I could make nothing of it and, much to Lynn's disappointment I simply shrugged my shoulders.

'Isn't that the baby crying?' I asked.

The baby monitor sat on the kitchen table, and I winced as the crying gradually built up into a piercing climax.

'Huh, he only went to sleep ten minutes ago.' Lynn left to respond to the howls, leaving me mulling over how everyone, even Carol Walker, found it easy to have a child without any hassle. Although motherhood looked as if it was taking it out of Lynn's hide when she returned with the bawling baby.

'Jeez, I think it must be colic again, he's not stopped crying for more than half an hour since five this morning. Am I glad to see you!' moaned Lynn.

There was no question, that my outstretched arms were the most welcome sight Lynn had seen since daybreak. I scooped up my nephew and paced up and down Lynn's kitchen as Holly got ready to go out on our walk.

'Ready, Angel Face?' I asked, stroking Holly's cheek. Holly let out an exasperated sigh, 'I'm *not* a baby anymore.'

I was getting used to Holly's recurring mood swings these days, sugar or shit, there was nothing in between. And today it looked as if shit was on the menu.

'Yeah, I know but even when you're all grown up, you'll always be my Angel Face,' I replied. Holly pouted, self-conscious in her skinny jeans and a crop top. This wasn't the child that was once happy to pose in her Minnie Mouse pants. The way girls seemed to speed through childhood these days, before very long, Holly would be insisting that she needed a trainer bra. I didn't want to visualise the image; adolescence would spoil everything.

'Okay, if you're such a big girl now, you'll know that you need to find a jumper to put on, and a scarf, and gloves and a coat. It's October and it's freezing out there. And because you're so grown-up, you'll be able to get it all by yourself.' I nudged her firmly nearer the door.

'Absolutely, it's far too cold to be going without wrapping up warm,' agreed Lynn.

'Whatever!' huffed Holly as she marched out of the kitchen.

Lynn leaned in close enough for to me to smell the coffee on her breath, Holly's hearing was dog-sharp. 'I hope you're being careful sis, I don't know the full story about Carol yet, but trust me, you don't *ever* want to end up a single parent.'

'What's all this about being a single parent? What's up?' I replied.

'Oh nothing. It's just with Chris always working late or away with the rugby club and business trips, I feel like I'm always on my own,' moaned Lynn. 'And it's really hard.'

'He's away *again* this weekend?' I asked.

'Yeah, he's travelling down to Newcastle for a conference on Monday. Says he needs to get there a day early to help set things up. You know what he's like, he can't say no.'

The recurring excuse of Chris being unable to say no to business trips and rugby commitments was now gossamer-thin. When Kirsty had suggested that I should intervene, I'd been adamant at the time that my sister's marital affairs were none of my business. But how long I could listen to Lynn's weekly moans? Should I even hint that there might be other pursuits out-with the office or the rugby club that Chris was finding it difficult to refuse? I had no solid evidence that he was unfaithful and it would be hard to prove. But maybe it was time to confront Chris and let Lynn know that she had to deal with an unfaithful husband or a selfish workaholic. Whatever was making Chris turn his back on family life needed sorted out, one way or another.

'I never get a minute to myself…'Lynn sighed.

I needed to break out of the suffocating atmosphere of the kitchen and get out into the crisp October air. With a cookie-cutter wife, a defiant eight-year-old, and a crying baby, I could understand Chris's need to escape the confines of his mock-Georgian box. Who could honestly blame the guy for making a bid for freedom whenever he got the chance?

'Right, well anyway, have an hour to yourself while I take them both for a walk.'

I strode back and forth, rocking James, my new nephew in my arms.

'Thanks Julia, I don't know how I'd have stayed sane without you taking Holly off my hands during these last few months. All those day trips tired her out. You're a life saver!'

'No problem, it suited us both.'

The motion of the pram was enough to send James off to sleep and I only had to contend with Holly on our walk round the woodland trail. I decided that we wouldn't go too far; we'd stick to our routine circuit. James wasn't the only individual that was shattered. I hadn't been sleeping well at all for weeks and sleep deprivation was really starting to make my nerves throb.

Weaving our way along the familiar path under leaden grey skies, the chill of winter was on the horizon. Nature's machine had flicked a switch, turning the yellows and greens of the leaves to withered oranges and browns. The end of a season, exhausted of energy and keen to rest and recover, before finding the strength to create new life in the spring. Mother Nature and I had a lot in common.

Where was the elation that I should feel right now after making my decision? The quick hit of euphoria had only lasted a matter of days. But when I came down from my high, I was left flattened, like the leaves underfoot.

Holly sniffed round me, an eager puppy, looking for a treat from a lethargic mistress. Claims of being a big girl now had been conveniently put aside and I hunted in my handbag for the bag of sweets that Holly knew would be there. We'd almost reached the Angel's Bench and James was now snuffling contentedly.

'How about we stop at the bench for treat time?' I suggested. Holly bounded towards our favourite stopping point, but instead of crashing down on the blackened bench, she suddenly stopped. Holly was staring at something attached to the upper slats of the seat. From a distance, I could only see a slight glint in the weak afternoon sunlight. There seemed to be nothing significant on or near the bench to cause Holly to stop so abruptly.

'Come and see this Auntie Julia!' cried Holly excitedly. Holly was as much of a drama queen as her mother, it wasn't likely to be that thrilling, and I didn't bother to quicken my step.

Parking the pram, I followed the direction of Holly's pointed finger. There on the backrest of the bench was a rectangular brass plaque, new and shiny. Holly read the inscription aloud:

'Miracles happen to those who believe in angels'

'Who d'ya think put that on the bench?' asked Holly.

'I've no idea, maybe an angel?' I wasn't prepared to give up hope that Holly was still willing to play along, even just for my benefit.

'Hmm. So what does it mean then?' asked Holly, thoughts of sweets momentarily forgotten.

'Eh, it means just what it says…' my voice faltered.

'Mum says James is a miracle so she must believe in angels,' said Holly.

'She's right, all babies are miracles,' I agreed.

'Why don't you have a baby Auntie Julia?'

Holly's directness almost floored me.

'You need to have a boyfriend or a husband before you can have a baby.'

'That's not true.' Holly raised an accusatory eyebrow. 'I heard mum and Annie talking about Carol Walker having a baby. So why don't you have one?'

Holly wasn't going to be fobbed off easily.

'Eh, because they cost too much.'

'But you don't have to buy a baby! Everyone knows that,' squealed Holly.

'That's very true but the things they need still cost a lot of money.'

'Why, are nappies really, *really* expensive?'

How could I get out of this, without digging a deeper hole? Not even when Holly was an adult could I ever explain to her that the cost of a baby was nothing to do with the price of Pampers.

Angels? Miracles? No, there would be no divine intervention to produce a baby for me. If I'd agreed to Peter's proposal, my deal would have been with the devil. My soul was no longer for sale. Everything can be bought at a price, but my integrity was off the market. And no amount of Paedo Pete's money could buy it.

There had to be a way to avoid Holly's inquisitive glare and kill this conversation. The answer was staring me in the face. I gave James's peachy skin a gentle nip and he woke with a start, and a howl.

'Oh, dear. I think we better get your little brother back home.'

Back in the warmth of the kitchen and chewing endlessly on a supply of caramels, Holly stripped off her jumper as if it had been knitted from barbed wire. She threw it over a chair as her mum pulled a postcard from the fridge door and handed it to me.

'This came last week. Did you get one too?' asked Lynn. I flipped the glossy photo of the Taj Mahal over and instantly recognized Maggie's handwriting.

Hope you're all well. Having a fantastic time! I've met two lovely English women who're also moving on next week to Thailand so you can stop worrying about me travelling on my own! India is an amazing place!!! I couldn't even begin to describe it in a postcard. The people are so friendly, even though most of them live in poverty, they seem really happy. Give Holly and James hugs and kisses from me.

Mum xxx

'Sounds like she's loving it, eh?' said Lynn, pinning the postcard back on the fridge door.

'Yeah, I got a postcard too,' I replied.

'I'm so proud of her,' stated Lynn.

'Me too, she was a bit nervous about all the travel details before she left but she seems to have managed without any problem,' I agreed.

'Listen, I know you were disappointed when you said that the investment deal fell through for you, but to be honest, I'm glad that you were able to give mum her money back.'

'You know, I could've invested the money into another renewable energy project I'd heard about. But I pulled out because I knew how much this trip meant to her.'

'Well, you only need to read that postcard to know you did the right thing. She'll be able to die happy now she's achieved her dream,' said Lynn.

'Yeah. Listen, it's time I headed home.'

'What's the rush? Stay for dinner. You're only going back to an empty flat.'

'No thanks. I've got a deadline to meet.'

'There's more to life than work Julia.'

It was tempting to reach for the kitchen cloth to wipe off her patronising expression.

'Don't I know it...'

I placed James safely back into his Moses basket and kissed his head.

'Bye, bye baby.'

I still had sleepless nights, filled with vile images of Holly photographed in ambiguous poses. I'd lain awake for hours thinking over Paedo Pete's proposal. Was he really suggesting that Holly could feature in amateur kiddie porn? Or was my cynical mind so polluted that I'd imagined the worst? Or maybe Peter was simply keen on photography and was looking to capture the innocence of childhood through Holly? The questions haunted me.

They say that your mind knows only some things but your inner voice, your intuition, knows everything. If you listen to what you know instinctively, it will always lead you down the right path. When my head and heart were in conflict and I questioned my sixth sense, I listened to my body. Any time I'd allowed even a fleeting image of Holly posing for Paedo Pete to enter my mind; it resulted in heaving sobs and acidic retching. I had my answer.

With my thirty-ninth birthday fast approaching, I reckoned that my gut feelings were as honed as they'd ever be. And for that reason I'd rejected Peter's proposition. The opportunity of acquiring the money from Maggie and Peter was now long gone. And as he'd promised, Dan had vanished too.

I sometimes wondered what had awaited Dan, when he had failed to raise the money. Were his hints of violent retribution for real? Or was it all a scam to pressure me into coming up with the cash? Maybe he'd managed to get the money he needed from another source? But, just like Carol Walker, he had disappeared into the night and I would never know. Unless of course Annie the Fanny knew something…

But I was only interested in hard facts and I had settled for being single, rather than being a single parent. I would never buy into the fantasy of heavenly intervention in shaping my destiny. Only someone Holly's age would believe the inscription on the Angel's Bench plaque. Miracles? What a load of bollocks.

CAROL

Dear Journal,

I'm sorry that I've neglected you for so long but I'm sure you'll understand that I haven't had a minute to myself since Marvella was born. Do you like the name? It's a bit fancy-pants for Portcullen folk but who cares? I'm the talk of the town anyway. I'd thought about calling the bairn Nadine, I've always loved my French pen pal's name, but this wee mite's all about the future, not my past. And Marvella is the French name for 'miracle' and that fits perfectly.

I planned to write about the birth, but I was too busy filling in the Peter Rabbit Baby Book mum gave me in one of her 'Helping Hand' packages. At least she doesn't need to post stuff now. Most of the parcels are for Marvella these days and my mum's forever knitting something for her, although I'm not that keen on the knitted roller skates. They're bootees with ribbon laces and four knitted balls sewed on to each sole. I suppose they're kinda cute but there's enough folk talking about me behind my back without giving them something else to point and stare at. I'll maybe put them on Marvella the next time mum comes round. I won't have to wait long cos she pops in at least once a day. I can't complain cos I'd never have coped without her help. I don't even feel like a single parent, not like I did when it was just me and Ben living in Shawbriggs. And Elaine comes up to visit every few weeks so I still hear all the gossip and I keep my magazines for her.

Mum's loving being a granny again and having me back in Portcullen. Don't get me wrong, I was nervous about turning up at her front door out of the blue with only a rucksack and Jinky. She kept looking down the street for the new car from the money she'd lent me. When my belly began to swell months later, it took her a wee while to get over the shock, but she soon realised that I was the happiest I've ever been since losing Ben. And she still hasn't asked for any details or her money back. She said it wasn't important how our wee miracle came into our lives, the main thing is that she did, and that's all that matters. Mum tells everyone who'll listen that we've been blessed. Poor Mrs MacWatt's ears must bleed with all the bragging she does about how lucky we are to have Marvella.

But mum's right, even when I'm tired and I'm up during the night when Marvella can't sleep, I don't moan. I'm a mum again, so what's there to complain about?

I stick on my Bay City Rollers CD down low, Jinky hates it, and we waltz around the living room with Marvella cooried in tight and me gently singing Bye Bye Baby. Marvella drifts off every time so she's either a born Rollers fan, or she's already worked out how to stop me singing. She's a smart cookie; just like her dad.

I've decided to make this the last time I write in this journal to concentrate on keeping the Baby Book up-to-date. I know you won't be offended that I've moved on, because that was why I was writing about my feelings in the first place. I hate to admit it, but I've got Charlotte's counselling sessions to thank for starting a journal.

She'd be chuffed that she was right all along; writing stuff down did help me. It wasn't easy being so open with you, but now I feel I can tell you anything and everything. But where would I start since my last entry? It would mean looking back and I don't want to do that anymore. I have a future now with my wee miracle and I know that's what you'd want for me.

You'll always have a special place in my memory box. Maybe one day, years from now, I'll go back to my Angel's Bench. Marvella will sit with me and you will help me tell our story - about her dad, and about Ben, the brother she never knew.

Bye bye from me and my baby.

xXx

ACKNOWLEDGEMENTS

Every writer knows that writing is all about rewriting. I wrote the first draft of Buy Buy Baby more than six years ago, but that version bears little resemblance to the one inside this cover. After being convinced that the story shouldn't be allowed to gather digital dust, I blew the cobwebs off the manuscript and set to work on a complete rewrite. And it's thanks to the insightful feedback and razor-sharp editing skills of Anne Glennie from Cranachan Publishing that the novel is now fit for readers.

Lots of other folk played a part too and I'm very lucky to have brilliant support, in real life and online, from sources such as the members of Book Connectors and The Prime Writers, my writing mentor and friend Karen Campbell, Diane Anderson for making sure the sections of Doric dialect were accurate, and Helen Fitzgerald for her generous cover quote.

At home, I have to rightly thank my best friend and beloved husband Donald, who has been my constant companion on the road to publication and made me believe my words are worth sharing.

Book Group Questions for Buy Buy Baby

1. The novel deals with the issue of motherhood; do you feel it gives a balanced view?

2. Which of the two main characters did you empathise with the most?

3. How effective was the author in creating two different characters chasing the same goal?

4. Female friendships and relationships were explored throughout the novel. Could you identify with any of the positive and negative aspects?

5. None of the male characters in Buy Buy Baby are likeable characters. Is this fair to portray men in this way?

6. Dan remains enigmatic throughout the novel. Did you feel frustrated or satisfied by this?

7. Did you find the plot believable?

8. How happy were you with the ending?

THANK YOU FOR READING

As we say at Cranachan, '*the proof of the pudding is in the reading*' and we hope that you enjoyed *Buy Buy Baby*.

Please tell all your friends and tweet us with your #buybuybaby feedback, or better still, write an online review to help spread the word!

We only publish books which excite and inspire us, so if you'd like to experience other unique and thought-provoking books, please visit our website:

cranachanpublishing.co.uk

and follow us
@cranachanbooks
for news of our forthcoming titles.

Lightning Source UK Ltd.
Milton Keynes UK
UKOW04f0910040816

279941UK00008B/44/P